DARKNESS IS AS LIGHT

DAVID B. SEABURN

PublishAmerica
Baltimore

First printing

ISBN: 1-4137-7729-5
PUBLISHED BY PUBLISHAMERICA, LLLP
www.publishamerica.com
Baltimore

Printed in the United States of America

To
MY FAMILY

Rita,

All my best to you,

Dave

1

I wonder how many minutes there are in a lifetime. I mean actual ticks of the clock. Figure there are over 1,400 minutes in a single day. So, simple multiplying tells you there's over a half million minutes in one year. If you live a long time, like 70 years, well, that's like 35 million minutes. That makes us all millionaires when it comes to time. Not as many minutes as Bill Gates has dollars, but a lot nonetheless, enough to do something. With all those minutes you could build a lot of pyramids or make hundreds of movies or be president. Usually those guys are all spent by the time they become president. I mean, they're on the gray end of life. But at least they're trying to do something with the time they have left.

Mostly we waste time. How much is spent watching TV or standing in the check out line or folding clothes or parting your hair? I heard that we spend one third of our lives sleeping. One third, for God's sake. That's millions of minutes. So I stayed up for days once to see if I could make my life better, but it only made me tired and irritable and I had all that sleep to make up. I ended up wasting time trying to figure out what to do with it. I guess you could say most of my life has been wasted time, like nickels thrown into a slot machine, gone forever with nothing to show for it. I keep pulling the handle and hoping, but it never comes up cherries.

It wasn't that way in the beginning. There's always a promise of something in the beginning. My mother told me there was a rainbow outside the hospital window the very moment I was born. She said she looked into my eyes and I looked back at her with a steady gaze, like I knew something really important, like I remembered where I came from before I came out of her and that it was a secret, a special secret about why we were all here. Then she would laugh and tell me that the very next moment my eyes were rolling every which way and my tongue had gone crazy trying to get out of my mouth and I didn't seem to have any recollection whatsoever about why I was here or where I'd come from. She would laugh every time she told me that story. Sometimes I would ask her to tell it to me when I was bored and there was nothin' to do. When the words came out of her mouth it was like she was making my life for me; the words themselves were my arms and legs and mouth and heart and everything. I could breathe deep and feel myself alive when she talked.

I wish I remembered more about my mother. I do have pictures, though. This one shows her holding me when she came home from the hospital. She's standing on the front porch and she looks cold. You can't see me because I'm all bundled up and she's about to go in the house. And this one is just of her sitting in the rocking chair, her head thrown back like she's laughing at the funniest thing. She has a beer in her hand and it's dangling down, all casual. And this one of her and my father. She's smiling at the camera, but he must not have been ready because he's looking away at something or someone, like he's not there at all or he's looking at someone else's camera.

My mother had blonde hair and was pretty when she was young. I don't remember that, of course, but I've been told. She was soft as a pillow at night. Her hands were warm and she screamed when she laughed. She didn't hit me very often but when she did, I always thought how strong she was and I was kinda proud even though it hurt. Mom grew up in a small town with her brother Harold and her parents. Grandpa worked at the tube mill and came home every day for lunch to eat and argue with Grandma. By the time he left for work again the house was in an uproar like a whirlwind had just dropped in for a few minutes leaving all the furniture in everyone's hearts mixed up and thrown about.

Grandpa liked to drink, so sometimes he didn't come home at all and that was worse, because everyone knew a storm was coming but they just didn't know when it would arrive. When it did, Harold was

6

the first one to feel the change in the weather. Grandpa would go right at him and knock him around until Grandma cried so hard that Grandpa would let him go. Harold never fought back. He just took it like he expected it, like some kids expect a hug at the end of the day. Grandma would keep my mother close so she could protect mom, or so mom could protect her, I don't know which, because it seemed like mom was a shield sometimes. Grandpa wouldn't touch her. He'd cry when he looked at her. He'd get all sloppy and sorry and then he'd get sick and mother would have to clean it up because by then Grandma was in her room, door locked for the night. I guess you'd say it wasn't a happy home.

One Friday night they got a surprise. They waited for Grandpa but he never came. He just never came home ever again. You'd think that was the happy ending that everyone was waiting for, that the sun would come out again and make things grow in their lives, but it didn't happen that way. Harold took a bad turn. His teachers worried about him because he was so mean and didn't seem to care at all what they said or wanted. He just stared at them with a look that made them afraid. Grandma didn't know what to do with Harold and threatened to send him away to reform school. So one day as Harold walked across the Ewing Park Bridge on the way to school he climbed up on the rail, glanced at the oncoming cars and jumped. He never said a word. The neighbor down the street saw the whole thing. She said he was calm as could be. He never flinched. He never hesitated. He never looked away. He looked straight down as he fell. Not a sound. Nothing.

I used to think about Uncle Harold a lot. He was about 13 when he ended his life. I've gone to the bridge many times myself and thrown things off, just to see how long it would take to hit bottom. It takes a good four or five seconds depending on the wind. One-Mississippi, two-Mississippi…well, you can do the counting yourself, but do it when there's nothing else going on and it's all quiet and you'll be amazed how long it is. I wonder what he thought about as he fell. Did he reconsider his decision? Did he think about my mother who was ten years old at the time? What did everything look like rushing by him? Did things come clear for him in those few seconds? Maybe it was the best thing he ever did? Maybe it wasn't a "waste," like all the old ladies whispered. Maybe it was the one bit of time that made the most sense in his whole life. Maybe it was the "fullness of time" for him, just like it talks about in the Bible. Maybe he came out the other side into some new mother's arms with a look on his face like he knew everything there was to know.

Why would you care at all about Harold and my mother, and me for that fact? Well, you may not care, but they suggested I write about whatever comes to my mind, so that's what I'm doing. They said it might be "therapeutic." I'm not so sure about that. Words can be mighty dangerous in the wrong hands, in the right ones, too. I've seen my own father tear a person to absolute shreds just with words, never laid a hand on him, just knifed him all up with nouns and verbs and adjectives and adverbs.

Maybe they want me to write so they can look inside me and find out what's wrong with me. I don't care much about that either. I used to ask myself what was wrong with me all the time. I been asking that question for as long as there's been questions to ask. It's like the first clear thought I ever had about my life was, Why aren't you doing this right? Never got an answer. I knew there must be a right way to do my life, but I sure as hell couldn't figure it out and there were no directions that I could find anywhere. It was like I showed up for the game and everyone around me knew what the rules were and how to play except me. I just went through the motions, hoping no one would notice that I didn't have a clue what I was doing or why.

My latest thought was that maybe there is nothing wrong with me at all, maybe I'm perfect, just perfect in a different way, that's all, like someone who's color blind sees perfectly, only a different kind of perfect, one without colors. Maybe I'm perfect, too, just different. Who knows.

So at first they said I could use the computer down the hall, when no one was on it. But it was too hard for me. My pointer fingers went stiff waiting for the words to come. Words got all backed up in my head like they were caught at some border crossing and couldn't find there way to the other side. They didn't have a passport or something. Then they'd get out of line and all jumbled up like a tossed salad, so that I spent most of my time staring at the letters on the little square keys, wasting more time. So they gave me a notebook and I've been writing in my room as often as I can. Sometimes I don't write at all, I draw instead, mostly circles and boxes. Sometimes I sit there and stare, too, but that's not because I'm jumbled inside, it's just because sitting and staring seems like the right thing to do at the time.

My room is very small. There is a single bed that's kind of bowed in the middle from all the others who've slept here. And there's this chair I'm sitting on and this little table. I can just about get my legs under it. I have a window, too. There's wire criss-crossed in the glass so it's almost impossible to break. I spend a lot of time at the window since it's so hard to get to the TV before the others and establish control over the remote. The window is my TV. Right outside is the roof and beyond it is the parking lot and beyond that is a cemetery where I can see life coming and going. The workmen come early and backhoe lots that they then cover with fake grass carpets. They put up the tent, which sometimes is an adventure. I'm surprised those old tents don't fall on the mourners, they're so flimsy. Then, of course, the mourners, some in black, but nowadays they wear almost anything they want. No one is afraid that their colorful clothes are going to make death take a shine to them. The hole gets filled up. The tent comes down.

Mostly there are joggers in the cemetery, running around in their spandex with the onlookers stretched out stiff as boards in neat rows, maybe smiling to themselves about how the runners can run but they cannot hide.

I also get some sun through this window. Between ten and eleven in the morning, there it is.

And about me. Looking in the mirror on my desk, I see a pale face with a mustache. It's supposed to be one of those fumanchu mustaches, but it's not quite thick enough so some of the mustache hair hangs down from above my lip and instead of making the mustache thicker it kind of slides into the corners of my mouth, which can be annoying. This may not seem important to you, but I have been trying to perfect this look for twenty years. So, I have the mustache. My eyes are kinda small. They're brownish I guess, although they look a little green in some kinds of light. Hair is brown. I'm sitting at the table, but if I stood up, you'd see I'm about 5' 8" if I straighten my back. I still say I'm average build, which is all relative. I heard that for the first time ever, more Americans are "large" than "average." So if that's the case, doesn't that change the definition of average build? Doesn't that mean that average is now bigger than it once was? I think so. I'm average build, but a lot more average than I was ten years ago.

I don't look much like my father at all, which is fine with me. I haven't seen him since I came here. We've lived together forever now. Not sure why. When he's not at work, he sits on the front stoop with his cooler of beer and watches the neighborhood and life itself go by. He has tomatoes in the back and he tends them from time to time, swears at them a lot, so they'll ripen up faster I guess.

I have a hot plate in my room at the house and one of those little refrigerators so that I can cook some meals and not leave if I don't want to. That way our paths don't cross all that much. We watch the WWF together from time to time, but actually, it's not together, we're just in the same space at the same time watching the same thing, if you know what I mean.

Carla comes around once a week to clean and put things in order so that we have something to mess up once she's gone. She cooks some meals for my father and freezes them. Sometimes they stay there in the freezer week in and week out. He drinks now more than he eats. And he sits most of the time, smoking his Camels and coughing. I tell him he ought to do something about his cough and then he says, "It's none of your damn business." I don't answer when he says things like that. Not that I don't have something to say, it's just that I don't want to waste my time saying it. Thinking it is good enough. "Go to hell you old fuck" usually covers anything I would want to say anyway.

By the way, I'm 43, kind of an old man myself some might think. When I look in the mirror, it is absolutely clear to me that I am at least 43, maybe older. There is a natural tiredness to my face that says, "I've been at this now for about 43 years straight without any break." But if I'm not looking in the mirror, I couldn't guess my own age. It could be anything. For example, when I sit on the toilet and look down at my feet, I often start rearranging the way my feet are, trying to figure out a better stance for hitting a baseball. I realize now that I never could hit very well because my stance was all wrong. I liked to copy my favorite players even though I couldn't hit at all when I stood like them. Now I understand what my limitations are. I think I could be a better hitter if I could only figure out my feet. And just when I think I'm close, I remember that I'm just a middle-aged guy sitting on the toilet. But I could just as easily be 18.

Eighteen was not a bad time in my life; I was playing American Legion baseball. I was a pitcher and when I didn't pitch, I caught. I was a pretty damn good pitcher, if I do say so myself. I was a flamethrower, but sometimes control was a problem. I was always trying the throw the ball right through the catcher's mitt, through the catcher, through the umpire and through the backstop. I thought if nothing was in my way, I could throw a ball so hard that it would never stop, that it would just go and go until it broke right out of gravity's pull and then it would go on forever. Unfortunately, that mentality often cost me. One headline in the paper said, "Legion Pitcher Fans 16 and Walks 16." I did win the game, though, 9-8. I even got a couple of hits, which made it all the better. A single and triple, I think. Yes, the triple was on a low outside curve that I just got a piece of. The right fielder tried to make a diving catch but ended up with a mouth full of dirt. By the time they tracked the ball down I was standin' on third. I can still feel that wind in my face in that long looping course around the bases, left foot on the inside corner of the bag so I could launch myself toward the next base, and then a slide into third, not just any slide, but down on my hip and back up on my feet as I reached the sack, just like in the majors. I could throw hard and run fast.

My father came to my games, even though I told him not to. He played baseball when he was a kid. First base. He never talked about it. He bought me a first baseman's glove when I was about six and I didn't know what to do with it. I just wanted a regular mitt. He got angry and yelled and sent me to my room. My mother came up afterwards to try and make things right. She always did that. My mother regularly traveled a well-beaten path between my father and me. That's when I found out he played first base. She told me. I guess he was good; all section team in high school.

So he came to my games no matter what I said, but he tried to stay out of sight. There was always a point in the game when I would hear him yell. I'd look around while I rubbed up the ball, expecting to see him by the dugout or hiding near a tree or sitting in a car near the road. His voice would come from nowhere and everywhere. I'd find him finally, but he wouldn't look at me. I don't know what he was thinking, maybe that I would figure he wasn't really there for the game, that he just happened to be at the park, just happened to be at the game, just happened to be my father. He was like that. He would be around, but never so close that I felt he was really there.

My father grew up without any parents. They died in a car crash when he was seven or eight and he went into an orphanage until he was grown. He used to say he was glad he never got adopted, that he wouldn't want some family to buy him like he was an animal in a pet store, but I never believed a word of it. His eyes told me a different story. I tried to think of him as a little boy. Maybe Sundays they let people come in to shop for kids, people who couldn't have their own, and he would scrub himself up good and put on whatever clothes he had and try to be as cute as he could and every week they would leave and he would stay. No, I never believed a word of it. His eyes looked too sad.

He never said much about his parents. I have a few pictures, though, that I stole from his trunk in the attic. His father was a big sonofabitch, I mean wide. He's wearing one of those straw hats that men used to think were cool for some reason. And he's looking at the camera like he's totally sure that the future will be good, like maybe he knows I'm looking back at him and he's smiling at me. I guess it was taken on a trip that he and my grandmother took to Niagara Falls. She's standing right beside him. When I look closely, I can see that they are holding hands, that they're hands are close to their sides, touching. I had to use a magnifying glass the first time I noticed it. My father isn't in the picture. Maybe he wasn't born yet, or maybe he's standing beside the person taking the picture. Anyway, my grandmother's head is tilted back slightly as she leans forward smiling, like maybe she was just about to laugh. I wonder what was so funny in their lives right then. I'm sure that no one was saying, "Hey, you're gonna die in a car crash someday and your son is gonna be raised in an orphanage and it's gonna fuck him up for all time and someday he'll have a son who will be almost as fucked up as him." I don't think they'd be smiling if they knew the truth of what was to come. Maybe that's best. Maybe it's best that we know almost nothing about almost everything. Then we can make up whatever we want to believe about the future, and we can smile into the camera with Niagara Falls in the background.

When I close my eyes and think hard about my mother and father, I can imagine finding a picture of them in the dictionary beside the word "incompatible." They defined it. At least when I knew them both. Maybe it was different before I came along. It's hard to imagine.

They never talked about what it was like before me. They were so quiet about their past that it wasn't until I was almost grown that it donned on me that maybe they did exist before I was born. There are a few pictures of them young. They do have that stupid innocent look about them that you must need in order to marry, in order to say forever or if not forever at least until someone dies. I wonder how long it was before one of them started to wish that the other would die?

I never saw them hold hands like my grandparents in the picture. Mostly they orbited each other. They could glide around the kitchen and never touch, not even once, and yet they were stuck together like glue. My mother would cry to me asking why my father was the way he was. He, of course, wasn't there to answer these crucial questions. Usually the car was cranking up just as my mother was asking me the $64,000 question. I was barely out of diapers, for chrissakes. I would stand there and just look at her, dumb as a stump, until she would yell at me, "Why!" Then I would cry and she would cry and my father would drive away. And that's the way it was and the way I always figured it would be. When you're a kid, you don't have any sense of time passing. The future doesn't even exist. It's like you have all the time in the world before you even have to pay any attention to it passing by. So kids never think things are gonna change; they figure, "This is the way it is." That's the way I felt. This was the way it would always be. I would always be watching my father's back as he left and my mother's hands over her face while she cried. Pass the mash potatoes and cole slaw, normal as can be. But I was wrong.

2

The guys at the shop sent me a card. I have it here on the desk, but I won't read it to you because it's one of those mushy cards that over states how people really feel. I think they picked it because they didn't know how I was doing and were afraid if they sent me something funny, I might take it wrong and kill everyone here with an ice pick. So they went for sincere instead. No one ever goes crazy over sincere. Everyone signed it, which is pretty nice considering most of these guys probably never wrote a letter in their lives. There are ten names on it, with little notes, like "Hang in there," and "Get well soon."

One says, "I'm praying for you." That one means the most, which would actually surprise a lot of people. I mean I don't go to church anymore or anything like that. I'm not a fanatic. In fact if someone asked me if I believed in God, I would probably say "no," because when you talk about it out loud it seems like the most foolish thing ever, right there with the Tooth Fairy and the Easter Bunny. I would say, "How can you believe there is some big old man in the sky who watches over everything in the world and is all powerful. Look around you for chrissakes, does it look like anyone is in charge? And if there is someone in charge, would you say he's doing a good job?" I mean if you hired someone to be in charge of the world and everything that happens, wouldn't you fire the sonofabitch almost immediately after looking around at all the wars and famines and petty bullshit that goes on day in and day out? It's just beyond all understanding.

14

But when no one's around and I don't have to talk out loud about it or try to explain it, I can't seem to shake the thought that maybe there's something out there or in here or somewhere. But it's a small thing that's hard to see and it needs to be held careful like, and not tossed around like a goddam baseball or something. It's not all-powerful at all. It's just this thing that gets up inside you and makes you wonder about things and makes you feel sad about the world and what a fucking mess it is and yet what a great thing it is all at the same time. It doesn't make any sense and I knew I wouldn't be able to say it right if I tried to write it. Maybe I should just be quiet about it. Maybe it's not for words at all. Maybe it's just a silent thing. I don't know. I guess that's the bottom line about God. Mostly, I just don't know, but I like to think that when someone says he's praying for you that it means something, that something gets stirred up in a different way, not that everything will be fixed but that everything will be okay, even if it's not better.

I've known some of these guys for more than twenty years. Billy graduated high school with me. We weren't friends or anything then, but we started here the same summer and have gotten to know each other pretty well. He was married there for a while, but his wife left him for the car dealer who sold them their new Saturn. Billy's got the Saturn, but he ain't got a wife anymore. She got the kids, too, which just about kills Billy. I've known Warren for almost as long. He's a biker type, with a big Hog that he parks in the lot. But he also does sculpture of some kind. He talks about it but I don't quite get it. Big metal things that he plants in his front yard. Looks like a bunch of tinker toys with glandular problems to me, but I'm no artist. And there's May, who's one of the guys, too, even though she's no guy at all. May's tough as any of the other guys, you don't fuck with May. She's a crane operator and they're just a little left of center to begin with. I saw her swing her hook into some guy once and sent him flying. He had been talking trash to her about sex and stuff and she just wasn't gonna take it. I like that about May, she doesn't take shit from anyone. And then there's Don. I knew him best because we worked side by side for so long.

Over the years you get to know a little bit about most all of them. When you write some of it down, it sounds like you know them real well, but when you think it's taken twenty years to learn this much, then you see you don't really know them well at all. I mean I don't know what makes most of them tick or what they dream about. Hell, I don't even know what some of them like to eat or what they do on the weekends. They could say the same thing about me. Still, I like that I know something about them and that we've been in the same place together for so long that we can't avoid knowing something about each other, even if it's only a little bit.

My father got me a job at Wilson's Manufacturing when I got out of high school. I hated him for it at the time. I didn't want to work. I didn't want to stay in this shit hole of a city, but I didn't have any other prospects, as they say, so I took it. He was a dispatcher at the time, working on the loading dock and I was working in janitorial, cleaning the crap off of toilets. I learned a lot about how filthy people are on that job. I hated it, but it paid me the first money I ever had and when I got that check every two weeks, I felt like Rockefeller himself. It was a good feeling. My father always said, "Money makes the man," and when my pocket was full, I knew exactly what he meant. I was a clothes hound in those days, so I would go downtown to Oswald's on Friday night and buy some new threads and then I'd hit the Oasis and slosh a few with whoever was there, maybe shoot some pool, get home around 2 and fall into bed dead tired, feeling like I had spent myself completely.

Times change. I don't work in janitorial anymore. And I don't go out to the O anymore. I work on the engineering side in the blue print office. It's kind of like a giant morgue with all these bins full of prints for different equipment that we make, mostly construction equipment. I don't work there, thank God, just pulling prints all day long. I work on the other side where the big blue print copiers are. When a draftsman or one of the big bosses calls down for a job, they pull all the prints and then send them to me with an order for how many copies they want. Then I make the copies. It's not as easy as it sounds. These are big prints, 24X36, and some of them look like shit, and I have to make the best possible copy I can. "You can't make chicken soup out of chicken shit." That's what Don would say. Don's the checker. After I make the copies, I slide the job over to him and he puts his rubber thumb on and counts the copies and stamps them all before they go back upstairs to the drafting floor.

The machines burn the copies using ammonia, which is pretty dangerous stuff if it leaks. I have to change the tanks in the back of the copier and it's more than a little tricky. Once I tighten the valve after rolling the new tank in place, I fold a piece of yellow copier paper over the valve. If it turns blue, I've got a leak and I have to start all over again. Sometimes when I'm hooking it all up, ammonia seeps out and knocks me completely on my heels. It gets in my throat and closes it almost immediately and if I don't either find the leak or get out of there in a minute or so, I could be dead meat. So it's kinda dangerous if you think about it. Putting my life on the line so that Wilson can keep building the machines and equipment that keep the money coming in that pays my salary. When I think of it like that, my job doesn't seem like such a dead end.

I always thought I'd get Don's job someday, which pays more even though he doesn't do much. Don is younger than me, but he can't hardly do his job because of the terrible arthritis he's got all over everywhere. Sometimes when I come in in the morning, he's just sitting there, bent over the table holding his head in his gnarled hands, counting out his pills and slowly taking them with his coffee. His body is all shriveled and twisted, pretzel-like. He looks odd because his feet haven't shrunk like the rest of his body; it's like he's wearing boats on his feet. They look hard to carry when he walks. Actually, he doesn't pick them up, he shuffles. He doesn't use a cane or nothing because he doesn't want to look "invalidish," as he puts it.

Looking back, I don't know if I'd say Don and I had been friends. We never got together outside work. He couldn't do much of anything. He always sat on his porch and listened to baseball on the weekend, while his family lived their lives around him. His wife was young and so were his kids. He just sat there and they were in constant motion around him. But if you added up all the words I have said in 25 years, I've probably said more of them to Don than anyone else. Fewer toward the end when his arthritis had got so bad he could hardly speak.

Don had taught me a lot of important things along the way, like how to make sure you always had work backed up on the table so when the big bosses came through, you weren't just doin' nothing. I used to work fast so I could sit and relax, even read a magazine, but he taught me not to get my work done so fast. Let a job sit on the table in case someone comes through, he'd say. Then it always looked like there was work to do. I resisted Don's wisdom in the beginning. I thought that it was better to get the job done fast so that whoever was waiting for the prints could get to their job faster. I thought the faster you worked the better, but Don convinced me finally that the faster you work, the less you have to do, so the more chances there are that you'll get laid off. Over the years he'd been right. Georgey used to work with us. He was a printer like me and he got laid off, just like that. No one upstairs gets laid off, for fucking sure, but the little people downstairs get laid off if they aren't smart. So Don taught me how to be smart, how to work steady, but work slow. How to stretch the jobs out so you're never empty of things to do. That way you look like you're not expendable, even though if someone watched you all day they'd know you actually were.

I always thought I'd get his job. Not that it's a giant leap up the corporate ladder or anything, but it was about two dollars more an hour and I would be like a boss. When the engineers from upstairs came down to check on a job, they never talked to me. They talked to Don even though I knew as much as him. He was in charge of the jobs and, I guess, he was in charge of me, although he never acted like it. He never treated me like I was his underling. If I was a little late in the morning or had to leave early in the afternoon, he didn't care. He always let me kind of run myself. I would have liked being a boss, even a little boss with only one person answering to me. I would have been fair, but I would have been the one that people talked to and asked questions. I would have liked that. Sure was a damn surprise when it didn't come down that way after Don died. Came as a kind of a blow, you might say.

My father must have learned the same lessons that Don learned about keeping a job, because he's never been laid off. He's had a job at Wilson's for nearly 40 years. He must be a good worker because everyone says he is. Your old man, they say, that sonofabitch is a hard worker. He even got an award for never missing a day of work for over 20 years. The Iron Man, they called him, a goddam workingman's Cal Ripken. Always puzzled me because of how little he did the rest of the time. Mainly he sat at home and drank. I don't know what his body was made of that he could drink so much and still work. Working so hard was like his protection against anyone saying he had a drinking problem. No one bothered him much about it, because he showed up. Showing up is most of what you have to do in life, he would say.

About the only one who would bother him about his drinking was my mother. That wasn't all the time, mind you. Sometimes she would sit at the table and drink with him and they'd laugh together and seem to be having fun. But I knew it wasn't so simple as that. I knew she was pulling some guerilla warfare shit on him. She was acting like she was on his side and then when the time was right, she'd want to stop. It was always before he wanted to stop, so she might sip on another beer and then try again. She would distract him with something on TV or talk about me or ask him to go for a walk. About then he'd see through the whole thing and start in on her. "I know what you're trying to do," he'd say. Then he'd laugh at her and go to the frig for another beer. She'd get quiet then. Sometimes it would stop there. She would give up and leave him at the table, looking all pathetic and alone. Sometimes she would make the mistake of saying something more, sometimes it was nasty, "You're a waste of a man," she might say. He'd laugh at her some more and then she might yell at him or she might knock over a chair. He'd get all calm while she was going off, but then like a cobra, he'd strike, maybe he'd hit her only once, but that was enough. She'd cry and head off to her bedroom, calling me to follow her, which I always did. He'd say, "Yeah, you go with your momma, little baby boy."

Other times it was worse. They would start in on each other and the yelling would get to be too much for me so I'd go to my bedroom and hide in my closet. I'd sit there until I couldn't hear any more hollering or crying or swearing, and then I'd sit there just a little longer to make sure. And sometimes I would stay there for hours and my mother would find me curled up, asleep on a bed of dirty clothes. And she'd say, "Honey, what are you doin' in here?" gentle and sincerely confused, like she didn't have a clue. She would smile at me and hold me and put me to bed and read me a story, just like normal. And I'd think I was the crazy one.

My father rarely lifted the shades so you could see him clear. There was the time after my mother died when he came home drunk and sad and was talking all in circles about my mother and how he'd done everything he could for her, how he'd given her a home and he'd made a life for her and how he loved her. And he said, "What was it, boy? Why didn't she ever love me? Why didn't she ever once just look at me for who I was and just love me without wantin' something different or something more?" I was a kid and didn't know what to say. I just looked at him, bent over like he was, all in tears and looking lost. I just couldn't bring myself to go to him, to touch him or even speak. I had heard and seen too many things in my short life that made it impossible for me to reach across the divide, too many to believe what my father was saying. But it did make me wonder about him. Who was he after all?

Even though I couldn't get close to him, I stayed interested in him for a time. When I was young, I would watch him from my bedroom window as he puttered in the garage with all his tools and the hood of the car open. He wouldn't let me near the car when he was working on it, but I'd watch him, curious, like I was at the zoo and he was some exotic animal, the only one in captivity, except he didn't know he was. I'd watch him and wonder how he learned so much about engines and how he knew just what to do. And when he'd get angry at the car I'd duck behind the shade and wait for the storm to pass and then I'd watch some more. Sometimes he sang while he worked, some old tunes I didn't know, but it made me think he was happy at least for a moment, and I wondered why I couldn't be a part of what made him happy.

My mother might come into my room then and see me at the window. She'd say, "What are you doin' little man?" and I wouldn't say anything at first and then she'd say, "What is it?" and I'd ask her why he didn't like me. Her face would turn all red and sorrowful and then she'd cry and bury her head in my shirt and I would pat her shoulder and she would eventually stop crying, but she would never answer my question. Sometimes I wondered if she was truly sad or was just falling apart on me so she wouldn't have to tell me the awful truth—my father hated me. When you ask someone a hard question like that and they don't answer, you have to figure the worst. So I assumed my father hated me, that he saw me as a piece of her, nothing more.

That used to bother me before all the really bad times hit. I used to watch other kids and their dads and pretend that I had the same thing. I would dive into my fantasy and talk about my father the way other kids talked about theirs—yeah, we played catch together all the time, and, *of course* we went to the amusement park and rode the Jack Rabbit and he held me tight so I wouldn't scream and I had to tell him to let go even though I secretly liked it. I played along with all the stories my friends told, even though I knew it was a lie. A lie was so much better than the truth. At least it made me feel better. Maybe if I wished hard enough, the lie would turn into the truth. That's how a kid gets all turned around and confused. Pretty soon you don't know what's true and what ain't.

I've passed some kind of safety test, because today they let me go outside on my own. I got to sit on the bench out front where all the other burnouts go to smoke and stare. The air had that early spring smell to it, like fresh wet dirt and earthworms. In the east the sun sat the rooftops and was soft and orange and so gentle you could look right at it without squinting. It rained last night and everything looked clean except for a pile of dirty snow left over from the last storm of the season. To the south I could see a steady line moving toward the northwest, snaking across the sky, the geese returning. Soon I could hear their wonderfully mournful sounds, their wings batting the air on the round trip that never ends. My father used to take me to the nature preserve west of here and we would watch the geese land in the water, so graceful. They would take the air into the pocket of their wings and reach out for the surface of the water and then, whoosh, they would sit down in the pond and settle in. I would hold my arms out, thinking I could fly, too, if only I could take the wind into my pockets like the geese.

I heard a story once about an American businessman who asked a famous Japanese artist to paint a picture for his office. It took many months before the painting was done. The guy had to fly the whole way to Japan to get it. He was very eager to see what the artist had done, but when he saw the painting, he was more than a little disappointed. Actually he was pissed. It was a very large canvas. In one corner was the branch of a tree in winter, all naked and craggy. On the tip of the branch was a small bird. That's all there was. Nothing more. The rest of the canvass was empty. The guy asked why the hell the artist didn't fill more of the canvas, and the artist said, "Then there would be no room for the bird to fly." The first time I heard that story, I thought, "Yes." I knew what he meant even though I couldn't put it into words. I just knew that my own life didn't leave any room for me to fly. I could stand on the limb and look, but I couldn't grab the breeze, and take off. I just couldn't.

My therapist, Jacob, asked me, "Why?" and I said, "How the fuck am I supposed to know." He didn't ask me that question again. I guess he thought I didn't want to talk about it, when all I was saying was, "How the fuck am I supposed to know?" Can someone answer that question for me? How am I supposed to know why my life never took off? It's obvious that I don't know. If I knew, I would do something about it. My life just stopped dead a long time ago and it's been like I'm just waiting now, waiting here at my own personal bus stop for a bus that isn't gonna come. Even though I know that, I still wait. It's crazy and so I'm here. When your life stops and you don't know how to make it start, they take you off the road, they take you in for repairs, they recall you because of a defect and you leave the world for a while to figure things out if you're lucky. Or you just leave the world, permanent, like Harold. He could fly. I need more canvas.

I really wanted Don's job. That would have made a big difference. Some days when Don was in a lot of pain and the workload wasn't large at all, he would ask me to stamp as well as copy. And I would do it. It wasn't a big deal, not a lot of extra work, actually. I liked Don and was glad to help him out. We had an old easy chair in the corner and I would help him sit down so he could relax and he would thank me like I had saved his life, "Jesus, thanks buddy, I really mean it." And sometimes he'd stay there all morning, although he tried not to. It was worse if he didn't move for long periods of time. I couldn't imagine it being worse because I saw him move and he always looked like he was walking on glass, the pain made him sweat and took his breath away. I'd ask him why he didn't get on disability. He sure as hell could get it if he wanted, but he'd say, "I'm not fucking disabled, you asshole!" It really pissed him off when I would suggest it. I just wanted to be helpful but he didn't want his family to be "no welfare trash." He said welfare trash like it was one word. "How much do you think my kids are gonna respect me if I stop working and we have to go on welfare?"

I wondered what his kids thought of him. I wondered if they understood what he went through or if it just pissed them off that he couldn't do anything with them. Don's son was 12 when Don died. He played baseball, which really pleased Don. Don was a fanatic about baseball, even more then me. He loved his Pirates even though they were so awful. "Bring back Stargell and Clemente and Maz," he'd say. But he was loyal and I admired that. His wife would drive him to his son's games and he would walk the hundred yards from the parking lot to the bleachers to watch his kid play right field. Sometimes it was the third inning before he got there, but he'd go, like every step was his way of saying, "I love you," to his son. I wonder if his son appreciated that? Who knows about kids? Maybe he was embarrassed that his old man looked so different.

Don's daughter was 13 and quite a looker for her age. I mean she made me turn my head a few times, looked at least 18, which made Don crazy. They fought a lot in recent years. She had a boyfriend and I think they got in a mess once, because Don had to take a personal day to deal with some "family matters," and I know it wasn't about him. I know he was worried about her getting laid. He hated the boyfriend. He knew all the kid wanted was to get in his daughter's pants, and why not? If I was that age and had her as a girlfriend, that's exactly what I'd want, too. But he couldn't see that about her. He couldn't see that despite her age, she was a damn woman. He just saw his little girl, the one who used to sit on his lap before his arthritis got so bad that no one could get close to him at all. What a terrible shame. Here's a guy who genuinely loved to be close to people and his body wouldn't let him.

It was just a few feet from where I stood in front of the blueprint machine to where Don sat behind the checking table, but when I was covering for him, sitting in his place, everything looked different. I could see the whole room, the tanks of ammonia in the far corner, the file room where Ellen and Jolene worked and the hanging files in the hall where the oldest prints were kept. And I could see my space in front of the machine in a way that I couldn't when I was in it. I could see how small it was. I could see the spot worn through the linoleum floor where I shifted my weight back and forth each time I removed a print. I could see how I was walking mile upon mile in the same place. I'd put the rubber thumb on and I'd feel like I had an important role to play. I had to stamp everything that left that room. My mark on each copy signified that it was done right and was ready to go. I was the gatekeeper. Every job that went back up to the engineering floor or over to the mill had to pass through my inspection. If a print was missing, who knows what problems it could cause. We could lose weeks on a job or maybe even lose a customer if we missed a deadline.

But if I checked things right, everything after me would go smooth. I was an important piece of the puzzle. If I were missing, someone would notice for sure.

So it never bothered me when Don needed to rest. In fact on some days I would ask him if he wanted a break. I'd tell him he was looking a little tired, did he need to sack out for a while. Usually he'd say, "No," but from time to time he'd take me up on it. It felt good knowing that someday I would get his job. Who else would want it? The ladies next door didn't know anything about what we did and they weren't interested in being near the machine. It was too loud and there was the constant smell of ammonia in the air. Georgey had been gone for five years and they never replaced him, so there wasn't anyone else except me to take it over. Anyone could learn my job, because I would be there to teach him, but only I knew Don's job.

About five months ago, Don's wife, Lorraine, called the office one morning to say that Don wasn't feeling well and wouldn't be in. I didn't think that much of it. Don had missed more work than usual in the last year because of doctors' appointments and being in too much pain. But one day turned into two and then three and I began to wonder what was going on, so I called his house to talk to Lorraine and she said he was in the hospital and it didn't look good. I thought, Jesus Christ. She said he hadn't been feeling well for quite some time, as if I didn't know. I wanted to say, "Look, I spend almost as much time with him as you do." She said he had developed pneumonia and wasn't doing well at all. She felt he was giving up. She talked like he was going to die or something.

When she said that, I couldn't imagine what she meant. Don never gave up. He was a tough little sonofabitch. Not long ago I had to yell at him for trying to unload the copy paper off the truck because it was going to kill him. He got royally pissed at me for that. He told me to go to hell and that I would never be half the man he was. I laughed at him as he shuffled back to his chair, but I knew he meant it. I knew he was not a quitter.

I never liked hospitals much, but I forced myself to go see him. I hate that medicine smell that gets stuck in your nose and throat, and I hate the white coats with the doctor's name embroidered on the pocket, everything is white, not just clean, worse than clean; sterile, antiseptic, untouchable, just like the way they treat you, untouchable. You're just a bunch of body parts to them. They look right past the person so they can see whatever part strikes their fancy. They don't give two shits about you, about how sick you feel or how afraid you might be, they just care about whatever numbers show up on their dials or whatever sounds they can hear through their scopes, but they don't really want to listen or look at all.

As soon as I walked into the lobby, I could feel things closing in on me. It felt hotter than hell so I stopped in the men's room and washed my face off. Then I headed down the corridor to the elevator. There were colored stripes on the floor and little colored tags on the ceiling with letters on them so you'd know where you were going. The light was piercing like they're X-raying you as you walk along. Passed the family waiting room with all the people sitting there looking at magazines, trying to pretend they were reading. There was an older woman at the desk with a telephone sitting in front of her. Everyone was waiting for a call, hoping that mom's gall bladder came out okay or Uncle Harry's tumor wasn't cancer.

There was one little boy lying on a couch with his head in his mother's lap. His mother was running her fingers through his hair very slowly and I could see that his eyes were sort of glazed over and he was in another world. When I was a kid and didn't want to go to sleep, I would ask my mother to scratch my back. She always sighed, knowing what I was up to, but she always did it. I would close my eyes and enjoy the feel of her nails and after a time, she would start combing my hair with her fingers and she would sing, "Hush-a-bye, don't you cry, go to sleepy little baby; when you wake, you shall have, all the pretty little horses…" I would breathe my mother in as she sang. The smell of cigarettes and coffee and maybe a beer and even some perfume or powder topping it off. Sounds pretty awful when I write it out like this, like she was some chain smoking drunk or something, but I loved the smell of her as I sank slowly into a world between sleep and being awake, a world in which my mother's hand was always on my back and I felt okay, like I could go to sleep and not worry.

I must have looked strange, because the next thing I knew, the lady from the desk was standing in front of me. "Are you okay, sir?" she asked. I said, "What?" kind of confused and offended that she was right there in my face. "Are you okay?" she asked again, her face all screwed up into a worry, her head tilted over slightly. She had the face of a woman who hoped that powder would hide the years, yet a kind face. "Yeah," I said, "I'm okay." My face was damp and she was handing me a tissue. I backed away and looked at her for a second and then I noticed that everyone was looking at me. "Are you waiting to hear?" she asked. "Hear what?" I said. "Are you waiting to hear about a loved one? Is someone you know having surgery?" "No, no," I said, "I'm just visiting a friend, no surgery, everything's okay. I mean he's pretty sick but he's not having surgery or anything." She just smiled at me strange, like I had asked her if the cafeteria served poop sandwiches. I said "Thanks," for no particular reason. It seemed like a good way to end the conversation.

I was sweating now and angry that I let that lady get under my skin. If she would have just stayed behind her desk, everything would have been fine. But she had to ask if she could help. Help ain't help unless you ask for it, and I wasn't asking. I hate when people assume you need help. Makes me feel small and stupid and incapable of taking care of myself. You see that look everywhere in the hospital; people ready to help whether you want them to or not. I see it everyday here, on my floor, too. The social workers and the interns and all the other little helpers who look at you with their long-suffering faces because they know they're superior to you; they know that they can walk out at the end of the day and go home to their boyfriends or wives and say, "I helped someone today" or "Working with these people makes me realize how good I have it." I wasn't put here to remind others how well they have it. I am tired of being someone else's scenery, tired of being someone else's background. I don't want to be the molding in someone else's game room. I might not know why exactly I was put here, but I know it wasn't for that. At least, I hope not.

Anyway, I got out of there and went back to the men's room. This time I took a seat and tried to get my head together. "What the fuck is wrong with you?" I asked myself. Not a question in search of an answer. Not really a question at all. It was more of a pull-yourself-together thing, an attempt to shake myself hard and wake myself up. "You've got to see Don, you asshole," just like my father might say it. I could hear his voice in mine, I could hear the hiss in "ass" and see the way his mouth turned up at the corners when he said it, and the way his eyes looked through me, like he was erasing me. I started to sweat again and the stall began to swirl. Before I knew it I was lying on the floor, panting for breath and soaked like I just came from a shower. I couldn't get up. I didn't want to. I knew I couldn't fall off the floor if I was lying down, so I just stayed there. It was steady and it felt cold and soothing. I thought I was going to throw up, but it passed. I could feel myself melting into the cracks in the tile. I thought I might trickle away and just be gone. I closed my eyes for a minute, but the door opened, so I scrambled back onto the john and sat for several minutes, my hands holding my head so it wouldn't spin away.

Whoever it was, he left and I was alone again. I had stopped sweating and was certain that I wouldn't pass out. My heart beat steady and hard, like it was trying to escape, like if it could break through my chest, it would and if it did, it would be free to go. It beat and beat and beat. I put my hand on my chest and felt the hard rhythm and knew that even though I might not be okay, I was still here. I also knew that I wasn't going to see Don.

I threw more water on my face and then stepped back into the corridor. The flow of people continued steady in both directions. No one seemed to notice that I was messed up, which was fine with me. They didn't need to know that I didn't have any emotional stamina. I'll bet some of them had enough to run a marathon, which is what having a loved one in the hospital is anyway. Some could probably sprint, but not last the whole race. But I felt like I could barely walk. Like I was limping but no one could see it, no one could see the crutches under my arms, the lame gait, the shoulders bent. I straightened my back, trying to seem upright. I took a deep breath and then headed for the front entrance. I was starting to calm down.

As I reached the lobby, a woman walking towards me smiled and I nodded. Usually people look away after such a small politeness, but she looked and even smiled more broadly. She said "Hi" and it donned on me. It was Lorraine, Don's wife. "Hi, how are you?" I said, surprised at how upbeat I sounded. Would she think I was happy that Don was so sick?

"Did you get to see him? Or was he too groggy to know you were there? He's in and out of it a lot because his breathing is so bad." She looked down at the floor, as if she was trying to figure something out.

"Yeah, I saw him," I lied. "But he was so tired, I don't know if he'll remember." I was ready to go. "Well," I said, about to take a step toward the door.

"How did you think he looked today? I mean his color is always so awful that I can't tell anymore how he's doing. I just don't know what a normal person looks like when they're sick. Don hasn't been normal for so long, it's just hard to tell. What did you think?"

What was I supposed to say? She was right. As long as I've known Don he's looked like shit. His skin is pasty and thin, like you could tear it away from the bone without any effort at all.

"I thought he looked pretty good."

"Really?" she said, hopeful. "I'm afraid he's getting weaker every day. I don't know what's going to happen. The doctors don't seem to have any answers. They just look at me real sad, but they don't tell me much and I can't seem to see things straight enough to judge, is he dying or what?" I was stuck now. I didn't know what to say and started fearing that I might never reach the parking garage.

"You know, he told me that you wouldn't come to see him. He said it would be too hard, something about not liking hospitals. I guess you showed him, though," she said with a nervous laugh. Actually Lorraine, I didn't see him. He was right. I almost passed out in the family waiting area and then I had to go to the men's room where I laid in the stall with my face practically in the toilet because I thought it was the only way to keep from collapsing entirely.

"Yeah, I guess I did." I laughed, too.

There was silence now and she didn't seem to want to go anywhere.

"Quite a guy, Don," I said. "You know I've probably had more conversations with him than anyone else in my whole life." Where was this coming from? "We just talk about nothing and everything, you know."

"He's a talker. He always thought of you as a friend," she said.

Really, I thought. I would never have guessed that. I mean, we got along, but being friends, I wasn't sure what that meant exactly. Maybe she was being nice.

"I've always thought of him as a friend too, a best friend in a way." I was learning this as it came out of my mouth.

She asked me if I'd like a cup of coffee and despite my best understanding of myself, I said, "Sure," so we went to the coffee shop.

We didn't talk while we were in line. For a moment I thought I could slip away and she wouldn't even notice. She'd get her coffee and go upstairs to Don's room and that would be it. But I didn't move. I waited in line until it was our turn. When she reached into her purse, I said, "I'll get this," and she smiled again and said, "Thank you." Next thing I knew we were sitting at a table talking.

She talked about their kids and a little about the problems with their daughter and I acted like I didn't know anything, because I figured Don wouldn't want me to let on that I knew their business. Their son wanted to take karate lessons and they weren't sure if they should let him. They didn't want to encourage any "violent tendencies." She seemed to relax a little. You could tell she loved her kids to death the way she talked about them. She smiled in spite of herself, because I could see that there wasn't really a smile in her eyes. I was surprised how easy it was to talk. Maybe because all I had to do was nod my head or smile or say "oh" or "really." That's all she seemed to need. It felt good to be with someone.

"You know, Don has already made plans for his funeral."

Not what I wanted to talk about. There was a long silence.

"He has?"

More silence. Her eyes were filling up now and I didn't have a clue what to do. I pulled a napkin from the dispenser, "Here."

"Thank you." More silence. I started feeling hot again.

"I'm sorry," she said, "I shouldn't be going on like this with you."

"That's okay."

"But he has. He's made his plans. He's picked out music and he wants some readings."

"Uh huh." We were in foreign territory now. I figured the less I said the less likely I would say something wrong.

"Did he ask you?"

"What?"

"Did he ask you about the reading?"

"The reading. What reading is that?"

"The reading for his funeral. Actually it won't be a funeral. It's a memorial service. He wants to be cremated." Now she began to cry. "I'm so sorry to be doing this. Here you are, you don't really know me and here I am crying away like some baby."

I handed her another napkin.

"No, it's okay. This must be hard." She cried some more. Now I didn't know what to do. Some people were starting to look. I should never have left the bathroom. I wished she would stop crying.

"Are you okay?" She sniffled like people do when they are trying to pull it together, like they can sniff their whole insides back into place.

"Yes. I'll be okay."

"You don't really think he's gonna...?"

"I don't know."

"I mean, he's been through so much it's hard to imagine that anything could, I mean, that anything could beat him."

"Yes. I know." There was a long silence and Lorraine looked like she was packing up inside, like she had shown me too much and now she was trying to put everything back in it's place.

"I'll do it."

"What's that?"

"The reading, I'll do the reading." I thought this might make her stop crying, but what was I thinking? I was making a promise I knew I couldn't keep. I guess I was betting he wouldn't die. "I mean, I don't really think it will come to..."

"You will? Really?"

"Uh huh."

"Oh, that will mean so much to him. Do you want to come back to his room and tell."

"No, that's okay, you can tell him. I wouldn't want to overwhelm him when he's so tired and all."

I did finally reach the parking garage where I sat in my car for the longest time wondering what the hell I had gotten myself into. I should never have gone there in the first place. I knew it. How was I going to get out of this? There was no way I could get up in front of a group of people and read some poem or some Bible passage. Shit. He'd better not die. Maybe Lorraine was just being hysterical or something.

I've never been good in front of people. There was a time when my mother made me go to church. It was during one of those periods when dad was trying to reform himself. Anyway, I was in the children's choir. We rehearsed for weeks so we could sing a song on Children's Sunday. I tried to convince myself that it would be okay even though each time I pictured myself in the choir loft in front of the whole congregation my legs got weak. I thought, this is stupid, it's just a dumb song and nothing more, stop making a big thing out of it.

On Children's Sunday we gathered in the basement where we put on Jesus robes and sandals and got in a line behind the adult choir and before I knew it we were walking down the aisle. The choir loft was up behind the pulpit where you could see everything and everyone could see you. After the first hymn, we were all in place and I looked around and thought, "This isn't so bad." But when it was our turn to sing, I started thinking about where I was and that everyone was looking at me and I started to feel sick. I stopped singing and just mouthed the words and then I stopped moving my mouth and just held the songbook in front of my face trying to breathe, but I couldn't get enough breath and I started to feel sick and suddenly I threw up all over the front of my robe and onto my fake sandals.

When the song was over we all sat down. I wondered what would happen next, but I must have hidden myself good because nothing happened. I just sat there in my puke. The service went on but I smelled so bad that one by one the kids around me moved away and by the end of the service I was sitting alone, no one within ten feet, my breakfast drying on my robe, my feet slippery from the mess.

I've never stood up in front of a group of people since. Especially not to say something because a dead person asked me to. How was I going to get out of this? He'd better not die.

When I told my father, he laughed and reminded me about the choir incident. "Don't eat anything ahead of time." I just looked at him. He was quiet then and after a minute or so he said, "So, do you think Don is really gonna kick it?"

"No, I think his wife made the whole thing up so she could have a cup of coffee with me in the coffee shop. I don't know."

"Hm. I remember Don when he first came to the company. He wasn't so crippled up then. He was always a likable sort, even though he rubbed some people the wrong way with his mouth. I always liked him though." He went to the refrigerator for a beer. "Think you'll get his job?"

I actually hadn't thought about it until right then. If Don dies, I'll get his job. What a terrible wonderful thought. All of a sudden his job seemed more important than his life. All of a sudden I wanted Don to die.

31

"What kinda question is that to ask? The guy's not even dead. And maybe he won't even die. Who cares about his job," I said.

"Didn't mean nothing, I was just thinking. You probably deserve it."

"Probably deserve it?"

"Yeah." He didn't say anything more.

"Why'd you say probably."

"Nothin'. Forget about it."

"No, what did you mean?"

"I didn't mean nothin'."

"What? You don't think I should get his job?"

"I didn't say nothin' like that."

"You don't think I should get it, do you? Is that it? Or is it that you don't think I can do his fuckin' job?"

"Sure you can, I was just."

"You don't think I can do anything do you, you old shit, sittin' there in your goddam beer."

"Now wait a minute."

"Don't 'wait a minute' me."

"Shut the fuck up. Okay, you want to know what I think? I think you can do his job all right, but I think you'll fuck it up, just like you've fucked up everything else in your life. Forty-three years old and you got the lowest fucking job in the place. You know why?"

"No, you tell me, dad, tell me why. Is it because I never got a fucking ounce of anything from you."

"Don't give me that shit, don't blame me because your life isn't worth a plug nickel. Hey, don't walk away from me, I'm still your goddam father."

"The hell you are." By then I was up the stairs and in my room. There's no end to the anger. It's like Hoover Dam back there inside my head and any time I need it, all I have to do is open the valve a little and let it go. It's the least I can do for mom.

3

Today they said I might get out of here soon, which is all right by me. I'm tired of people asking me how I feel. I'm tired of sitting around in circles and listening to people whine about their shitty lives. I'm even tired of listening to *me* whine about *my* shitty life. They say I'm doing better, but I don't really know. I guess I am. I can get up in the morning now and I don't sleep all day long. They've got me on some drugs and they let me take it on my own now.

I wonder what it will be like to be outside? Not that I want to stay here, but it's like any prisoner who gets used to the shape of his cell. Going beyond the boundary is tricky. Will the canvas be too big to handle? It's brand new, in a sense. Not new, like, I've never been out there before, but new, like it's been so long that I wonder if I'll remember how to do it. I've been on the grounds a lot. They think that's a good start because I'm beyond the walls, but even I know it's not the same. The walls are still there and if I need them, I can go back. I can play at being "in the world" like a regular person, but it's just an act so long as the walls are still there to protect me or to remind me that I'm not strong enough yet.

They asked me if my father would come to pick me up and I said, "yes," but I don't know. He tried to visit me once, but I wouldn't see him. I told the nurse I didn't want to see him at all, so he never came back. I guess he called a few times, but only left messages, "Tell him his father called," things like that. He said he was sick once, but I don't know what that was all about. I hate to go back there, but I can't stay here. I don't want to see him, but, at the same time, I'm curious to see him, like feeling the need to look when you're driving past an accident.

Don used to ask me why I still lived with my father and I never found an answer that suited. I would tell him it was for financial reasons, or that I was saving up to buy a house of my own one day, or that my dad needed me around to do things, but these were mostly lies. I didn't really have an answer, I guess. I tried to leave a couple of times. Found an apartment and moved into the city for about eight months, but I hated it. I came home every day to this empty place, no one around. So I got a cat and the damn thing ran away on me. I got to know my neighbor but then he moved. I was working at a bakery, which made it almost impossible to have social life. I was working all night and into the late morning and then sleeping the rest of the time.

Somewhere in there, my father broke his leg at work and I came home to take care of him for a weekend and I just never left. I kept the apartment until the lease ran out and then I didn't renew. It wasn't like I announced that I was coming home or that my father asked me to come home, it just happened. Before that I went away to college, but that only lasted a semester. I drank my way through four months of higher education and flunked out. After a while, living at home just became a habit. Everything is so familiar and easy in a way, even though my father and I don't get along. Anymore I can't imagine living anywhere else.

There's still a lot of my mother around the house, too, even though she's been gone so long. I have my pictures and I have some of her jewelry in my room and there are still some of her clothes in the closet. For a time after she died, I could smell her in those clothes, but not anymore, not in a long while. But her clothes are there, and I like to think that I am keeping watch for her, not like she might come back, or anything crazy like that, but just keeping watch over where she was. Keeping watch over the space and making sure no one forgets. I'm glad I still have the pictures. I used to practice closing my eyes to see if I could remember her face, just like I used to listen for her voice. I felt all scared when I couldn't hear her voice anymore, so I worked hard on being able to see her face. For a long time I was able to and then for an even longer time I pretended I could still see her face, but eventually I was left with only her pictures. I would study them until

I could remember what she really looked like, not all motionless, like in the picture, but breathing and moving around. I felt better when I could. I still can every once in a while.

So I don't know if my father will pick me up. I may just call a cab.

I got two cards from Lorraine, which was very thoughtful. She must still be going through hell, now that she's a widow with two kids, so it was nice that she thought of me. She said in one note that she might move back to Massachusetts where her parents live. Probably a good idea. I still think about the memorial service a lot even though it's been a few months.

It was just as hard as I feared. Don lingered for another week or so. I didn't even try to go back, but I did call his room once. Lorraine acted all excited to hear my voice, like I was a long lost friend calling to say "Happy Birthday!" She muffled the phone, but I could hear her talking to Don and encouraging him to talk to me:

"He's called to talk to you, Don, not me...I know you're tired, but I think you should talk to him.Come on, just for a minute, it will make you feel better.I didn't say *get* better.Are you going to talk to him or not?" And then suddenly he was on.

"Hello." He sounded like he was calling from the bottom of a barrel on the other side of the moon.

"Don?"

"Yeah."

"How you doin' pal?" I was cheery because I didn't know what else to do. I couldn't see him so it was hard to know how to gauge things. I figured "cheery" was safe.

"What do you mean, how am I doin'? I'm doin' lousy, that's how I'm doing."

"How they treating you?"

"Okay, I guess, if they'd stop waking me up all night and poking me all the time." Then he started to cough and his voice trailed off. I waited, not knowing if he was coming back or not.

"Don? Are you still there?"

"Yeah, I'm here. Not goin' anywhere, I guess." I didn't know what else to say.

"How's the food? Is it as bad as they say?"

"Don't know. Haven't eaten much. They bring it, but I'm not hungry. The smell bothers me."

"Oh." Another long pause.

"Don, everyone's pulling for you down at work, you know."

"Yeah, I'm sure. Tell 'em thanks, but not to waste too much energy, I don't think I'm coming back."

"You never know about these things."

"Well, I think I know. I can see it on the nurses' faces. I can see it in my wife's face. The kids have been in but they have to leave because they get all upset and then I can't." He started to cry. I thought, Shit, what do I do now?

"Come on, Don, hang in there. I mean, you gotta keep pluggin' away, just like you always told me when I got down."

"Yeah. Yeah. I suppose." More silence.

"Well, I better get going. I imagine you're tired and all."

"Yeah."

"Take care of yourself, Don. I'll be thinking about you."

"Okay."

"Maybe I'll get over there again."

"Uh huh."

That was it. I never talked to him again and within a few days he was gone. Lorraine called me at home around 10 PM. I knew it was something bad, because no one calls the house that late. Actually, no one calls the house. She told me he just sort of slept away. The kids were with him and they held his hands and he just closed his eyes and was gone.

It was hard for me to imagine Don dead. It shouldn't have been so hard, though, because he was always very sick, but I got used to it. It seemed like the normal state of things. He would always be sick, but I never really thought about him dying. I just thought he'd go on and on the way he always did.

I hoped Lorraine would forget about the reading, but before we hung up, she asked again if I was going to do it and I said, "Yes." She thanked me and then she said she had to go. She and the kids were having a private viewing before Don was taken to the crematorium. Then he'd be really gone for good. Just a pile of ashes. I don't know what they're going to do with his ashes, if they'll sprinkle them somewhere or keep him on the shelf in the house. I read once in the "Star" that a woman slowly ate her mother's ashes over a whole year. After she was done, she said she started to behave like her mother.

She took up smoking just like her mother and she developed diabetes like her mother and she was also "visited" by her mother. Not like visions of ghosts, but inside her head. She would hear her mother talking to her, telling her what to do. Strangest damn thing I ever heard of.

I couldn't imagine eating my mother, although I guess there are some places in the world where they do eat each other. I guess the Catholic Church does that, in a way. The little Styrofoam wafer they give you is supposed to be the real live body of Jesus. Isn't that kind of the same thing, a little like cannibalism? Of course, no one really believes that the Styrofoam is actually Jesus, maybe that's the difference. It's kind of, "This is the Body of Christ," wink, wink, because you know for a fact that it's not, but you eat it anyway. And you drink the blood, too, but it's just wine, or if you're some kind of Protestant, it's grape juice, Jesus's blood-lite.

Anyway, I would have to do this thing after all. They scheduled the service for the following Saturday so that some of Don's relatives could come to town and the people who worked with him could come without missing work. On Friday Lorraine called me again and asked me to come to the church a little early to meet with the minister, so he could show me what I was reading and where I had to go.

Now I was really worried.

My father said I should have a drink or two ahead of time.

"Yeah, a couple of hits and you'll feel okay, aware enough to see what you need to read and not so drunk that you can't read it."

"That sounds like you. 'Get drunk, that solves everything'."

"Look. It's just a suggestion. You said you were all nervous and I thought a drink would help. What's the harm?"

"The harm is this is Don's memorial service and what would it look like with me showing up with alcohol on my breath. I know that doesn't matter to you. You don't have to smell yourself, but I don't want to go in there like that. Don deserves better. His wife and kids do, too."

I knew I was going to take dad's advice. It was the only possible way for me to get through this. If I had to do it with eyes wide open, I'd never make it. I'd be standing there with puke all over me again and I didn't want that to happen. I would try to stay away from people so they wouldn't be able to tell, especially the minister. I would sit somewhere by myself on the end of an aisle and I would just stay to myself like I was deep in thought or something, then no one would talk to me and no one would know. Don would appreciate the dilemma. He'd say, "Do what you have to do."

I was up early Saturday morning. The service was at 10. Actually I didn't sleep much at all and when I did I wished I hadn't. I had dreams, more like nightmares. I was at the service, but I got there late so I didn't know what I was supposed to do. The place was filled and when I walked through the door, they quickly ushered me behind a curtain up on the alter where I could stay until it was my turn. No one could see me, which was fine, but I could hear what was going on. I could hear the minister talking about the "dearly departed" and I could hear the sniffles of people in their pews and I wondered when they would call my name.

Then I heard Don's voice and I wondered if they had a recording or something, but the harder I listened, the more it sounded like Don, for real. At first I couldn't hear exactly what he was saying, but then his voice got louder: "...never recovered from his mother's death; lived his whole life with a father that he hated. He was a fair worker but he never went too far. His life stalled out early and he never lived out the promise that his parents must have had for him when he was just little, before life took over..."

I couldn't believe this. I tried to call out, but I couldn't speak. I wanted to say that Don was the one who was dead. Don was the one whose life got stalled by all his illnesses, but the words wouldn't come. I struggled to get out from behind the curtains but they fell on top of me like a shroud, and I couldn't escape.

That's when I woke up all in a tangle with my sheet. I was soaked and so was it. I looked at the clock and it was only 2:16 in the morning. For a moment, in the darkness and silence, I felt a wave of relief, like the day might never come. It was still hours away and I could sit there in my bed and watch the clock to make sure that each moment's passage was noted. That way it would all go slowly and maybe even stop, if I watched closely enough.

But, of course, the morning came.

I sat in my car across from the church parking lot for about twenty minutes trying to harden my resolve with a bottle of vodka. The first sips made me warm. It wasn't long before I felt a little numb and stupid. I watched as the minister arrived and then some other people, mostly women who were probably preparing the lunch. Lorraine arrived with the kids. She talked to them continuously as they moved slowly into the church. They looked a lot older all dressed up, especially Don's daughter. They disappeared into the front of the church. Soon a few other cars arrived, well-wishers, some people from work, others.

It was time for me to go in. When I opened the door the air hit my face and startled me. I didn't notice the curb and I stumbled, but caught myself, and figured that was a good sign that I was in charge of my faculties. In the back of the church I saw Lorraine, so I walked up to her, "Hi Lorraine," sounding a little more friendly than I expected. She looked a little worried, "Are you okay?" she asked.

"Sure, I'm fine. How are you doing today?" She didn't answer as she directed me through the sanctuary to the back of the church where the minister was waiting. I didn't really notice if there were many people in the crowd. I was feeling pretty confident at this point, feeling like I could carry this off easy as anything. The minister was friendly in a way that makes you feel like you aren't good enough or that he knows something about you that you don't want him to know. He shook my hand.

"So you're Don's friend from work who is doing the reading today."

"Yessir," I said, clear as I could. He was a little hard to follow after that. He seemed to use ten words for everyone word that was absolutely necessary. Finally I decided I didn't need to listen, I just had to look like I was listening. I shook my head whenever it seemed called for.

"Are you sure you understand? Are you okay?"

"Yep, Reverend, I'm ready to go."

"Well, let me show you the reading first," and he pulled a Bible down off his shelf and opened it somewhere in the middle. "Here it is. Psalm 139. Are you familiar with this passage?"

"Not lately, no, but I'm sure it will come to me."

"Well, you don't have to memorize it, you just have to read it. Slowly."

He handed me the big book and suggested I sit for a minute while he checked on one thing or another. So I sat. At first I couldn't find what I was supposed to be looking at, but then I saw it—139. I started to read, although the words didn't make a whole lot of sense. But I could say them and that's all that mattered. I had to get through the reading and say all the words. So I kept reading, ".Whither shall I go from thy Spirit?" it said, Whither shall I go? I didn't know what that meant but the sound of the words was soothing. I wished we talked like that all the time, all thee and thou, I'll bet we would be nicer if we did. Hard to say something like fuck thee. Doesn't sound right. It wouldn't work, so maybe we'd stop saying it.

"Whither shall I go from thy Spirit? Or whither shall I flee from thy presence? If I ascend to heaven, Thou art there! If I take the wings of the morning and dwell in the uttermost parts of the sea, even there thy hand shall lead me, and thy right hand shall hold me. If I say, 'Let only darkness cover me, and the light about me be night,' even the darkness is not dark to thee, the night is bright as day; for darkness is as light with thee." For darkness is as light with thee. I kept saying it over and over until the words didn't make sense any longer, like a child says a word over and over until it sounds like a foreign language or a joke. For the darkness is as light with thee. I couldn't figure it out and my head started to hurt from trying. I just knew I had to read it, not explain it. That was up to the Reverend.

He was back. Lorraine was with him and they both looked worried. "Are you all right?" they asked in unison. "Yes. I am fine," I said, very calm, pronouncing every word clearly. And I wasn't lying. I did feel fine. I felt like I could do anything they wanted me to do. In fact that's what I asked them, "This doesn't seem like much at all. Do you want me to read more? I could do it without any trouble," and I stood up and starting reading another passage for them, but they didn't want me to read. They said, "That's fine," and suggested I sit down again. Now they were talking between themselves and I couldn't hear exactly what they are saying. Finally Lorraine knelt down in front of me. Her eyes were very wide, her eyebrows raised.

"You know how important this is, don't you? Don wanted you to do this and I want you to do it, too, but if you're not feeling well enough..."

"Don't worry, Lorianne," I said, "I am very, very fine and I can do this." I tried to be as confident as possible, but her expression didn't change. She talked some more with the Reverend, who was patting her arm and talking in his soothing voice now.

Finally he turned to me: "Okay, this is what we'll do. Why don't you wait in my office and when the time comes for your reading, I'll have someone bring you in. That way you can sit here and relax." Someone came to the door with some coffee. "There you go, have some coffee." This was great, I thought. "Thanks!" Then they left. I could hear the organ start and I figured the service was beginning. I leaned back on the leather sofa and thought what a good deal being a minister was. You have your own office, with lots of books and shelves and great furniture and everyone looks up to you. For a minute, I thought I should have gone to church more, the way mom wanted me to. I could have been a minister, except I hated church. Maybe it was different when you were the boss. Maybe that made it more interesting because everyone had to pay attention to you, like you were a junior God. They had to do what you said because they didn't know for sure if you had the inside news on what God really wanted. Like those Jonestown people, poor bastards, who believed what that guy told them and now they're all dead.

I wouldn't do anything like that. I would tell people to do good things to each other, especially to their kids, and all, and not to lie and hold grudges so long that you can't hold anything else inside, like the only job you got in the world is to hold some weight against someone else, even someone close to you. I could do a lot of good, I'll bet. It would be great having everyone look up to me and I could smile at them and they would feel all good. And I'll bet the women would do anything for me that I wanted. I mean, I'm a Reverend, right, so if I told them to go to bed with me, they would, maybe. They might let me touch them real soft and gentle and maybe they would smile at me too and want to hold me close and their skin would smell sweet like some damned incense or something and I would lay there like I was in heaven. And I wouldn't be alone.

There was a knock at the door. A woman poked her head in.

"It's time."

"Okey-dokey." I was ready. I stood up a little too quick and for a minute the room was spinning. She reached out for my arm, but I told her, No, I was fine, and she just looked at me like I peed my pants or something.

I followed her down the hall and the organ music got louder until we reached the big oak doors at the back of the sanctuary. They ran the whole way to the ceiling and creaked when you opened them. I half expected to find Vincent Price on the other side, but instead there was a whole lot of people and they all turned to look at me at the same time, like someone told them my zipper would be down and they should take a good long look. I smiled at them and stood there for a moment getting my bearings. The altar was to my right and on the other side I could see Rev. sitting in his black robe, hunched forward towards me, his glasses on the end of his nose. He smiled timid-like and nodded to me like I should come up, so I did.

I stood in front of the pulpit, holding onto the sides, just like I'd seen preachers in the movies. The Bible was already open to my reading and the words were frighteningly big, like they were jumping off the pages at me, so big I had a hard time taking them all in. I looked around and behind me the singer and the organist were sitting in the choir loft. The organist smiled and I smiled back and she nodded and I waved. Then she stopped smiling.

I turned to the crowd and couldn't tell exactly who was who except I could see Lorraine in the front with her kids, one on either side of her. She had her arms around them and they leaned into her like they fit just so. I smiled at her, too, and she smiled back. Her smile was real, I thought, not just a trick to make me feel okay, but a real smile like my smile had touched her and she had to smile, too.

I looked at the passage again and cleared my throat.

"I been asked to read from the Bible for my friend Don who died. I never done this before. Stand in front of people and read something. But it's not so bad. I thought I wouldn't be able to do it. But I think I can."

So I started: "Weather shall I go. No, wait...Witter, no, wibber, whit, whit-her, with-er, that's it. With-er shall I go from thy Spirit?" The words began to float, making me dizzy. I looked up and then back to the book. I figured I would just say the words I could see clearly: "Let only darkness cover me...even the darkness is not dark...for darkness is as light with thee." I stopped here because the words didn't make sense anymore.

"I'm not sure what this is all about, these words about dark and light and all that. I don't think Don woulda picked these words. He wasn't much for this kinda thing. He was just a guy who suffered a lot and tried to make the best of it. He had two kids, there they are, and he had Lorraine and he had work. That was about it. He had just a few things in this world and a whole lot of pain and suffering to go along with it. A lot. He used to break a sweat some mornings just trying to climb up on the stool where he checked the work I did. He would have a hard time just with that, he would. So, I don't know much about these words, about darkness being light and such talk as this. Don had a lot of darkness around him, I guess, but it didn't seem like it gave him light, it just made his life all dark. And that's an awful thing to have your life be all dark so that sometimes you can't even spot a thing that's standing right in front of you. Not that I know anything about the Bible. My mother tried to teach me but she died and there was no one then, so I didn't learn. It was all dark and it was hard to see and sometimes I miss her awful." Shit, I thought, there was a drop of moisture on the page and I figured I must have spit, but it wasn't so. Then there was another and it got harder to talk. "I will miss Don. My friend. He shouldn't have died so young."

I couldn't think how to end so I turned to the Reverend and nodded and then I stepped off the altar and went through the door and down the hall and out to the street where the sunlight was so bright that I could only squint and stand still hoping to see. I took in the air, which was cool and let it soak into my skin and one breath after another I started to wake up to where I was and what had happened. I thought of Lorraine and hoped she wouldn't hate me and I hoped her kids weren't embarrassed and I hoped I hadn't said anything too foolish. It was finished. There was nothing I could do to change it. I hoped Don wasn't laughing somewhere.

I sat in my car across the street from the church parking lot where I could watch people come out through my rear view mirror. For a moment it was like I was watching a movie. I felt calm and distant and what I was watching didn't have anything to do with me at all. It was just a day when someone who died was being memorialized and that was all. Could be any day anywhere, cause someone is always dying and what does it matter after all. Lorraine came out with the kids finally. I thought about our talk at the hospital, how she talked to me like no one had warned her that I was just some guy who never quite made it anywhere. She talked to me like I was a person in this world, just like her.

Dad was sitting in his chair when I got home, a bottle of Genny at his side. He was watching one of those live police shows they have

43

on. Some cop had stopped a guy along the road and the guy had gone crazy on him, beating him to the ground and driving away. The cop got into his car and the chase was on.

"Jesus H. Christ, you shoulda seen the segment before this one. They were driving right through the backyards of this neighborhood. You shoulda seen the looks on the faces of all these assholes standing at their grills and shit. My God." I didn't answer. I just stood there.

"What?"

"Nothin," I said.

"What are you all dressed up for?"

I didn't answer.

"That's right, today was the service wasn't it."

I went to the kitchen, opened the frig and stared. He called after me.

"How'd it go? I mean, what happened?" I could hear him struggling to get out of his chair. He had a hard time breathing because of his smoking and all. Sometimes he could barely get around. Of course, a lot of the time he couldn't get around because he was drunk. I couldn't tell if he was today.

He was behind me now.

"Did you do the reading alright? Did you take my advice?" I turned to look at him. He looked at my eyes and started to smile.

"My God, you took my advice, didn't you? You got drunk." He started to laugh. "Jesus, did they stop you? I'll bet Rev. whatshisname went nuts. Holy shit." If I had discovered a cure for cancer he couldn't have been any more pleased. He always had a deep dislike for churches and ministers. Never trusted them and thought they were all fakes and that all they wanted was your money. He watched the evangelists on Sunday morning just to rail against them and he loved it when one of them would get caught doing some scandalous thing.

"Yes, I made an ass of myself. You would have been proud."

"What's that supposed to mean? You feelin' sorry for yourself, are you?" I was. I felt a deep kind of sorrow for everything about myself and I hated it. "You feel bad about what you done? Well don't. They're just a bunch of Bible totin' hypocrites, is what they are and you know I'm right. Jesus, to think Don being laid out in the church is a hoot. Don never set foot in a church his whole life. It was just for that wife of his, she's so much better I guess than he was, or so she thinks."

I didn't like him saying anything about Lorraine. As far as I could tell, Lorraine was as good a person as you could find. It must have been hell being married to a cripple all those years and yet she always had a smile and a good word.

"No need to say anything about her."

"Why's that? You got something for her. You got *feelings* for her, do you?"

"No, I don't. I just don't think its right for you to talk about her that way."

"She ain't perfect, you know."

"What's that supposed to mean?"

"Just what I said, she ain't perfect."

I decided not to answer, but it was too much for the old man.

"Everyone at the shop knew she was doing it with one of the big bosses. She would come around every week or so all dolled up and she'd go into the office and wouldn't come out for the longest time. That's what everyone said. Everybody know'd what she was doing. How else do you think old Don kept his job so long?"

"That's bullshit."

"Is it? Didn't you ever wonder why they kept him on so long, him missin' all that work the last couple of years? Didn't it ever strike you as odd? Hell, you did all his work and she screwed his boss. Not a bad deal as far as I can tell."

"Shut up."

"Why you tellin' me to shut up. I'm just tellin' you the truth, that's all. If you can't take it, that's your problem."

I was walking away by then. I didn't want to hear anymore. Could this be possible? How could I have missed this? I just figured they were doing right by Don. I never thought anything else. I never saw anything else and I never heard anything else. So, what the hell's he talking about? I would have heard something, I'm sure. The way rumors fly, I would have known. They did keep him on a lot longer than they kept some other guys on. They didn't seem to have much trouble lettin' people go. Old Georgey was out the door after about 20 years and no one gave him a second thought. And he was still working hard. They just said there was a down turn coming and he'd have to go.

So why did they keep Don on so long? Shit, he would die a whole second time if this were true. I think he'd be more pissed off about them keeping him for no reason than anything about his wife. He used to tell her to find someone else if she wanted to, but just not to let him know about it. He knew he couldn't satisfy her and he wanted her to be happy, although he was glad each time she would say, "Who else could I find? You're the one for me." But was she being truthful or was she just doing what he told her to do, keeping a secret?

He would hate the idea that they kept him on even though he wasn't valuable to them anymore. He always prided himself on being productive, on being able to work even though he was in such pain all the time. He was a man because he was still a worker. That meant a lot to him. He would hate this whole thing, if it were true.

But Lorraine. I kept thinking of our talk in the hospital coffee shop. She seemed like a person that you could see right through and not find a single dark spot or sharp edge or anything. She just seemed like what she was, nothing more. She looked right at you, not like some people who can't look at you because they have something to hide. She didn't seem to be hiding anything. She just seemed like Lorraine. It pissed me off that my father had put this notion in my head. It was the kind of thing he would do. Just when you finished digging a well, he'd come along and take a piss in it.

4

My performance at Don's memorial service was news for a week or so. And although my having been drunk was talked about a lot, most people said they heard that what I said was good, that Don would actually have liked it. It was like my drinking was okay because I was so sad over Don dying. I didn't tell anyone at work that the reason I drank was because I didn't want to talk at Don's service and the only way I could keep my promise to Lorraine was to go in there feeling no pain. I wish it were the grief, but it wasn't. It was fear, pure and simple.

I even got a note from Lorraine. I couldn't open it for several days, though, because I hadn't been able to get my father's story out of my mind. It confused me and I was afraid that reading a note from her would confuse me more. I didn't want to judge her, but I couldn't help feeling odd about the whole thing. Even if what my old man said was true, I wasn't sure anymore if what she did was wrong or not. I just couldn't figure it out. I didn't want to think of her as unfaithful to Don, he worshipped her so. But was she being unfaithful? Or was she being faithful in some different way that was hard to explain but meant she might have to do something bad in order to keep faith with something that most people wouldn't understand? I guess I just didn't want to be confused about Lorraine. I wanted her to be simple.

I finally opened the note:

"I looked for you after Don's service but I couldn't find you. I wanted to tell you how much I appreciated what you did for Don. I know it was hard, but he would have liked it. I think you know that Don wouldn't have chosen a service like that, but I felt he deserved something special. There wasn't much in his life that was special. He would have appreciated what you said, so I want to thank you again for doing it. I hope you are doing well. Stop by to see us anytime."

Yours,
Lorraine

I read her note several times. Then I put it back in the envelope and stuck it under the organizer on my dresser where I knew no one else would find it.

5

I was doing both jobs at work now and was falling into a routine. I didn't mind because it gave me time to think about how I would run the operation once we hired someone to do my job so I could move permanently into Don's. I realized that there were more efficient ways to layout the room so that work could be done on more of an assembly line basis. I even found a way to regulate the ammonia better so we didn't have to use as much without messing with the quality of the prints. I knew the big boss, Mr. Conner, would like these ideas. All they cared about was the bottom line. Throw the word "efficiency" around or "cost savings" and they'd go nuts.

I told Conner that I had some ideas and he said we'd meet sometime to discuss them. I wasn't in a big hurry, but I wanted to get things settled soon so I could make some other plans. With the raise from getting Don's job, I could move out of my father's house and get a place of my own. Maybe this time it would work.

This time I was thinking. I was planning. I had found an apartment near work in some old lady's home. The rent was dirt cheap and she seemed to like me because she said she would hold the place for another month until my situation got sorted out. I didn't tell dad. He used to make fun of me when I would threaten to leave. He would laugh and say, "Where the hell would you go? You don't have no idea how to make it out there on your own, so talk all you want, you ain't goin' nowhere." This time he would be wrong. One day I would walk into the house and up to my room. And I would pack my bags and walk out and he would be left at the door, his jaw wide open. I had played that scene in my head before. At first I thought I would tell him off, but then I thought the better thing would be to say nothing, just leave him speechless. And if he called after me, I would keep on walking. I might even turn and smile as I got in my car. That would drive him crazy for sure, because he would see that he couldn't touch me anymore. He would see that I was my own person.

The day of my meeting with Conner finally came. I sat in his waiting room for about fifteen minutes reading the magazines. He had good ones, like "The New Yorker" and "Atlantic Monthly," ones I'd never buy. I looked through them but I didn't read anything. The stories were always about some political thing or some war in Africa somewhere, stuff that didn't really matter at all. They were mostly too long anyway.

The furniture in his waiting room was nicer than the furniture in our house was when it was brand new. Real leather and floor lamps like you'd have in a game room or something. His secretary was young and pretty and kind of stuck-up, the way people get when they work for someone who is real powerful, like now they're powerful too. She answered the phones just like you'd think she was a recording. She looked up from her desk every once in a while and smiled at me. Asked if I wanted some coffee and I figured, what the hell, so I said, yes. She asked what kind and I figured she meant regular of decaf, so I said regular. She smiled and asked if I wanted the Colombian-something or some other fancy sounding stuff. I said yes to the second one. Funny, the coffee didn't taste any different than what we had downstairs. She served it in a real mug, though. No Styrofoam cup.

I felt ready for this meeting. I would tell him my ideas and he would see that I knew what I was talking about. I thought if I impressed him enough he might even throw in a small raise since I had been covering for Don so long. I'd earned it, for sure, although I wouldn't ask for it. I would just talk to him in a way that would make him realize how valuable I was. Then I could be all surprised and appreciative when he made the offer. If he didn't make an offer, then I wouldn't have made a fool of myself by asking for more money.

His secretary's phone rang. She answered and then looked at me. "You can go in," she said, as polite as anything, just like she was talking to an executive.

"Good morning Mr. Conner." I spoke confidently. I wanted him to think of me as someone who knew what was what. I wore a suit to the meeting, the only one I had. It was a little old and the lapels may have been a tad wide, but it was okay enough. I bought a new tie at Ames and some black shoes that were shiny as hell and I trimmed my moustache. I wanted him to see that I was a take-charge person and that's often reflected in how you look.

"Good morning." He was looking at some spreadsheets and didn't look up at first, but when he did, he smiled. "So, how's it going?" He seemed in a good mood and I thought it was a good sign that he asked how I was doing, like he was interested in me.

"Well, I'm doin'."

"So we're here to talk about Don's job, right?"

"Yes, we are and I been doing a lot of thinking about it, sir." This was my chance to show him I was a go-getter. "As you know I have done Don's job off and on for a long time and I've had a chance to think about what needs to happen downstairs. Don't get me wrong, Don was a great guy and a good worker, but I realize now that we could do some things differently. We could be more efficient and we could probably save some money in the process. We just gotta work smarter and do some stuff different, that's all." I had almost memorized these lines. I wanted to bowl him over, if I could, and I wanted to use the important words that all the big bosses liked. They didn't really know what the work was all about. I just had to convince Conner I was on the team and understood things, then I could basically do what I wanted.

"It will help terrifically when we hire someone to do my job and then I can start making some of the changes that..."

"Let's talk about that."

"What's that?"

"About the changes that we need to make."

"Okay, you're the boss, as they say." I laughed but he was back at his spreadsheet again.

"Look here," he said. "Look at this." So I got up and walked over to his desk. I looked at the spreadsheet with all its graphs and lines and arrows. It was just gibberish. "Now look here. See this trend, this downward line. You know what that is."

"I think so." No clue.

51

"That's our profit margin for the copying operation." I never thought of what we did as an "operation." Sounded like a bigger deal than it was. We just did some copying.

"Uh huh."

"Look at this. See how things have declined in the last four years. We've lost money in each of those years."

I didn't know what he was getting at. Maybe he wanted to show me how things had gotten worse since Don had gotten sicker. Maybe he wanted to show me that I had a challenge to meet. That was fine. I'd figure something out.

"Uh huh."

"That's not good." He smiled for the first time, one of those, "you don't really get it" smiles. He crossed his arms and sat back.

"I guess I don't get it. Don and me, we worked hard." He jumped into action again, laying another spreadhseet across his desk.

"That's true, that's true, let me show you." he was pointing again and I was looking but I wasn't seeing it. "Right here, look, you're right, both of you worked hard and produced at a steady level, but, look, here, see what I mean?"

"No."

"Look, cost has gone up for paper and maintenance not to mention salaries." Now he was pissing me off. I know I wasn't making shit at that job and Don didn't make a whole lot more.

"What do you mean salaries? I'm not making…"

"Don't get me wrong. I'm not saying that your salary is out of line. You are making what you should be making after your years of service." Okay, this sounded more reasonable. Maybe he was getting it after all.

"But that's part of the problem."

"What do you mean, part of the problem."

"I mean both you and Don stayed in your positions for well over 20 years and so your salaries went up accordingly. The problem is that those jobs were never meant to be career jobs; by that, I mean, jobs that someone would stay in for an extended period of time. They were designed as short-term jobs, maybe 2-3 years and then whoever had the job would move up in the organization or move out. That way the salary for those jobs would stay at a lower rate because new people would always be coming in. That's the only way we could keep the cost of the operation reasonable: if the salaries didn't become inappropriately high."

I just looked at him at this point. I didn't know what to say. He was telling me that I was too costly for the job, that it was costing him too much for me to do my job because the job was something that anyone with no experience could do. But I knew that wasn't the case. Not just anyone could do the job. It took some real knowledge, not just to make a good copy, but to work with the engineers and deal with their stupid ass shit all the time. There was a lot to the job that made it more than just some entry-level bullshit that any asshole could do. I just couldn't think of a way to explain it to him. He could see I was stuck.

"So, we were committed to helping Don out because of his, his situation and all." Don would have loved this. He would have shit a brick if he knew his job was just the big boss's version of a pity-fuck. "But we've been losing money and even if Don hadn't passed away, we would have been faced with making a change soon. But now that he's gone, we have to move in a different direction. Times are hard." He said this with a slight tilt of his head and raised eyebrows, as if to say we were all in the same boat. I wondered if his tie was made of silk.

"What the fuck...I mean what does this mean? Are you firing me or what?"

"No, no, absolutely not. We will just be reassigning you."

"So, you're going to move me somewhere else and hire two other guys to come in and do what Don and I did?"

"Not exactly. We are closing the department down."

"Whatdaya mean, closing it down? If there aren't copies, there's no way to do the jobs."

"That's exactly right. We're subcontracting that out. The work can be computerized and done for almost half of what it currently costs us. Because of our projected volumes, which now will increase, we negotiated a very reasonable deal with Techtronics. Even if we only hit 75% of capacity next year, we will still save money."

This was unbelievable.

"What about me?"

"Yes, what about you. That's really why we're meeting. I don't want you to worry about this. You've been a loyal employee with a pretty good record for a long time and we want to do right by you, so we're holding another position for you if you want it."

"What's that?"

"Well, all we have right now that is unskilled is janitorial. But I think that within a year or two you could move up to supervisor and you'd be back to the hourly rate you have now. It might mean a little belt tightening for a while, but at least you'd have a job. We wanted to do that much for you. What do you think?"

What did I think? I thought this was the worst fucking thing I had ever heard. Janitorial. That's where I started forever ago and now I'd be back cleaning shitters and taking crap from every asshole in the place. Not to mention a fucking cut in pay. What the hell was he doing to me?

He was still smiling like he had just surprised me with a Christmas bonus. I looked at him, at his close shave and his manicured nails. The fucker never did a day of real work in his life.

"This is about Lorraine, isn't it?" I said.

"What, what are you talking about, what, who, who is Lorraine?"

"You know what I'm talking about. Lorraine, you fuck. Don's wife."

"I don't know what…"

"He's dead and you can't screw her anymore so now you're gonna screw me."

"Now wait a minute. I don't know what you're talking about."

"Everybody knows about it, everybody."

"What are you…this is ridiculous…I've never heard…look, I'm trying to help you."

"Don't give me that crap. I know about it all."

"You better be careful. You better think long and hard before you say another word, you little shit. I didn't have to find a job for you at all. In fact, if it weren't for your old man working here so long, I would have dumped your ass long before this. So I think you should just take a deep breath, smile and say 'Thank you, Mr. Conner,' and get the hell out of my office."

"Why don't you go fuck yourself," I said with complete calm.

He took a deep breath, placed both hands on his desk and began to stand. He was calm, too. "Okay. We're done. And you're finished. I'll hire some high school kid to do your job or, better yet, maybe I can find another retard. Whoever it will be, it won't be you. One more thing. If I ever hear you spreading any rumors about me again, it will be your old man's ass that's on the line. Not only will he be gone, but I'll see to it that he doesn't get a pension, that he doesn't get a plug nickel to drink with. I don't think you really want to fuck with me, now do you? Do you?"

I didn't answer.

"Where's your smart ass mouth now?"

I still couldn't speak. I stood up, though. He had already turned his back and was doing something on his computer. His secretary told me to have a good day in that empty sing-song way that people wish each other well. When I reached my car and got behind the wheel, I just sat there. I couldn't think of what to do next and when I tried to put the key in the ignition, my hand shook and shook and I couldn't find the hole.

6

From the hilltop where the cemetery was located you could see all of Ellwood. There was the main street with its toy buildings in two neat rows and tiny cars running between them. There were the three bridges that crossed the creek. I could see the pillars of Lincoln High School where I graduated. There was the tube mill, still closed after all these years, a rusting dinosaur lying in the dirt. I used to stay awake at night with my head out the bedroom window listening to the third shift. The noise carried so well in the summer breeze that I could hear the voices of men taking their lunch break a mile away as clearly as I could hear metal on metal. When it rained, the tin roof outside my window sounded like a sizzling skillet and if I thought about it real hard I could see my mother cooking bacon on a Sunday morning.

A voice called out my name and when I turned, there was Alvin Coppler waving to me from across the way. Alvin and I went to school together and for a while were friends.

"How you doin'?" he said.

"Okay, I guess. You?"

"Pretty fuckin' good, I'd say. My lady's still good in the sack and she keeps the kids off my back. Hey, how 'bout that, I made a fuckin' poem," he laughed and smacked my arm and doubled over. I realized why I hadn't stayed in touch with Alvin over the years.

Alvin had gone into the service right after high school, but something went wrong cause he was back in about six months. It was all hush-hush, but some said he went a little nutty when they were about to send him to Vietnam, who wouldn't, and they let him out. Of course, that's not what he said. He told everyone that he volunteered to go to Nam, but they kept him from going because they thought he was too wild, that he might not follow orders in the field because he was so gung ho about killing gooks. I always thought that was the dumbest story I had ever heard but I never said anything because I wasn't convinced that I wouldn't have done the same thing. I was lucky. My lottery number was 348. The only bit of luck I ever had. Once Alvin came home he took a job as a gravedigger for the summer while he sorted things out, and he's been here ever since. Now he's the chief grounds keeper, which means he supervises a few high school kids.

"So you still living with the old man."

"Yeah."

"Man, I don't know how the fuck you take it. What a crazy fuck he was." I wished he wouldn't talk about my father. I mean he was right but who was he to be right about anything.

"Remember that time?"

"What time?"

"You know, the time. The time, for chrissakes! Jesus, it was such a big fucking deal, remember? You and Billy and me was going down to the river to sleep out one night and you had to stop home to get your stuff. Jesus, don't you remember this? And your old man stopped you in the garage while you were getting your sleeping bag and shit and he says, Where do you think you're going? And you says, I'm goin' with Billy and Alvie, and he says, The fuck you are. I'll never forget that. Only dad I knew who wasn't afraid to drop the f-bomb. I'll give him that much. But then, just like it was nothin' to him at all, he hauls off and slugs you right in the fuckin' kisser. I thought, What a fuckin' maniac. Jesus man, don't you fuckin' remember?"

Yes, I remembered. I remembered the day pretty well. It started slow enough. He wanted me to go to the lumberyard with him to get some plywood paneling cause he wanted to do something to the walls in the basement. I think the paneling is still rotting down there. While he was talking to Mr. Yahn, I was trying to help the guys carry the sheets out to the car so we could tie them on the roof. I lost my balance and the sheet I was carrying slipped out of my hands and cracked on the pavement. My father said, "Jesus Christ, can't you do nothin' right?" and he started laughing and telling Yahn what a general fuck-up I was, how I was soft and how maybe I had been too much of a momma's boy and how he was sure I wouldn't ever amount to anything.

No one said a word to me. The other guys just looked on while I picked up the sheet and tried to carry it back to where I got it. My father wouldn't let up, though, and by the time we got home, he was riding my ass like crazy. Finally I told him to "shut up" and he must have been startled because he didn't say a word. He just looked at me, his eyes narrow like he was looking down a gun barrel at some animal he found digging in the garbage can. When we got home, his fist came from nowhere into my stomach so deep it felt like he hit my back. The wind left me in a flash. I fell to the ground, my mouth wide open hoping air come find my lungs without me having to draw it. He stood over me and said, "Don't you ever say that to me again. Ever."

I should have kept my mouth shut but I didn't. As he walked away I said, "I know what happened with mom." I knew I was going to speak but I was shocked at the words that fell out in the space between us. "I know." He turned. His face was red and his mouth was twisted up toward one ear and he walked to me slowly and stood over me.

"What did you say?"

"I...think...you...heard...me," I said, still trying to draw a full breath.

"You sonofabitch. You think you know everything don't you. You don't know a goddam thing. Nothing! If you did, you wouldn't even think of talking that way to me. I am ashamed to call you my son. Did you hear me? I said, I am ashamed of you," and he leaned toward me to make sure I could see his mouth shape each word. "Go to your room and don't come out."

I never told Alvie what was going on when he and Billy stopped by the house. I never told him that he was walking in on something that had started long before we had cooked up the plan to sleep out at the river. What my father did may have shocked Alvie, but it came as no surprise to me. And when he hit me, I didn't even care. I didn't even feel it. When my mouth started to bleed, I tasted it, I drank it down, the salt of myself, like drinking the blood of your enemy to make you strong. Cause that's what I felt like. My own enemy. I was as ashamed of me as my father was, but for other reasons. He could do the hitting for both of us.

"Yeah. I remember."

"Wow, what a crazy fuck he was."

"Look, Alvie, I gotta go."

"Goin' to see your mom?"

"Uh huh."

"Yeah, I figured. You're pretty good to her, God rest her soul."

"I guess."

"Look, I'll take extra good care of her spot for you, okay, keep it real nice, just for you and your mom."

"Thanks."

"Take it easy now and don't be no fuckin' stranger, okay?"

"Yeah, right."

"Can you find it from here okay? The place has really filled up. Do you want me to show…"

"No, I got it okay, I know where to go alright."

I walked slowly across the stone garden, trying not to step where bodies might be at rest. Just beyond the rich graves with the giant monuments I turned left and walked down the hill a few yards. I hadn't been here since Christmas when I brought a potted poinsettia, which I intended to plant in the spring. Spring planting time came and went and now all that was left were dry leaves that crackled in my hand. The grass had grown around the stone, too close for the riding mower. I pulled the plant out of the pot and high grass from around the stone. It was a modest stone, about a foot or so high. I had always wanted her to have something better, but I guess it fit okay. It was a modest life after all and maybe should be marked that way, too.

I ran my fingers across her name and felt the depth of each letter and the smooth space between them. The wind picked up and the sun sat on the ridges in the west where the old strip mines had been. The grass was stiff. The ground was flat on her grave, losing its characteristic mound long ago as the dirt settled in on my mother's coffin. I leaned against the stone and stretched my legs out wondering how much room the box took up.

The ground was covered with an artificial grass mat and we sat under a tent. I was 10. My mother was 39. The coffin was suspended over the hole by large straps. On top was a bouquet of flowers with "Mother and Wife" ornately written in the ribbon. About ten folding chairs sat opposite the coffin. I didn't want to sit, so I stood near the head of the coffin trying to imagine my mother asleep inside. My father was in tears and kept calling for her. He was drunk and the minister looked nervous. He tried to console my father but the booze had really kicked in by then and nothing could stop him. He called for my mother to come back and not to leave. He apologized and whined like a baby. I didn't look at him during all of this. I didn't move a muscle. I didn't cry. I didn't blink. I barely breathed. I stood guard, making sure that my mother was safe and nothing more could happen to her.

That summer I had tried out for Little League baseball for the first time. In those days you weren't assured a spot on a team when you tried out. On try-out day, all the 10 year olds went to the Little League Field and took turns batting and catching and throwing while the coaches of the various teams watched. It was hard to stand out in the crowd, but I tried my best and hit the ball well enough and was picked by the coach of the Moose team. Then the real tryouts began. I went to practice every day after school for a couple of weeks while the coach watched us do our thing. We had inter-squad games and infield practice. I was put in centerfield because I could run fast and I caught the ball on the fly pretty well for my age. I wasn't much good with grounders. After about a week, the coach started taking kids aside after practice and giving them the bad news. They were cut from the team and would have to try out next year.

For the first few days his choices were no-brainers. Some of the kids had no talent at all. They went out just because their friends played or because their fathers mistakenly thought they would be the next Willie Mays or something. But after that the cuts were more selective.

I was surprised when Donny Adams was cut because I thought he was a better player than me. I figured I had it made by then. The final night of the final cut finally arrived. I figured it was between me and my friend Richy. We were the only 10 year olds left. He was bigger than me, but I thought I played better than him. After practice we stood together as the coach came over to talk to us. It was short and sweet. He looked at me first and I knew what that meant. He said I was pretty good and should make the team next year, but this year he'd have to cut me. And cut me he did. It hurt like hell and I cried the whole way home. I was pissed and embarrassed and humiliated. When I hit the front door, my mother was on the phone and she called out to ask me what happened and I screamed through my tears that I had been cut.

When she finally caught up with me, I was in the backyard furiously throwing a rubber ball against the side of the house, practicing already for next year. She walked over to me slowly and I didn't look at her. She put her hand on my shoulder and I stopped, my head down and I began to cry again.

"I'm sorry," I said, surprised that those were the words I chose. I looked up at her and she had the saddest smile on her face, like she had a deep cut herself and knew what it meant to be bleeding inside over something that no one else could understand. The wind blew her hair across her face, but her eyes were steady as she looked at me, never blinking.

"I love you," she said. "Always remember that I love you. It doesn't matter to me if you never make a baseball team, ever, I would still love you." I was puzzled why she said that, but I remember how settled I felt inside, like every part of my body fell right into place for the very first time.

Three months later she was dead and I was standing in the funeral parlor trying to see right through the lid of that box, wondering if she was still smiling or not, wondering if she still loved me from somewhere far away or was she just gone, her love gone with her.

For a long time I was angry at her, as well as sad that she was gone. I never said goodbye. I never had that final moment, a chance to put into words all of what someone means to you, some few words that have to last forever. She had done that for me at a time when I didn't even know there were such things as endings.

"I still wonder where you're at," I said to no one. "I wonder if you are anywhere at all. I wonder if you are okay. I want to believe you are. If you are somewhere and can see what's going on, then you know I'm not okay. And I hope that doesn't hurt you. I hope that you are somewhere where you can look down at the hurting and see that it's not important at all. Like you know that all this hurt down here is really nothing compared to the big picture. I hope that's the way it is because I don't want you to worry. You had enough worry when you were here. I am 43 now, mom, older than you. I will take care of myself so you don't have to give it a thought."

The sun disappeared behind the hills and the grass grew chilly.

"I love you." I kissed my hand and patted the stone.

7

Dad wasn't there when I got home, which was fine enough with me. I could smell him, though, the beer cans in the trash bag and dead Camels in the ashtrays. His chair sat directly opposite the TV, which he had perched on top of a phone book so the sun wouldn't hit it wrong on Sunday afternoons when he watched the races. It was an old recliner that had been in the same spot for as long as I could remember. Like him, it was worn and tired looking and dirty brown. If you hit it hard it billowed with decades of his dusty skin. There was a pillow deep in the crevice between the seat and the back. It was there to protect his hip, grown weak over the years from working on the loading dock.

On the table beside the chair were a reading lamp and a small picture of my mother, framed in silver. The lamp was turned on. It was his night light when he couldn't sleep and his daylight when he read the paper, and otherwise, it was just a light, always on. The picture of my mother was from a happy time, a time before they married, before they knew each other, for surely they would never have married had they known each other, I mean really known each other beyond the airs that men and women put on to capture one another. She is wearing a skirt and a red cardigan and her hair is curled and she is smiling and the wind has blown her hair away from her face like she has been running and she looks happy. I look hard at her face sometimes because it is so different than I ever knew it to be. So young and without care.

She would be in her 60s now had she lived. I wonder what she would have looked like? I can't imagine her face looking wrinkled, like a bed sheet in the morning. Maybe she wouldn't have made it this far. She did drink, not like my dad, but she drank often enough and it worried me. I remember holding her hair back as she puked her guts into the toilet bowl. I was crying and she was sobbing and it didn't make sense at all for me to be standing over her like that and yet, there I was. And I asked her never to drink again and she swore she wouldn't and she held me tight and cried so hard into my pajama top that I had to change into a T-shirt for bed. But it wasn't more than a couple of weeks before I heard her again. This time she was bent over the washtub in the basement, trying to hide from me, I suppose. I watched her but I didn't help her, and I didn't let her know I was there in the dark behind her. I wanted to, but something inside me said, "Let her be," and so I did.

Maybe I was afraid that if I touched her I would get the curse, too. That's crazy talk, I know, but I couldn't figure out any other reason why she kept doing it, except that she was cursed somehow. What else would make her do what she hated so much in my father, what she had suffered through with her father, the very thing that made her brother jump the bridge. If it were a curse, maybe she could throw it up and out and if I wasn't near by, maybe I could avoid being touched by it. So I just stood in the dark and watched and hoped the demon would spill out and be flushed away.

The kitchen floor was re-tiled shortly after she died. Just plain white blocks. But I remember the old tile. It was swirled like sand after the ocean has swept in and left tiny stones and shells behind. The pattern was no pattern at all, at least I could never figure it out. And it was smooth to my feet when I slid across it in the morning before school and my mother would tell me to watch myself that I didn't fall, but she would be smiling, nevertheless, like it was just fine that I was sliding by, like maybe she wished she could slide along, too.

The tile was gone before the funeral. They couldn't get the blood out. The blood left its own tidal mark that wouldn't go away, so my father had the whole thing pulled up and thrown out and he replaced it with this tile, the same tile that is on the floor today. Plain white blocks, only it's not white anymore, not after all these years. It's gray like my mother would have been by now had she lived.

When I stood at the door to my bedroom, it looked different, smaller, and quiet, like people are when they're sitting and waiting. I have a single bed in the far corner. I can't remember the last time I made it. Shoes scattered underneath and my clock radio on the floor, covered in dust. A small lamp on the bed stand with a picture of mom and me when I was about two. She is bending over as if to encourage me to smile at the camera. I am squinting into the sun. Newspapers underneath the stand. Throw rug pushed off to the side. Closet door open and old shoeboxes piled in the back. Nothing on the walls. A dresser in the opposite corner. One window.

I looked into the bathroom mirror, not glancing, but really looking at what was staring back at me. I never looked at myself much, except to shave or trim my mustache, but never at my face as a whole, just the parts that needed tending to. My teeth were yellow like old scrimshaw and I still had a pimple or two in the same places I had had them when I was a teenager. My hair was receding more than I realized. I could see the old line where the hair once peaked on my forehead. I started letting my hair grow long enough to part it when I was in ninth grade and I have been parting it in the same place ever since. It is the only thing I can do easily with my left hand.

My eyelids were puffy and swollen underneath and even when I opened them wide, like I was surprised, my whole eyeball never completely saw the light of day. They hid there behind my lids, plain and brown and not really revealing much of anything. I noticed that the corner of my mouth pulled up to one side, pinched back in my cheek. It was a small movement but I knew it was a sign of displeasure or disappointment. I had seen it often enough on my mother's face and now I could see it on mine. It just pulled up like that automatically whenever I saw something that didn't satisfy me or that didn't meet some expectation I had inside that I couldn't even speak of.

I took a step back and looked at the whole picture. My shoulders sagged like an old man and my chest wasn't really much of a chest at all, caved in as it was between my shoulders. Even though I was on the last hole in my belt, my stomach spilled over my pants a bit. "Jesus," I said, "Look at you."

I opened the medicine chest. There were bottles of prescription drugs that had long since passed their expiration dates. There was the pain medication from the last time my father injured his hip at work.

And there was a bottle of sleeping pills he probably bought at Rite Aide. I took them down from the shelf and closed the door. I held them up in front of my face and studied them for a minute, unsure whether or not to take them all. I then realized that the bottles weren't full and that taking everything would be the wisest choice. I poured the pills into the palm of my hand and rolled them into a mix.

I looked at the mirror again and for a moment everything came clear. It was like driving out of a tunnel you had been in so long that you didn't even know it and suddenly, as you come out, you can see it all; you can see out over the landscape and everything is clear like it is before dusk when the sun shines parallel to the ground and the trees are stark and distinct and crisply defined. Everything else falls away and that moment is the only thing that matters or even exists. It didn't matter that Don had died or that I had lost my job. My mother's death didn't even matter anymore, and neither did my father's life. I felt the cool breeze of freedom that must have caught Harold when he jumped off that bridge so calmly that it sent shudders down the spines of those who saw him leap.

I filled a glass with water and started to take the pills. In four swallows they were gone. I walked across the hall to my room and cleared my clothes off the bed. I crawled in and pulled the covers up because it was cold. I closed my eyes and went to sleep.

8

Liberation day was coming and I still didn't know where I was going. I hadn't spoken to my father yet, even though he dutifully left messages for me every few days. I don't know why he kept it up. I don't know what he was trying to prove. My therapist offered lots of explanations, like he cared about me or he felt guilty or he did it just because he was my father and that's what fathers are supposed to do.

None of this rang true for me. I tried to think of him in those ways, wanted to think of him in those ways. It would have made everything one hell of a lot easier. But I couldn't. Maybe he got so drunk that he became totally disoriented and called me, forgetting that I had already made it clear I didn't want to talk to him. Maybe he didn't realize he had called so often. Maybe he forgot each call, so that every time he picked the phone up in a stupor, it was the first time. Who knows?

I knew I would have to call him sooner or later and I had put it off as long as possible. My therapist said something about a halfway house or apartment. No way in hell was I gonna live with a bunch of other head cases. There was no other option than going home again. I knew it. I bet my father knew it, too.

The thought of going back made me edgy. Sometimes I could smell the place, like it had left some residue in my nose, the scent of dad and cigarettes and stale bed sheets and frayed carpeting and cold ashes in the trashcan. I could breathe it in and be home no matter where I was.

At night in the hospital when my room was still and no one was asking me questions and no one even knew I was awake, I could go home if I wanted to. I could close my eyes and tour the house. I could walk up the four cracked cement steps where the chipmunks lived onto the front stoop with its rod iron railing and its wicker rocker turned gray from the weather and the welcome mat that read "we ome" from the wear. The outside door and the inside door with its three long beveled windows. I'd have to kick the door for it to open. Small entry with a plastic mat. A pillar to the right of the door looking embarrassed for being so out of place in this less than palatial setting. The living room to the right and the kitchen straight ahead and the stairs dividing them and the small pantry beyond the kitchen where my mother used to iron and can things and do whatever she did. It's a junk room now. We throw things in there and that's where they stay. No exit. Everything stays.

In the corner of the kitchen is a narrow door to the cellar with a drawstring single light over the steps. Half the cellar floor is dirt. The other half has a table saw piled with old magazines and two saw horses with a plywood board between them, full of boxes and a broken table chair. I used to play down here when I was a kid. I loved the cool air in the summer, the dampness, the quiet.

Across the kitchen and around the corner is a narrow staircase overlooking the living room. Each step played its own creaky music, sounds I had heard forever. At the top landing my bedroom was on the right and his was on the left and the bathroom was between us. There was a throw rug on the wood floor. Home. It was cozy and poisonous and warm and deadly.

So, I called my dad.

"Hi."

"Hello."

"It's me."

"Yeah. Hello."

"It's me I said."

"Okay, yeah."

"Well. How are you?"

"Okay."

"What you been up to?"

"Nothin' much. The usual. Workin'."

"The usual, yeah."

"Uh huh."

"How's work?"

"Same."

"Everything the same, huh?"

"Yeah. The same."

"Well, okay. Just thought I'd call."

"Okay. Did they tell ya I been callin'?"

"Yeah, they told me."

"Okay." Silence.

"I don't know. I'm pretty busy in here, you know, going to groups and stuff, weaving baskets and hangin' out with the other lunatics."

"I wondered how you was doin'. I mean I didn't know since when you..."

"Yeah, I know. I'm mostly okay."

"Okay."

"You know I'm getting' outa here in a few days or so."

"That so?""Yeah."

"Well that's good."

"Uh huh."

"Yeah."

"Thought I'd come back to the place, you know."

"Okay, yeah."

"Just to get my feet on the ground, you know. I probably won't stay, but I thought it would be best to come home. I don't know."

"Yeah, no, that would be best."

"Okay."

"Okay."

"So."

"So when will that be?"

"Uh, not sure exactly. Sometime this week. Depends on what the doctors say."

"Okay."

"Yeah."

"Yeah. Did you hear about Carla?""No, what's that?""She quit.""She quit?""Yeah."

"When'd that happen?""Two weeks."

"Jesus. What happened?"

"Her mother's sick or something, anyway, she went back to Texas."

"So you're on your own."

"Yeah, I'm trying to keep up."

"Uh huh."

"Yeah, she's gone."

"Yeah. That's too bad.""Yeah."

"Okay, well, I better get going."

"So you're comin' home."

"Uh huh."

"If that's what you want."

"Well, it's just what I have to do right now."

"You don't have to on my account, if you don't want to."

"I'm not comin' home on your account."

"Okay, that's okay. I'm makin' out just fine, you know."

"I'm sure you are. Okay. I better go."

"Okay."

"Bye."

"Yeah."

When I hung up the phone there was a moist handprint on the receiver. I paced back and forth in my room and I couldn't settle down. It was like my idle had been turned up and even though I wasn't going anywhere I couldn't get there fast enough. Did I make a mistake calling him? Maybe I shouldn't go home after all. Maybe I should try something else. But what? Shit. No fucking job. Why the hell did I go off on Conner? Goddammit, why did I wake up? What the hell am I going to do when I get out of here?

I talked to my therapist about this and he said it was normal to be afraid to leave the hospital. Everyone feels like that just before they leave. Not to worry.

There's that word again—normal. It's meaningless. I'm sitting in a locked hospital ward afraid to go back to my own fucking house and my own fucking old man; afraid, in fact, to set foot outside the grounds and he says it's normal, like my temperature is 98.6 even though my fucking head is burning up and I'm delirious inside. What the hell is normal? I wouldn't know normal if it bit me in the ass. I'd settle for semi-normal or very-nearly-normal or if-I-stand-on-my-tiptoes-I-can-almost-see-normal. Normal is not a mother bleeding to death on the kitchen floor or a father pissing his pants from drinking too much or a son locked up in a fucking cracker factory. There's not a damn normal thing in the whole picture.

69

Why the hell did I take those fucking pills? And why didn't they work? I have tried not to think about what I did, even though my therapist thinks I need to "come to grips" with it. In some ways it seems obvious. Everything was closing in on me. I couldn't move. I couldn't breathe. The only way out was to exit permanently, get out and away to whatever was on the other side and I didn't much care if it was something or nothing, at least I would be gone. In other ways it doesn't make any sense at all. To do something that would make everything inside stop, every movement, every beat, every pulse, every thought, every memory, every twitch and grimace and smile and tear and everything. To absolutely stop after going so long; and not because anyone or anything else made you stop, no disease, no accident, no gunshot, nothing else except yourself. To go to the one place that everyone wants to avoid, the dark place that most people pretend doesn't exist. To choose it. To say *that* would be better than *this*, than this sunrise or this tree waving in the breeze or this hot tar on the summer pavement or this pimple on the end of my nose or this newsprint ink on my hands, better than any of this. It seems so odd to feel that way and yet that is how I felt.

I made the choice to leave, and I failed. My therapist says I succeeded by failing. They all talk like that, twisting the words and waving them around in the air hoping some magic will come out that will open the poor devil's eyes. But I failed as far as I can tell. I haven't done very well staying in the world and I haven't done very well trying to leave it.

Not as well as Harold. That's for sure. What was he thinking? Or was he thinking at all? Was he planning to kill himself when he walked onto that bridge? Or was it just an impulse? And if someone had come along and said "hi" to him or waved at him from a passing car, anything that might have broken the momentary spell and made him think, would he have gone ahead or would he have just walked on across the bridge and never given it another thought?

There was a crazy guy who lived just outside town, I mean really crazy as in hearing voices and believing the government was out to get him because he could read the pope's mind. Crazy. He was on all kinds of medications and one day he overdosed. They found him out on the New Castle Road dead. Turns out he believed that his true love was calling to him from the afterlife. He'd talk to her and she'd comfort him. I guess this went on in secret for months until he told his shrink, who convinced him that there was no reason to hurry to be with her. He accepted this, or so they thought. He didn't talk about her anymore and told everyone she was gone, but she wasn't. She was planning a way for him to come to her.

One afternoon his parents went into town to shop and he told them he didn't want to come. He said he had a headache and wanted to take a nap, so they left him at home. Shortly after they left, he took every pill he could find. And waited. Like me.

At some point, though, he got nervous. He must have started to feel something inside, something that scared him, something that made him realize what he had done. Or maybe his true love turned on him and said she didn't care. Who knows? But something changed and he got scared and left his house and ran down the road, stopping at houses along the way, beating on doors, but no one answered, so he kept on running until he finally collapsed on the road. They found him with an empty prescription bottle in his hand, his front teeth jammed up into his gums from when he hit the pavement and his glasses shattered. I guess several cars went by before someone stopped. Jesus.

What made him run? I figure he got sane for a moment and realized that he was dying and he didn't want to go. I think he was trying to run away from the pills inside him, away from whatever was going on in his head that told him he was on his way out. It was that terrible Woody Allen joke all over again, "It's not that I'm afraid to die, it's just that I don't want to be there when it happens." He knew he was going to be there when it happened and he tried his best to get away. But couldn't.

As for me. When I left the cemetery and headed for home, I knew what I was going to do even though I didn't really know at all. I knew that it was possible while another part of me felt confident that I would turn away before I did anything. But the closer I got to home, the less fearful I was. In fact, the closer I got to home, the less I felt anything. I was a shadow walking without anything inside to guide me or to question me. When I stood in front of the medicine chest, I realized I didn't care anymore, I didn't feel a thing. That made everything easier. And after I took the pills and laid down, I convinced myself that I was just going to sleep; only I wouldn't have to wake up. That was the clincher for me. I wouldn't have to wake up.

Of course, that's not how it turned out. My dad finally decided something was up and here I am.

"So, why haven't you tried to kill yourself again?" My therapist has asked me this question several times since I've been in the bin. At first I thought he was just being a prick, rubbing it in and maybe making fun of me because I was such a fuck-up that I couldn't even off myself. Like he had the right to punish me for my stupid decision or point out to me what a fool I was.

"No, really, why haven't you tried again since you've been here? I'm serious. I'd like to know." I started to believe him. He really wanted to know why I hadn't given it another shot. Actually he wanted to know why I was still alive. How was I supposed to know?

"I don't know. There's always someone around. It's impossible. Believe me, if I thought I could get away with it, I would try again. But, there's no way."

"Sure there's a way. If you really want it bad enough, there's always a way."

"What are you talking about? You fucking with me or what?"

"No, I'm just curious."

"I told you. There's no way you can get away with something like that here with all the nurses and staff and other people around all the time. Case closed."

"Okay for now. But I'm not convinced. I just don't understand, unless you really want to live." Sometimes he talked like that. Like he knew there was something inside me that I was totally unaware of. That really pissed me off.

I thought about it a lot. Why didn't I try again? It would be hard here, harder than walking into my own house with no one around to lift a finger. That's for sure. It would take a lot of effort to do it here. It would take a lot of thought and planning. It would take days to figure out how to do it. At home I didn't have to plan at all. I felt comfortable at home where I was away from the world, where the smells and the sight of everything were so familiar. Home reached down deep and warmed the sadness inside me, this lost and found feeling deep down that was so strong that I could taste it; cinnamon toast, rotten eggs and me. At home everything awful was possible. Where else would I go to end things than where they all began?

I thought about killing myself almost every day. It was a good thought, like remembering you have $10,000 hidden in your room when you think you're broke. It was my life insurance policy. It insured that when life became too much to bear, I could leave it all behind. I liked having that thought, but I didn't seriously consider doing anything. I don't know when that change occurred.

"How you doing today?"

"Okay."

"Okay? What's 'okay' to you? I mean 'okay' to me is whistling on the way into work while I'm listening to Dave Brubeck on my CD player. Is that the 'okay' you mean? Or is it something else?"

"I don't whistle much." I wasn't sure how to answer his question. I just said, "okay," not because it meant anything but because I needed to answer him.

"You don't strike me as a whistler."

"No. My mother could whistle."

"Is that right? Your mom, huh? Did she whistle for you?"

"Yes, she did. She would whistle kid songs and lullabies and stuff."

"When she whistled, did it make you feel okay?"

"I guess so. I don't really remember." My mother's whistling was like the "all clear" after an air raid. If she was whistling, I new it was safe to come downstairs. I knew that either my old man was at work or was too drunk to do anything. I knew that mom was feeling good, and when she felt good, I felt good, too. She'd grab me by the hands when I came into the kitchen and dance around with me. I would pretend I didn't want to, but I always did. And she'd laugh and both of us were light as air. I'm sure our feet were still on the floor, but I had no proof that they were. We were floating.

"What do you remember of your mom?"

We weren't going there as far as I was concerned. He was always trying to get me to talk about my mom.

"Not too much."

"Nothing?"

I didn't answer.

"I know you were young when she died. I have wondered what that must have been like. I try to imagine what it would have been like for me and I think I would have felt lost and sad and pretty afraid. And maybe angry. Did you feel like that at all?"

"Probably."

"Probably. I'll bet more than probably. What happened to your mom?"

This was the first time that Jake had asked such a direct question about my mother. I almost answered him, but I could not find a way to make a decent beginning to the story. To tell the truth I had had the story in my mind for all these years, but I had never tried to organize the words so that they could come out if needed. In the beginning, I didn't even have any words for what I felt and thought. In the beginning it wasn't even in my mind, it was in my gut and sometimes in my head. The words pressed on the inside of my skull and made my head ache so badly that I had to lie in a dark quiet place for a long time. Or it would ball up in my stomach and I would throw it up in the schoolyard. The doctors didn't know what to say. "Just a little nervous, I guess. High strung, but there's nothing wrong with him. He's perfectly healthy." In fifth grade, some of the kids called me "Puke" because it happened so often. My teacher looked at me with worried eyes and kept me after school on occasion to help out. She would talk with me and ask if I was all right and I would say "yes" because the words weren't there to say anything else. "Things will get better," she would say and I would hope she was right.

At times I would look at my dad and wonder if he had anything to say about it, but he never looked like he even gave it a thought, which seemed odd, because mom's dying was such an awful thing. And he played such a part in it. How could he not be thinking about it? How could he think of anything else? I knew I couldn't. My grades went to hell and there were meetings and my father just seemed more and more angry. I genuinely couldn't see why they were all so worried about school. How could school possibly matter at a time like this? I guess they finally figured that out for themselves, because they gave me a social pass to sixth grade and then to seventh.

Toward the end of seventh grade a new family moved in next door. They had a daughter my age that limped a little because she had had polio when she was very young. She also wore thick glasses, which didn't help matters and only gave kids at school more ammunition for their taunting. They all seemed relieved to have someone to heap their malice on, other than each other.

She came by our house with a pie one day. She smiled at me when I opened the door and said, "We thought you might like a pie. It's cherry. My mom made it for you and your dad. She thought that since you don't have a mother, you might not get pie very often."

No one my age had ever said anything directly to me about my mother's death and here she was, someone I didn't know hardly at all, talking right out loud on the front porch about me not having a mother.

"Thank you for the pie." She was right. I hadn't had a piece of pie in a long while. "But you must be thinking of someone else. My mother is alive."

"Oh, I'm sorry. We never saw her and my mother heard that she had died a year or so ago."

"Well, your mother's wrong. In fact my mom is here right now. She's just lying down. She gets tired and has to lie down. I'd let you in, but I don't want to wake her. She doesn't go out very much. Maybe that's where your mother got the idea. That's not a very nice thing to say, that someone's mother is dead."

I left her standing there on the porch empty-handed. I took the pie to the kitchen and cut myself a large piece. Truth was that my mother never baked at all. The only pie we ever had was Mrs. Smith's, but now that mom was dead we didn't even have that. My dad just never thought of it, I guess, when he shopped.

At first I was offended that she had brought the whole thing up, but after a while, I was more impressed with how bold she was than anything else. It must not have donned on her that no one talked about my mother anymore, that her name was never spoken in our house at all, except when I talked to her at night after the lights were out. But never a word between two people. I wished I could say it right out loud like that. "Yes, my mother died last year and my life just isn't the same. I can't think of anything else. I wish she was alive again and she could hold me in her arms so I wouldn't feel so awful inside." But I could never say that out loud. Never.

"Why do you think you're father never talked to you about your mother?" asked Jake.

"I don't know."

"Come on, you must have thought about this."

"I don't know, maybe he didn't care. Maybe he was glad she was gone. Maybe he wished I were gone too. I don't know."

"You don't like your father much, do you?"

"No, not really."

"Is that why you won't let him come to see you here?"

"I don't want anyone to come see me here. Would you?"

"Why would your father be glad your mother was gone?"

"I guess you'd have to ask him."

"If I asked him, what do you think he would say?"

"I don't know. Maybe he'd say he didn't love her anyway and it didn't matter if she was dead. Maybe that's what he'd say."

"Is that what it seemed like to you, that your father didn't love your mother?"

"I'd say so."

"Did your mother love your father?"

This was harder to answer. I always hoped she didn't, but sometimes she behaved like she did. Most of the time, it was just her and me, but sometimes they'd be laughing in the kitchen and then they'd go to the bedroom and I'd be told not to come upstairs. Of course, at the time, I didn't know exactly what they were doing except that she was choosing him over me, which was hard to believe since she never had a good word to say about him. I felt certain that she loved me more than him, but then there were times when the only person she could pay attention to was him. I never figured it out.

"I don't know."

"You don't know?"

"No, I don't know if she loved him or not. I hope not."

"You hope not."

"Right."

"Why is that?"

"Because of what he did."

"What did he do?"

"A lot, he did a lot of things."

"Like what? What did he do to make you hate him so much? Did he hit you and your mother?"

"Sometimes."

"How often is sometimes?"

"Whenever he was drunk, which was most of the time."

"He hit you and your mother when he was drinking."

"Yes."

"That must have been awful."

"Yeah."

"How long did that go on?"

"All my growing up. Less when I got old enough to defend myself."

"Did your mom try to protect you?"

This was another hard question, because she didn't do that much to keep him away from me. She would try to distract him, but lots of times he was like a locomotive coming down the track and she didn't want to step in front of him. She always looked sad about it. She would comfort me and tell me everything was going to be all right, but it just kept happening.

"She couldn't."

"What do you mean?"

"Once my old man was drunk, there was no way to stop him if he was angry. He just did what he wanted."

"Does your dad still drink?"

"Does a bear shit in the woods?"

"I'll take that as a 'yes.'" He looked at me for a long while. I couldn't tell what was in his mind. I didn't want him to ask me anything more. But I also didn't want him to stop.

"Why don't you tell me what happened?"

I started to feel warm and my face tingled as the sweat began to bead. I looked down at the coffee cup Jake had put on the floor. It said, "World's Greatest Dad." I wondered what that meant. I wondered about his children and what he did with them and were they afraid when he came home and did they ever wish they could disappear.

"How many kids you got?" He opened his mouth but then paused. I could tell he was thinking this through. Was I tricking him? Should he tell me anything about himself? He hadn't before. It's a rule, I guess. The therapist is not supposed to be a person at all. The patient is not to be trusted with any personal information about the therapist. We are so defective that such information might drive us stark raving mad. Maybe I would get jealous of his children or want to be his child or maybe I'd want to fuck his wife and eat his children or whatever bullshit they thought up about what would happen if we knew anything about them.

"Three. I've got three kids."

"Three."

"Uh huh."

"What are they?"

"What?"

"Boy, girl."

"Two boys and a girl."

"Good for you."

"Yeah, the boys are 12 and 10 and my daughter is just 4."

"You love 'em?"

"Of course. More than anything."

"So you're a good father."

"I try to be."

"Maybe you can answer me this, then, since you are a 'good father.' Maybe you can tell me why someone would have a kid if they had no intention of ever loving that kid." I waited but he just looked at me. "I mean, when a man fucks a woman, does he ever give it any thought? I mean about maybe being a father, that maybe he's squirting out a son, you know. Or is he just thinking about his dick and how he'll feel when he starts to come? What does a man think about? Tell me."

"I don't know how your father felt. I don't know if he wanted you or not. I don't know if he loved your mother or if he loved you. But I do know that he's got a hold on you and you've got a hold on him and it doesn't look like either of you can let go. Unless one of you dies. And even then, I don't know if it will be over. I don't know if your suicide would have solved anything."

"It would have solved a lot for me."

"What would it have solved?"

"I wouldn't have to feel like this anymore. I wouldn't have to feel like I'm just here. Alone. And for no good reason."

"You blame your father for this, don't you?"

"Yes, I do. I blame him because he's to blame."

"For what? What did he do? What do you remember? What happened to your mother?"

I didn't know if I wanted to tell him the whole story. It was the only thing I had left of my mother. It was mine. I didn't know if I wanted to share the one thing I had left in the world. What would it sound like anyway? Would the words erupt in my throat? Would it come out as words at all, or as howling or screeching or silence? Would my tongue bleed, would my vocal chords melt, would my lips crack? Or would it come out as a tiny, middle of the night whine or a sigh or a groan?

Would the words be wet with tears or dry and raw and wasted away? The room was so damn warm. Couldn't he feel the heat? Couldn't he feel it?

"I was out for a month."

"Out?"

"Of school. I was out of school for a month."

"When your mom died?"

"Yeah. The kids in my class sent me a card they made in art. It had a rainbow on the front and a sun coming up inside and everyone signed it. It was funny because no one in my class liked me. I mean none of them were close friends. I can remember making a similar card for another boy in the class when he had his tonsils out. I remember how everyone moaned when Miss Loss told us what we were going to do that day. They made faces and one kid had to stand in the corner because he threw his paper on the floor. I don't know how she got everyone to sign my card. Some kids wrote things like, 'Sorry about your mom.' Another kid wrote, 'Too bad.' One girl wrote 'Happy Birthday.' I can see her coming in late to class from the nurse or something and the card coming around and she just signed it with what she figured was going on. She never asked anyone. She never looked at what the other kids wrote. She signed it and passed it on and not even the teacher caught it. She took her time and wrote each letter with a different color. And put little eyes and smiling mouths in the 'Ps.' It wasn't like it wasn't noticeable, but the teacher never noticed. She brought it by the house and gave it to me and said the kids wanted me to have it and that they were thinking about me and hoped I would come back to school real soon. At that point I wasn't talking yet, so I just looked at her and she smiled and then she left."

"You weren't talking?"

"No, I didn't talk at all for almost two weeks, maybe more, I don't remember."

"You were out of school for a month, is that right?"

"Yeah. I couldn't eat anything and when I did, it came right back up. The doctor came to the house. He was cheery and told me I was fine and that I really should go back to school and then he looked at my father and shrugged his shoulders. My father didn't say anything. It was the neighbor who called the doctor. She came over almost every day, Mrs. Simmons, I think it was. She came and looked in on us and she got worried because I wasn't going to school and I wasn't getting out of bed. So she called the doctor. My dad didn't seem worried. I couldn't tell at all what was going on with him. I don't remember him paying much attention to me at all. He stayed in his room or sat in his chair and drank all day. And all night sometimes. We were both on our own. And it stayed that way. It just happened that we were in the same house."

"After a month you went back to school?"

"Yeah. I went back to school. My teacher had me stand up in class and told the class to say 'Welcome back!' and they did. For art class they were making Mother's Day cards and Mrs. Olin said I could make something for my grandmothers. But they were dead. So she said I could make something for my father since Father's Day would be coming in a month or so. But instead, I sat and cut the paper into tiny strips and then cut them again and again until all that was left was confetti. And I cut my finger and the blood dripped onto the floor and Mrs. Olin got upset and sent me to the nurse's office."

"Sounds awful. You must have felt all alone."

"I don't know that I felt much of anything at the time."

"What else do you remember?"

"In those days the kids went home for lunch. I went home, too, but there wasn't anyone there. The door was locked so I would sit on the front porch until it was time to go back to school. When I saw kids coming down the street, I'd go out back so they wouldn't see me and then I'd come around just as they were passing, like I came out the back door."

"Didn't your father know?"

"He was working and we didn't talk much. He worked, came home, sat in his chair and drank until he fell asleep. I usually went to bed on my own. He must have gone up to bed sometime during the night because the television was usually off when I got up and he was usually gone for work. I was on my own pretty much."

"Hm. Sounds pretty rough to me."

"I guess it does when you say it out loud, but it didn't seem like that when I was a kid. It just seemed normal. My mother was gone so all the things she did were gone with her."

"You said it was almost Mother's Day when you went back to school. So did your mom die in April sometime?"

80

"Yes, April 19."

"April 19."

"Uh huh."

"Had she been sick?"

Now he wanted more. I wasn't sure I wanted to give him more, but I also wasn't sure I wanted him to stop asking.

"No. I mean she always had something wrong. She'd stay in bed some days. But I always figured it was to avoid dad. But she would go to the doctor's a lot. She had a bad back or something, I'm not sure exactly, but she always came home with some pills. She was always taking something, sometimes even when she seemed perfectly fine. But I don't know if you'd call her sick. But if you mean, did she die from being sick, no."

"So, as far as you know, she wasn't sick."

"Huh uh."

"Hm. What did happen to your mother?"

"I don't remember exactly." I started to feel warm again. I couldn't look at Jake because if I did the whole damn thing would just throw itself up onto the floor. And then I wouldn't be able to get it back.

"Do you remember much about that day?"

"Some."

"What do you remember?"

"It was school day. A Tuesday, I think. We were going to the zoo that day. The whole class."

"Uh huh."

"Mom made me a bag lunch. It was a ham and cheese sandwich with that brown mustard on it. I didn't like brown mustard but it was all she had. I got angry and she told me I'd have to learn to give things a try." She was always telling me to give things a try. I was very picky about what I ate. Sometimes dinner was carrot sticks and celery and maybe a bowl of Cheerios. She told me I'd waste away to nothin' if I didn't watch out, but I never felt hungry. My father would yell at me for not eating and then yell at her for not making me eat. Pretty soon he'd say what a terrible mother she was and she would ask him how he knew since he was never around. They'd forget about me by then. When my fork hit the plate, it was like sounding the bell for Round 1. I'd sit at the table and move the food around with my fork and then I'd go to my room and lay on the bed until it was over. By then no one cared anymore if I ate at all. It was forgotten until the next mealtime or maybe the one after that. You'd think I would have just taken a bite of something, just to shut them up, but I couldn't.

"Anything else?"

"What?"

"Do you remember anything else?"

"About the lunch?"

"Well, the lunch or anything else. The zoo."

"I remember that I hated going to the zoo, because the animals were always asleep and the ones that were awake always looked sad or bored. The lions were right across from the open area where they had antelopes and stuff, but the lions never moved a muscle. They hardly even looked at the antelopes. It was like they had forgotten who they were or they just didn't care anymore. Nothin' seemed right to me about the zoo. We got to ride on the elephants that day and I remember how coarse the hair on their backs was. We ate our lunches near the snack bar, away from most of the animals so it wouldn't stink. You could watch the prairie dogs from the picnic area. The teacher sat with me and we laughed at how jumpy and busy they were. I remember her smile was so relaxed. I had never seen a face look so unused by life as hers. After lunch we went to the petting zoo and they had a python that each of us got to touch. And then it rained but instead of leaving we stood under some trees like we were in a jungle and waited for the rain to stop. I stood by my teacher who talked almost continuously but her voice sounded like a song so I didn't mind. Her name was Miss Handleman. Yeah, Handleman."

"Handleman."

"Uh huh."

"I'm amazed that you remember so much."

It was important to remember. It was important to go back and walk through the day, looking for cracks or creases in time where something else could have snuck in and turned things in an entirely different direction. I didn't want to go to school that day. What if I had convinced my mother that I was sick and had to stay home? You know they say a butterfly flapping its wings somewhere in the world can change the direction of just about everything. I don't know if that's true, but what if it was true? What if things happen for the least significant reasons? And if you could change just one thing it would all be different. Maybe time isn't one long straight line from here to there. What if you could stand high above it all, and you could see every minute at once, from ten million years ago to ten million years from now and you could reach down and move a minute here, an hour there, and maybe reshuffle a few days so it would all turn out different? Is it odd to remember a single day? Maybe I am the keeper of just one day. Maybe that's my job. Just in case it can be changed. Instead of lost.

9

"Hi, how are you doing? Thank you for letting me come to see you."

Lorraine had a tired looking smile, like those muscles had lost a battle with the rest of her face.

"Okay enough, I guess." She was the first person I had seen from the outside. Outsiders make a difference. They smell different, their eyes take in more, you can see them breathing, they're more alive. They make a person see this place differently, as well. I had grown accustomed to everything here, the smell of the unit, the smell of people sitting in their own sorry situations, the smell of stale air pressing against the permanently locked windows. With Lorraine sitting there in front of me, I felt ashamed of where I was, who I was. I felt ashamed for being unable to live in the world without someone watching over me, someone making rules for me that I had come to accept and count on.

"How are you?" A stupid question. It had only been several weeks, maybe a month. She smiled and looked down at the keys in her hands.

"I'm doing okay, actually. I mean, it's not like it isn't hard without Don being there. But we're doing okay." She smiled again but she wasn't looking at me anymore. She was looking at something that I couldn't see.

"The kids and I went to my parents' for a while, which has helped. They're still there, but I had to come back to take care of some things."

"Uh huh." She was looking at the keys in her hands again and I was looking at the roster on the wall. I had never noticed it before, the list of nurses and social workers written in and erased over and over again. I kept looking at it, hoping that when I looked back at Lorraine she would be gone. I had been told things about her, things I didn't understand, things I didn't know what to do with. Things that she didn't know I knew. I tried to imagine her with Conner and I couldn't see it in my mind. It just didn't fit, and yet who was I to understand these things.

"That's why I came to see you."

"What's that?"

"I met with the lawyer about Don's will. We read it just the other day and there was something in it about you, or for you."

"Something for me? I can't think what Don would…"

"Its nothing very big, but it's something he wanted you to have, something that he felt you would want." She put a bag on the table in front of me. "Go ahead and open it."

"Lorraine, I don't want anything of Don's. It's not right."

She didn't say anything.

I reached across the table for the bag and looked inside. There were two boxes and an envelope. I pulled the larger box out and recognized it immediately. It was Don's old chess set. He kept it in a drawer beside his checking table. On lunch breaks and when the work was slow we would play. He taught me the game when I first started working there. Georgey had never been interested, so Don was delighted when I told him I'd like to learn. He took the game very seriously. We usually sat in silence, Don hunched over the board while I ate my sandwich. I never got the tricks of the game and moved my pieces with little or no thought, while he sat for minutes sometimes, sighing and thinking and finally moving. If I moved too quickly he would get mad and make me take it back. "Think, for chrissakes!" he would say. "Don't just move like you're playing checkers. Give every move some thought. When you move, you should move only when you know what other moves you want to take. You should always be four or five moves ahead." I'd listen and when he was done, I'd stare at the board while I counted to thirty and then I'd move a different piece. "There, that's better," he'd say.

I seldom won but he still looked at our matches as a competition of equals, a true test. It made him feel strong to beat me. We stopped playing several years ago when we lost a white pawn. I came in one morning and he was on his knees beside his table looking under a filing cabinet and swearing, "Chicken shit pawn!" We looked everywhere and couldn't find it. He got madder and madder.

"Don, it'll turn up. Don't get so pissed about it."

"Fuck you," he'd say and back down on the floor he'd go, groaning from the pain. I told him we could get another pawn easily enough, but he wouldn't have it. "No, that's the pawn. That's the one." He put the chess set away and we never talked about it again. And we never played again.

"Jesus," I said, smiling as I thought of Don all pissed off about how poorly I played. "We used to play a lot."

"I know. He told me."

"Not in a long while, though."

I pulled out the other box. It was a cube with no hint of what was inside.

"I wonder what this is?

"I don't know. He didn't say. He just wanted you to have the contents of this bag."

I pulled on the corner of the box. Inside there was a brand new dating stamp, the kind he used when he checked all the prints we made.

I opened the letter:

> *I wanted to thank you for all the time we spent together over the years. They were good times.*
>
> *The stamp is for you to use at work. I imagine that when you read this, you will have my job and I wanted you to know I approved. Congratulations. I know you'll do good with it. Just make sure to ink it before the weekend so it doesn't dry out or crack.*
>
> *Do you remember the other thing, the chess set? I thought you might like to have it, although Bobby Fisher you're not. I know you can't really use it, but I wanted you to have it anyway. I couldn't think of what else to do with it.*
>
> *Your friend,*
> *Don*

I was caught completely off guard by this. He was trying to look after me, passing things on to me that a father might pass on to a son. I didn't know what to say. What would he think about what's happened to me since his death? I felt awful that I would never get to use the stamp, that I wouldn't fill his shoes. But I was glad that he never learned the truth of why Conner kept him; that he never had to face it head on. I think it was better that he died than to have learned he was a pawn in a larger game that he didn't know about. He would have been devastated no matter what explanation Lorraine would have offered.

Lorraine laid a tissue on my hand. I looked up at her and she smiled. I wiped my eyes.

"Don thought the world of you."

"He was a good man. He deserved better."

"He would be happy to know that these things mean so much to you. You know he may not have acted like it, but he was very sentimental and he wore his feelings right out there for everyone to see."

"Oh, I know that. I don't think he ever had an unexpressed feeling." We both laughed.

"Even if sometimes we wished he had."

"Yeah, that's true." We were silent again. Don was our only link. And he was long gone now.

"What will you do?" I asked.

"Well. I'm not sure yet. My mother wants me to move back to New Hampshire. But I don't know. There's something about this place. Maybe it's just Don. I don't know if I could leave knowing he was still here. I know that must sound crazy. He isn't really here. But he is, for me. I can see him any time I want in all the places he touched. It's like this town is a map of him. The gas station, the grocery store, the park, the ball field where he watched our son. Everywhere. And I don't know if I can give that up. So, I can't say what I'm going to do."

"Yeah."

"What about you?"

"Well, I may just stay here at the Hilton." I tried to laugh. "I don't really know. I'm getting out soon, but I don't know beyond that."

"Are you okay? I mean from the…"

"I think so. My therapist thinks I need to 'work it through' more, as they say, but I think I'll be okay."

"I felt awful when I heard. I mean, I'm sorry that it got so bad. I heard about work. I knew it was hard and all, but I didn't know."

"I guess I didn't either."

"When I was young. When I was ten actually, my father did this. He didn't come back, though. He was gone. I came home one afternoon from school and, well, it was awful. I never quite got over it. I mean, I didn't get a chance to say anything to him. I was so sad. I couldn't imagine that he would want to leave me. I was just a kid. I didn't know what people go through. I just kept thinking, 'Why did he leave me?'"

I didn't know what to say to this. I never thought of my mother as leaving. I felt she was taken, so I didn't have the same questions that Lorraine had. But maybe that's how my mother felt about her brother. I know she missed him terribly. I was too young to understand much about him before my mother died, but I wonder what her last day was like with him? Did she see him that morning? Did they have breakfast together? Did they talk? What were his last words before he left the house? Who did he say them to? Was there any clue in what he said?

I think we hope that the ties are strong, that there are invisible strands that connect us with the ones we love most and that those strands are as strong as a spider's web and that they will hold. It is shocking when they don't. Makes you wonder if there are any ties at all or is it just in your own mind. When someone close makes a choice to die, it kind of makes you unimportant, inconsequential, in a way, because they could do something so absolutely final and never give a thought to you.

"Why do you think he did it? Do you know?"

"I don't know. He didn't leave a note or anything. It drove my mother almost crazy. I mean, she would sit in the bedroom with one of my father's suits in her lap and she would smell the suit and cry. I didn't know what to do for her. I didn't know anything at all about what to do, so I just stayed away from her and hoped she'd be okay, because if she weren't, I didn't know what I would do. I tried not to make any problems. I never ruffled her feathers or gave her any reason to want to leave. I knew I couldn't risk that."

"I lost my mother when I was young, too."

"I didn't know that."

"Yeah, I was ten, too."

"I'm sorry. What happened?"

"I don't know exactly. She died." Lorraine waited expecting me to say more, but I didn't.

"I'm sorry."

"Thanks." There was a fly in the corner of the window buzzing furiously, confused by the light outside and unable to reach it.

"I guess we're two sad sacks," Lorraine said with a slight laugh. "I mean, I'm sorry."

"No need for you to apologize. You didn't do anything. Things just happen, don't they? They just happen and we are left to figure out why. But maybe there isn't a reason. Maybe we just think there's a reason for stuff like this because we want there to be one. You know what I mean? I mean we want one because it's just too hard to think that something so bad could just happen, just like that."

"I don't know. I like to think there's a reason behind everything. I don't know if I could go on if I didn't think there was some purpose or something, even if I don't understand it. There must have been a reason my father killed himself and your mother died and Don had so much suffering and you...I mean there must be, don't you think?"

"I don't know." We were both getting uncomfortable. She fingered her car keys and smiled at me.

"Well, I better let you go."

"Okay," she said. "I hope you feel better."

"I will. Thank you for coming to see me. I know you are busy with the kids and all the stuff with Don and everything. I mean, it was nice of you to come here. It's not exactly a place people want to visit."

"I'm glad I came. Please stop by the house when you are home."

"Yeah, okay." When she turned to the door, I wanted to ask her to stay longer, but I didn't know why. I didn't know what to say or how to explain myself.

10

"Nice chess set."

"Thanks." Jake was back, bright and early.

"Where'd you get it?"

"Belonged to someone I used to work with."

"Don?"

"Yeah."

"Nice. Was that his wife the other day?"

"Uh huh."

"Did you know you're missing a pawn?"

"Uh huh."

"Lost?"

"Very."

"Okay. So. Where were we? I think you were talking about your mom when we met before. Right?"

"Uh huh."

"You were telling me about the day she died."

"I know what I was telling you."

"Okay. Can you tell me more?"

"Why don't you back off?"

"Because it's important."

"To who?"

"You. It's important to you. It may be the only thing that's important to you. Maybe that's why you won't talk about it. Maybe you don't want to give it up."

"Wow, that's pretty fuckin' good, you have it all figured out." I was tired of Jake. Tired of his mosquito-like presence every day, buzzing, buzzing. But he was right. This was the only truly important thing in my life. The only matter of substance, this story about someone who died over a quarter century ago. It was a rare day that I didn't think about my mother. It was so common that sometimes it was like she was still alive. I never thought of her as getting any older. She still looked like she did on that last day, her hair pulled back as she rushed me along, an apron around her waist. We fought but I never left the house without a kiss from her, even if I didn't want one.

She was different in those last weeks. One night I found her in the kitchen alone, just sitting. Another morning I found her out on the front stoop, trying to hide a beer from me. Yet another morning she was in the bathroom. I know she was throwing up but she looked at me odd when I asked her and then she laughed and said I had quite an imagination. It was like she was waiting for something. I don't know what. Even my father seemed more attentive. I heard him ask her several times if something was wrong. She never looked at him and he would walk away.

"What happened when you came home from school?"

"Nothing."

"Nothing?"

"I just came home from school. That's all."

"Was your mother there?"

"No. She wasn't."

"Was that unusual?"

"No." But it was. She was always there when I came home. But that afternoon when I reached the front door, it was locked. I figured she was inside, so I knocked but there was no answer. I knocked again and again, but still no answer.

"What happened next?"

"Nothing much, I went to my room. I don't remember what I did." I sat on the porch for almost an hour. By then I was worried. I didn't know what to do. My father was working and I thought of trying to find him, but I wasn't sure if he would get mad at me. I knocked on our neighbor's door, but no one was home. I went around to the back of the house and stood on the gas meter so I could look in through my parents' window. The bed wasn't made and there wasn't any sign of my mother. But when I came around the house again, she was there on the porch unlocking the door. Her voice was all cheery as she apologized for being so late, but her face didn't look right. She looked like she had been sleeping or crying. Her face was puffy, but she didn't smell like she'd been drinking. She kept talking in her masquerade voice. She had been to the store and ran into so-and-so and lost track of time and then the traffic was bad and she kept talking the whole way into the kitchen. But she didn't have anything in her arms, no bags, nothing. She said they didn't have what she wanted after all, so she came home and that's when the traffic got bad because of an accident.

Finally she said, why am I telling you all of this? She looked at me. It's not for you to worry about, she said. I didn't know what that meant and I asked, but she told me to stop questioning her and I said I didn't mean to question her.

"So, you were in your room after you got home?"

"Yeah."

"What happened after that, after dinner, for instance? Could you tell that something was wrong?"

"No, it was a normal evening." Dinner was quiet. Each of us stared at our plates. No one spoke for the longest time. My father asked my mother about her day and she said, "What do you mean?" And he said, "I mean, how was your day?" My mother said, "Okay," and that ended the conversation. My father looked at her and huffed. My mother got up and started to clean off the table while we were still eating. I couldn't figure out what was going on and neither could my father. He looked at me and shrugged his shoulders, but I looked away from him, not wanting to look like I was on his side. I stopped eating and asked my mother if she needed any help, but she said, "No," almost like she didn't hear me. Then she looked at me and smiled, saying, "No thanks, honey, why don't you go upstairs and do your homework." My father kept eating.

I worked in my room for a long time. When I finished, I went to the top of the stairs. There was the low hum of voices, but I couldn't make out a thing. I wondered why there wasn't any yelling. There was always yelling. Or there was nothing at all. It must be something serious if they couldn't yell about it. I mean they yelled about almost everything and said the most terrible things to each other so loud that half the block knew that my mother was a "fucking bitch" who did "nothin' but ruin" my father's life and that my father was a "goddam drunk" who couldn't "get it up if his life depended on it." If it's okay for the whole world to know these embarrassments, what could be left to secrecy? If they were yelling, at least I knew they were okay. But this, this I couldn't figure out.

"Had your mother been ill?"

"No, not that I know of. She went to the doctor's a lot, but she never seemed sick. She just seemed nervous a lot of the time. I mean she felt sick, but wasn't sick, if you know what I mean."

"Yeah, I think I do."

She went to the doctor's almost every week. When I'd ask her if everything was okay, she always said "yes" and that she was just going in for a routine check, nothing to worry about. Sometimes she took me with her, especially if I was missing school. She'd talk about my stomachaches and the doctor would listen, but he seldom talked to me. He didn't really even check me, now that I think of it. He would just listen for a long while and then he'd start to get up or close his chart and that was a sign that the conversation was over. Usually my mother left with a prescription, but I never took any medicine. I just figured she had a bad case of my father.

"What else can you tell me about that evening."

"I don't want to get into this now." After a while my father went to the garage and my mother went to her bedroom. I watched television. It was as quiet as I ever remember the house being with everyone home. I didn't like it at all. I didn't understand it. Didn't know what to do with it.

"You really should. I think it may help you."

"How would you know what will help me?" My mother finally came downstairs around 8:30 and told me that I should take a bath and get ready for bed. She went to the kitchen and got a beer for herself. She called outside to my father to see if he wanted one and he said "yes." I felt better that they said something to each other. As I went up the steps, they were in the kitchen drinking, my father leaning against the refrigerator and my mother looking out the window over the sink. They didn't say anything to me so I just kept going.

"You're right. I don't actually know what will help you or anyone, for that matter. But my impression is that you are in a lot of pain and that a lot of it stems from what happened to your mother. The fact that you are so reluctant to talk about it after all these years makes me wonder all the more."

"Should it get easier to talk about your dead mother, is that what you're saying? Did you learn that in some book? Well-adjusted people should be able to talk about their dead mothers with anyone who wants to listen?"

"I think you know that's not what I'm saying at all. I'm just trying to understand."

"If I don't understand, how could you?" When I came downstairs after my bath, mom was still in the kitchen. There were several bottles on the table. Where's dad, I asked, and she said he had gone to bed already, that he had to get up early. She smiled and told me to come to her. She pulled me close and said she loved me and that I was her boy and that I should never forget it. Her breath was strong now, but that didn't really matter. I was glad to be her boy. You'd better go up, she said, it's past your bedtime. I asked what she was going to do and she said she wasn't tired and that she had some things to do, but she just sat there and took another drink from her glass. When I went upstairs, I could see that the light was still on in my parents' bedroom. I went to the door and was going to knock, but didn't. I went into my room, turned out the light and went to sleep.

"Does anyone understand what you have gone through?"

"No."

"Why do you think that is?"

"I don't know. You're the therapist, why don't you tell me."

"Are you pissed at me?"

"I'm not pissed."

"I think you are."

"Think what you want."

"I think you're pissed because I'm trying to get in and that scares the shit out of you. No one has ever tried to get in, have they? Not your dad, right, and with your mother gone, there was no one else, so you've had to carry this thing alone."

"Everybody carries their own shit around by themselves when all is said and done."

94

I don't know what time it was when I heard the first scream. All I know is I sat bolt upright and it was totally dark and my mother was screaming, calling, moaning. I couldn't see and for a minute I didn't know where I was. I sat there and it was quiet, but then she screamed again. I ran to the door and across the hall to the top of the stairs and yelled, "Mom!" But my father yelled, "Don't come down! Don't come down!"

I didn't know what to do. My mother was crying and talking and saying she was sorry and then she called my name. This time I ran down the steps to see what was going on. My father was standing over my mother in the kitchen; his hands were all bloody. My mother was lying on the floor with her legs pulled up to her chest. I couldn't tell what was wrong. She was breathing hard and her face was all twisted up in pain. She looked at me and tried to speak but she couldn't. My father looked like a madman, "Goddamit, boy, get upstairs! Now!" I hesitated, but he yelled again. My mother turned over and I saw something gleam. I looked again and her hands clutched a sharp piece of glass, like she was trying to pull it out of her stomach. Her white robe was crimson now and there was a slow trickle of blood moving across the linoleum. My father yelled again and I ran up the stairs to my room and slammed the door. I got into bed and pulled the covers up around my face and I stayed there for the longest time, listening.

"You never know. Maybe talking might help. Maybe getting some of this out where we can look at it together might make a difference."

"Maybe." Everything got very quiet for a while as I lay still. My mother stopped screaming and I couldn't hear any of the shuffling that I had heard before. All I could hear was the sound of the third shift at the tube mill across the river. I turned all my attention in that direction and listened for the voices of men, some of whom were on lunch break in the middle of the night. Every day on the way home from school the men would be coming and going at the mill. On hot days, the great doors at one end would be thrown open to make a wind tunnel for the men who were sweating over their machines inside. I always envied them with their hard hats and dirty clothes and protective shoes. It looked like play and they acted like it, too. They'd wave or call out to me as I walked home from school. It made me feel important that they noticed me across the street and I imagined that I was a friend of theirs.

So their sounds in the middle of the night were comforting. I imagined that I was one of them sitting at the picnic table inside the fence, opening my lunch pail and laughing at some joke. I imagined that I was high up on a crane running along the tracks at the top of the mill, everyone watching out for me so the hook at the bottom of the chain didn't hit them and knock them down dead in an instant. And I settled into position and gently lifted some great bundle of tubing and set it down on the flat bed truck so easy that the truck didn't even shutter under the weight. And the men smiled and shook their heads as if to say, "How does he do it?" And I would just wave and head back down the track, knowing I was somebody in this world and that everything was okay at the end of that long chain and that heavy hook.

"They're real men, aren't they?" my mother would say to me and I'd look up into her face and smile. "Maybe that's what you'll be when you grow up."

"You think so?" I'd say.

And she'd say, "Why, of course, you can be whatever you want," just as easy as that and I'd believe her because she said so. She said it with such a casual confidence that she might have been telling me the sun came up this morning. And in those brief times that were nestled between my parents' fights, I felt safe about what was coming even though I didn't know what it was.

I lay there on the windowsill listening until I was jarred out of my dream by the sound of the car door slamming and the car screeching off down the street. I wonder what my father has done now, I thought. Where does he go when he just leaves us? My mother used to stand at the door and look for the longest time, but she stopped doing that. In fact, she'd tell him to get the hell out and he'd go and she'd cry and then the house would be still for a while, like things are still right after a storm has passed and the trees are dripping dry. They were still that night and for a moment I thought things must be okay.

They got away from each other like they always did and now things would fall back into place and we'd go one just like we always did. That wouldn't be so bad, I thought. I had almost gotten used to my father's tirades and the back of his hand. And mother was strong. And actually dad always came home and we always had food on the table and I could always watch my favorite TV shows if dad didn't mind and mom and I had our times together. It would be fine if things just stayed the way they always were. I didn't care to make things change. Maybe things would get worse. Maybe there was something worse than my life and I didn't know it. Why take that chance? Let's just leave well enough alone.

Before I went upstairs I said to her, I said, "Are you okay, mom?" and she looked up at me but she didn't answer. It was like she couldn't speak. She just looked at me; her eyes all surprised and bewildered, like those mothers in the Disney cartoon movies that always seem to die.

"I think he killed her."

"He?" Jake asked.

"My father."

"You think your father killed your mother?"

The only light on in the house was the reading lamp beside my father's chair in the living room. It had a ruffled shade that glowed like a firefly in a jar and made everything look soft and pale yellow. My mother's slippers were behind the chair, half way under, and her robe was in a pile near the kitchen table. A kitchen chair had been turned over and it lay on its side. There were hand towels everywhere, folded into themselves and strewn around the kitchen floor, also larger bathroom towels because the smaller towels couldn't hold it all. There was a broad swipe of blood across the refrigerator, like an artist had studied his canvas for a long while before making his mark. My schoolbooks were still stacked on the kitchen counter, although one had fallen on the floor. It lay in the middle of a large pool of blood. There were bloody footprints leading to the back door, my father's I guessed, and beside them the marks of someone who must have tried hard to stand but who slipped and fell and finally was dragged to the door.

I don't remember feeling anything. Not a thing. I told myself this was a terrible mess and my mother would be upset when she got home. I stood still at the entrance to the kitchen for a long time until I noticed something beyond the light, something lying in the middle of the kitchen floor near the stove. I walked over and picked it up. It was one of my mother's shoes. It was black and it had one small dot of blood on the toe. I went to the sink and ran water over the toe, but the blood had dried around the edges, so I got a napkin and wiped it until the spot was gone. Then I held the shoe against my stomach and rubbed it over and over again with my shirt until I could see the shine again, even in the pale light. I found the other shoe and put them both by the back closet where my mother usually left them, one right beside the other, like they were standing at attention.

"Why do you think your father killed your mother?"

"Because of what I saw."

"What did you see?"

"I saw my mother and my father. Maybe a knife. I saw blood."

"You witnessed this?"

I remember thinking that if the blood dries, we would never be able to get it off the floor. So I went back upstairs and opened the hall closet where we kept the bath towels. I grabbed as many as I could and went back to the kitchen. I didn't know where to start. There was blood splattered across the floor and droplets sprinkled against the cupboards like someone had waved a wet paintbrush in the air. There were smears in almost every direction and, of course, footprints leading to the door. There was a single dark pool beside the kitchen table, though, right where I had last seen my mother. That's where I began. I threw a towel over it and stood on the towel to help it soak up the blood. Quickly I felt the cool wetness on the bottoms of my feet and I jumped off the towel, leaving my prints in the middle. I washed my feet off and continued my work.

It took several bath towels of blood before the pool was gone. I didn't know what to do with the towels, so I took them out to the garbage can. The floor was starting to look better already and I remember feeling proud that I was making progress. I put detergent on another towel and ran water over it and then began to scrub the cupboards. First the blood spread out in long arcs as I wiped, but soon enough the cupboard was clean again. I did the same with the floor, following a path to the back door. There was some blood under the refrigerator that I couldn't reach even when I wrapped a towel around a yardstick and poked it under. But, by and large, the kitchen was looking more like itself and everything seemed almost normal again.

I washed the chair and sat it up beside the table and pushed the other chairs in as well, just the way my mother liked them to be if we weren't eating. "There's not enough room in here to have those chairs scattered all over," she'd say. I knew she would be happy with what I had done. I knew she would smile to see everything back the way it was.

The sun was coming up now. Its light always hit the living room first and carved a path across the floor, stopping at the edge of the kitchen. We had a woodpecker in the neighborhood and he was already busy looking for breakfast, busy like I had been busy. I felt an odd sense of accomplishment as I stood in the living room admiring the job I had done. For the first time I felt tired. I went back upstairs. I sat on the edge of the bathtub and washed my feet and watched the pinkish water swirl down the drain. I washed my hands and arms at the sink, as well, and cleaned the basin, too. Then I crawled into my bed. I pulled the covers up just as I had done hours before.

The house was quiet and still again. The image of my mother lying on the floor came to my mind and I turned quickly as if to shake it out of my head. I closed my eyes and I could hear her voice, not really a voice at all, but sounds, not any sound that vocal cords could make, but sounds that come from somewhere deeper, sounds that come long before words. I felt a chill and I rolled over to look at the picture of my mother beside my bed. Gone, the pain on her face. Gone, the anguish, the frightened look, the helpless gaze. It was her again, whole and smiling and almost happy. I looked at the corners of her mouth and counted tiny creases, three on each side and lines on her forehead, three as well, not worry lines, but lines of expectation, maybe even of hope. And her eyes, if she could turn just slightly, she would be looking right at me, and so I imagined it as hard as I could and then she was looking at me, smiling, and I felt safe again. Then I fell asleep.

"Yes. I witnessed it," I said.

II

I couldn't tell Jake the story, not really. I told him some of the facts, but not the story. It was too hard to say it all out loud. And so much of it was still somewhere in the silence. I didn't tell him about the morning after. There wasn't a sound in the house. I could hear the woodpecker at the tree in our neighbor's yard and the sun was shining through my window and for a moment I tried not to think about last night. It was far away now, like Monday mornings are far away when you're coming home on Friday night. I made my bed. That was a good way to start. I made my bed and I washed and got dressed. This would be a surprise for sure. I never got ready like this in the morning. I always dawdled, that was my mother's word for it. "You always dawdle," she'd say, but with a smile, like it was a joke that only we understood. No dawdling today, though. When I stood at the top of the stairs, I was smiling. I looked down, hoping to see my mother's shadow as she worked in the kitchen. "Mom!" I called, but there was no answer. I called again, "Mom!" but nothing.

I went down two more steps and leaned forward as far as I could to peek into the living room. I could see my father's chair and one of his arms on the rest. He didn't move. "Dad?" But nothing, so I went a few steps further. I could see the back of his head, tilted over like he was asleep. He was still wearing his work dungarees and a T-shirt. There was a can of beer cradled between his legs. Now I could hear his breathing, unsteady like he was fighting not to choke. As I came round the corner, I saw two six packs of beer torn open beside his chair. Empties were scattered on the floor in front of him. I felt oddly comforted by seeing that he was no different today than any other day. Surely if something was wrong, he wouldn't be the same old shit he always was.

I stood beside him now and could see the dried blood on his fingernails and a stain on his shirt. He wasn't asleep after all. His eyes looked dead, though. He didn't blink and he didn't look at me or at anything, for that fact. He just stared. I touched his arm and he startled which scared me and I pulled back. He looked at me finally and his eyes were red and swollen like someone had punched him. He opened his mouth for a long time like he was waiting for words to crawl out, but they never came. He looked away.

"Where's Mommy," I asked, but he didn't answer. "Is she okay?"

He still didn't answer, although he took a deep breath and shifted in the chair, looking for a more comfortable position. I waited. Maybe he was just trying to put his thoughts together. Maybe he was going to answer. Often there were long silences before he spoke and you'd better not interrupt those silences. So I waited, but then I could tell his eyes weren't busy in thought. They were empty.

"Is Mommy okay?"

"No. She's not okay."

"What do you mean? Is she okay? I cleaned everything up and I wanted her to see what I did. What do you mean?"

"She's gone."

"Where has she gone?"

"Away. She's gone away where she can't come back."

"What do you mean, she's gone away and can't come back?"

"You know what I mean. You stood right there and saw her, didn't you? Didn't you!"

"Yes, I saw her. She looked like she hurt her stomach bad."

"Yes."

"Where did she go? To the doctor's?"

"Yes, we went to the hospital. I took her in the car last night. To the hospital, but they couldn't do nothing. Said we were too late."

"Too late?"

"Yeah, too late."

"But she's okay, right? I mean, mom's okay?"

"No, she's not okay. That's what I'm trying to tell you. Your mother's not okay. She's dead." He looked down at his hand and noticed the blood on his nails and he rubbed them with his thumb, but the blood wouldn't come off. I looked at the top of his head and noticed how little hair he had and how matted it was.

"What do you mean? You're making this up."

He was getting angry now.

"Like I told you. Your mother's not coming back. Ever. I tried. I tried to do something, but it didn't work. She couldn't hold on. I told her, hold on, I said, but she didn't do it. I tried to talk to her, to keep her going and she didn't answer. She didn't breathe. Not one fucking breath. They rushed all around doing nothing at the hospital. All them machines didn't do a damn thing. They just. She wouldn't come back. They tried, I guess. They kept pushing hard on her chest over and over, then they pumped with a bag, but the air just came back out. It didn't stay, she didn't want it."

Never coming back was all I heard. This didn't seem possible and I didn't believe it. I couldn't get the idea of "never," and my father couldn't make me believe it. He got angry at me and asked if I was trying to make him mad with my questions, but all I had were questions.

The police came and I didn't understand why. All they had were questions, too, and I could tell that their questions also made my father mad, but he didn't show them. I could tell, though, by the way he sighed and never really looked at them when he was looking at them.

"So, what exactly happened?"

"I told you already."

"I know this is hard on you, but we're trying to understand. Can you tell us again?"

"She was yelling and I was upstairs getting ready for bed. I ran downstairs and she was lying on the floor in the kitchen and there was blood."

"Was she conscious by the time you got to the kitchen?"

"What do you mean?"

"Was she awake? Did she speak to you?"

"Yes."

"What did she say?"

"I don't remember exactly. She was kinda drunk."

"Had you been drinking too?"

"What's that got to do with it?"

"What did she say to you?"

"It was all crazy like. She said she was afraid. She kept saying it over and over, I'm afraid, I'm afraid. I didn't know what she meant. She was bleeding everywhere. It was a mess. It got on everything."

"What happened to all the blood? You said there was a lot of blood, but the kitchen looks pretty clean."

"I don't know."

"I cleaned it," I said. My father looked up at me for the first time. There was surprise in his eyes.

"You cleaned it?" The officer's eyebrows were raised.

"Yes." I was afraid now. Did I do something wrong.

"Did someone tell you to?"

"No. I just did it. I knew mom wouldn't like all the..."

"Did you see your mom and dad before your mother died?"

"Don't bother the boy," my father said, which surprised me because it sounded like he almost cared.

"I know you and your son are going through an awful time. We're just trying to understand." He turned to me again. "Did you see your mom and dad?"

"Uh huh."

"What did you see?"

"Mom was laying there on the floor all hurt and dad was leaning over her."

"Anything else?"

"No, not really."

"Did your mother say anything to you?"

I wished I could have answered yes, but she didn't say anything. She just looked at me and there were words in her eyes, but I couldn't read them.

"Huh uh."

"Did your dad?"

"Yeah."

"What did he say?" I looked at my father and he looked at me like he was holding his breath. I wasn't sure how to answer. Should I say he yelled at me and that he looked crazy and that he smelled like a beer can?

"He told me to go back upstairs."

"That's all?"

"Uh huh."

"Is that all officer?" my father said.

"Just one more thing. When did you clean all this up?"

"I don't know what time. It was still night. I don't know."

"Did your father tell you to clean it up?"

"Now hold on, what the hell…?" I was afraid now, because I could see that my father was going to explode. I wanted to tell the policeman that he better watch out, that he better not piss my father off too bad. I answered quickly.

"No."

"No?"

"No. It was my idea. He wasn't here."

"Do you remember anything else?"

"I don't think so," I said.

"Are you sure?"

"Uh huh."

"Okay."

He turned back to my father.

"Did you and your wife get along?"

"Yes, we got along. What kinda question is that? Jesus Christ, my wife just fucking died."

"There are police reports that the two of you didn't get along that well, that your wife called on occasion for help. Is that true?"

"All marriages have problems. What the fuck are you trying to say?"

"I'm not trying to say anything. Try to stay calm. Your wife died with a knife in her abdomen and we are trying to understand how it got there."

"It got there because she put it there." My father started to cry. I had seen him cry before but he was always so drunk that I never thought much of it. I mean it wasn't like he cried about something, it was just that he would cry after a while when he drank. But this was different. He was crying about something. He was crying about my mother. I thought, Jesus, it must be true. She must be dead. What else could make him cry? So I cried. I sat on the stairs listening to my father and I cried while the police kept asking him questions.

My mother's funeral was at Porter's funeral home down the street. The Porters lived there and when there was a funeral, they cleared out the front room for viewing. I had been in their house before. My mother's casket was right where the Porter's usually had their TV. It didn't look exactly like a living room, but I couldn't help thinking about the Porters sitting there, watching TV, laughing at some stupid show. I wondered if the Porter kids got angry when there was a body in the room, or did they have a TV somewhere else in the house. I wondered if they came in the room at night and looked at my mother. They knew her. She yelled at them all the time when they ran through her garden, but it never stopped them. Now they wouldn't have to worry about where they ran.

I had never been to a funeral before. I didn't know that's where we were going when my father told me to get dressed in my Sunday clothes. We just got in the car and went. The police hadn't come back again, but my father had gone to the station a few times. He drank hard when he came home after those trips and I would find him in his chair in the morning. He went to see the doctor a couple of times as well. And so did the police. But he didn't seem sick. I didn't know what the doctor could do for him. My mother always came home from the doctor with medicine, but my father just came home from the doctor's with more beer. He was drinking more and more. And he drank a lot that morning when we got in the car and drove down the street to Porter's.

I had never seen a dead person before. I had seen animals that were dead, like a squirrel crushed in the street. Once I had seen a deer beside the road. It was all bloated and its neck was turned almost entirely around and its eyes were open and staring, just like they look when you see them mounted on a restaurant wall. Except its tongue was hanging out. But I never thought of them as dead. They just got hit by a car and never knew what happened and never knew they could die and it probably didn't matter. But a person is different. I mean dying is what we most want to avoid. You don't want to be like an animal along the side of the road, looking like you didn't know what hit you.

I worried about what my mother would look like.

My father didn't say a word in the car. He had his only suit on and his blue tie. He had shaved and put some cologne on that didn't mix well with the smell of beer that was his permanent aftershave. His white knuckles clutched the wheel. His eyes never wondered from whatever he was looking at, perhaps the road.

When I saw my mother from across the Porter's living room, I was surprised how good she looked. I had never seen the dress before, but it had flowers and was bright and she would have liked it. She was holding a bouquet of pink roses and she looked, for all the world, like she was asleep, nothing more. I was encouraged by this so I stepped slowly forward until I was standing right beside her, looking down at her face which was pale white. Her mouth was pressed down and stretched into a permanent semi-smile, kind of like her real smile. Her hair smelled like roses.

I looked at her for the longest time until it donned on me that she was not going to move. At all. I don't think I expected her to move. But I didn't expect her not to move either. I didn't know exactly what I expected, but one thing was certain, this was not just sleep. I watched her dress and her chest was still, like she had taken a deep breath and was never going to let it out. Her hands weren't holding the flowers at all, they were stiffened into a pose and the flowers were laying on them. They were manikin hands, except you can move a manikin's hands into different positions if you want to. You couldn't move these hands at all. No, this was not sleep. It wasn't even a distant relative of sleep and everyone who says people go to sleep when they die should have to stand here in front of my mother. This was something else all together, something startling in its absolute, undeniable permanence. Go, went, gone.

I reached out with one finger and touched her right hand and it felt like frog skin stretched over a cold stone. I began to cry.

The police came a couple of more times, but that was it. I didn't understand what was going on and when I asked my father he wasn't any help at all.

"It's nothing. They're just doing their job, that's all, nothing to worry about."

"But they said something about the knife…"

"Like I said, it's nothing. Your mother died peculiar, that's all."

"But they were asking you…"

106

"Look, let's just drop it. It doesn't matter now. It won't bring her back."

I knew by then that she wasn't coming back. I wanted to understand how and why she left in the first place. It didn't add up. Why would the police come at all unless they thought something was wrong? Did they think my father had something to do with my mother's death? I'd lay in bed at night thinking about what happened. I'd close my eyes so I could see it again and again, hoping I would see something that I hadn't seen before, something that would give me an answer. I'd watch myself walk down the steps. My mother would call out. My father would yell at me to go back. She would be holding her stomach. I would see the knife again and again. Each time it ended as it had the very first time.

Did my father kill my mother and get away with it? Was she calling out to me for help? I began to wonder why I listened to my father when he yelled at me to go back upstairs. Why didn't I go to her? Why didn't I do something?

12

I stood at the entrance to the psych ward with all the methadone addicts huddled under a tree smoking. It was already hot, the kind of beating sun that slows you down and makes you squint at the dry pavement and brown grass that is reflecting the haze. The cicadas were grinding the air.

"Got a light?" He was a young guy, maybe 22, 23, that I had noticed over the weeks. He went to his group each morning, part of the deal to get his hit of methadone.

"Yeah, sure." I lit him and he drew it in like he was making love. Everyone who comes to the program smokes most all the time. But I guess that's an okay addiction cause no one seems to make them stop. I wonder if they give them a carton of cigarettes on the first day.

"They lettin' you out?"

"Yeah, I guess."

"Good, man, what were you in for?"

"I don't know."

"Everybody's here for some reason. What's yours?"

"Fucked up, I guess."

"Yeah, we're all fucked up, but what's you're particular fucked-upness? I mean, you hear voices and shit like that?"

"No, no voices."

"That's cool, I'm glad for you. I mean I been coming to this program for two years and I seen a lot of fucked up people walking around the halls talkin' to, like, nobody, you know what I mean. I mean they weren't just fucked, they were totally fucked."

"Uh huh." I wondered what Jake's diagnosis of me was. Partially fucked? Half fucked? Totally fucked? I realized I didn't have anything in common with this kid and I didn't care to. It got quiet.

"So, cool, I'm glad you're gettin' outa here, you know."

"Uh huh."

"Waitin' for your lady?""

"No."

"Yeah, I hear ya. That's a bitch. Why bother, right? Why wait for the bitch, you know?" He bobbed with each phrase like he was shadow boxing. "I'm happy for you, man, I mean, you're movin' on, right. I don't know what your thing was and I don't need to know. I seen you around and you looked like a long-timer first time I seen you, I mean, you looked fuckin' whipped like a dog; your face was, like, absolutely no where in this world. I saw you in the hall a couple of times and, shit, you didn't look like you knew which end was up. You were gone and I thought, he ain't leavin' this place, no way, you know? But here you are. You're lookin' better, I don't mean, like, all better, but you look a hell of a lot better than you did."

I guess I was a mess when I got here. No one had said it quite like this, though. They never told me what I looked like. They told me I seemed depressed or anxious or withdrawn, but they never acted like that was odd or that it was particularly worrisome. That doesn't make sense, I know, but being messed up was so commonplace to everyone in the hospital that after a while it all seemed kind of normal in a screwed up way. Jake was always trying to get me to talk and insisting that talking would make me better, but he never acted like I was a total mess. He just accepted what I brought to the game, which is his job, accepting people that is, but sometimes it seemed unreal that I was here, or that there was anything wrong. Life got so routine and normal here after a while. Not much different than being outside. I mean I got up and ate and talked to the same people pretty much about the same stuff, and I did the same things each day, just like I did on the outside when I was working and all, except here I lived where I worked and worked where I lived and everyone else got to go home.

Jake asked me if I felt like I was ready to leave. I told him I was but I don't know if I am or not. Going home, I don't know. Home's a place where I can go and I know that I can stay there and that my stuff will be there and that everything will be basically the same, which is good and bad. Home is where I can go when there's no place else for me. But that's not really enough. My home doesn't feel like home, whatever home is supposed to feel like. It's familiar, but not the kind of familiar that makes you lean back with a sigh because it feels so good or because you know you can walk around in your underwear and you can say what you want and do what you want and no one is gonna make you stop.

Home can be dangerous; there can be land mines if you're not careful. Maybe what makes it home is that although it's dangerous, I know where the danger is and how to walk around it, I know where to step, what to say and not say, when to say anything at all, which is mostly never. But it's home nonetheless.

Maybe home is a place you have to go to because there is no other place to go. And if you don't go there, you won't fit anywhere; and if you do go, you'll understand why you don't fit anywhere else.

He was still there beside me.

"Well, good luck, man."

"Thanks."

"And remember, you know, when things get hard, just fuck 'em if they can't take a joke."

Jake said I should see a therapist when I left the hospital and he gave me the name of one, but I doubt I'll go. I don't even have a job for chrissakes. How could I pay for a therapist? My father brought my mail to the hospital last week and there was a "Thank you for your years of service" letter and my final check. The letter said that my whole department was being closed. They "regretted having to make this cost saving move" but felt that I "would understand that the welfare of the entire Wilson family had to be the number one priority." It ended with a cheery, "Good luck!"

That letter knocked me on my ass for a few days. When I thought about it, though, working at Wilson's had been a total dead ender. I never moved forward at all, not a single inch. If it weren't for Don being there, I might have left years ago. He made it sane and I felt like I had a place of my own, a place where no one would bother me and I could do my work and I had a friend. I didn't even feel like I wanted to go back at this point. Although, if the job were still there, I probably would.

So I wouldn't be seeing a therapist. All I had to fall back on was a bottle of pills and three refills. Once that was gone, my lifeline to the hospital was gone as well.

The other piece of mail was a letter from Lorraine, which came as a surprise. It was addressed to my home, so she obviously thought I would have been out of the hospital by the time I got it. It was very chatty about her kids and how the end of school went and how her son was giving her trouble and how her daughter was doing okay although she was very quiet and how Lorraine's parents had been great although living with them was awkward and how she missed Don but felt like she was doing the best she could with the help of a grief support group.

She also said she was coming to town again, something about Don's "estate." She said she would give me a call and maybe we could go out for coffee again. At first I didn't think much of this. But then I read and re-read her letter trying to figure out why she wanted to see me. I wondered what was on her mind? Was it something about Don? Or his estate? Maybe I was going to get something. No, I knew that wouldn't be it. There was nothing to get. Maybe she just felt sorry for me and wanted to see how I was doing. I wasn't sure I liked that idea. I didn't need her pity. I didn't need to feel any smaller than I already felt. If that was it, maybe I wouldn't respond to her call or if I did maybe I would tell her I couldn't make it. I would be real friendly so she wouldn't suspect anything and then maybe she would think I was doing fine and she wouldn't pity me. Or maybe I needed her pity, maybe that was okay, maybe I needed to roll up inside of it and hide away in her sympathy for a while.

I couldn't figure it out. All I knew was that I couldn't get her letter off my mind. I never expected to hear from her again and then this. I told myself that she probably wouldn't call so I wouldn't dwell on it so much, but that didn't seem to make a difference. I kept wondering. In a way, it gave me something to think about instead of thinking about leaving the hospital and going home again. I guess it was something I could look forward to, even though it might not happen. I could keep it there in my mind for hope's sake, but keep it away a little bit, too, so that I wouldn't hope too much.

The methadone crew was heading back into the hospital now. Must have been time for group.

I took a seat on the bench near the bus stop, the smoke still filling the air. My cab was late. There was one other thing in the mail, a note from my father: "I haven't been feeling so good, but if you need a ride from the hospital I could maybe pick you up. Call if you're needing a ride." He wrote down his work number and our home number, like I would have forgotten by now. I thought about calling him. I even went to the pay phone on my floor, picked up the receiver and then thought about it one more time and hung up. I appreciated that he wrote me the note and that he offered to come, but he had made so many offers along the way and never came through, that I didn't want to take the chance. There were the baseball games when the coach would have to stay long after everyone was gone because he forgot to pick me up; there were the open houses at school; there were the times I was stranded at a friend's; there was even the time that my mother and I walked the whole way home from the super market pushing a grocery cart because my father went to the bar after he dropped us off and got so drunk that he couldn't remember where he had left us. My mother tried to make a game of it. She let me sit inside the cart and we pretended we were on an adventure. But I could tell she was embarrassed when friends drove by and offered us a ride. They always looked worried, but she would pretend it was normal as could be, as if she had planned to come home by grocery cart all along. And when we'd get home my father would be sitting in his chair with a Genny, yelling about why she was late getting home and where was she and why wasn't the dinner ready.

Most times mom didn't say anything, but I couldn't keep my mouth shut.

"Where were you? We waited and waited and you never came to get us!"

"What the hell's he talking about?" he'd say to my mother, but she wouldn't answer and then he'd get really angry. "Where were you?" he'd ask her. His tone was quiet, but his eyes were dark and his jaw was set. His questioning almost always led to suspicion about whether or not my mother was seeing someone. I wanted to say, "Yeah, she fucked him the whole way home while I pushed the cart." But, of course, I was just a kid and wouldn't have said that. At least I wanted to say, "Why are you being so mean?" But I couldn't say that either. So I cried and went upstairs to my room and the battle shifted to me. "See what you did!" my mother would say. Then they'd fight about me. And that's the way it went.

So I decided to pass on my father's offer to pick me up.

"How long you been in? I hope you don't mind me asking. But I guessed you didn't work there when I saw the bag over your back." I had all my clothes in a Hefty bag.

"A while." The cabby checked me out through his rear view mirror. It was quiet for a few minutes, but his curiosity got the best of him.

"Did it help? Being in there?"

"Don't know." And I didn't. I felt a little like a drunk coming out of the hospital. It's pretty easy to do okay in there when you have all those walls and rules and people and everything around you. But what happens when you leave and the first friend you meet says, "Good to see you. Come on, I'll buy you a drink." The hospital is all rehearsal. It's not the real thing. I seen several people come and go and come and go during the time I was on the unit. They'd leave full of hope and then get sucker punched by the world and have to come back. I wanted to tell him, "Talk to me in a month or so, or in a year." Did I feel better? Not really, but I didn't expect to feel better. I didn't think being in the hospital would make me feel better. How could it? I mean it's the hospital, for chrissakes, it's not the world.

I did feel different, though. I felt less casual about my life. When I took the pills, it was easy. I mean I didn't care at all. It didn't matter. If I'd been dead when I woke up, I don't think I would have been sad at all. I would have been relieved, I guess. But now I felt a little vibration inside, a little hum, like my idle was running a little high. I felt like I used to feel before a ballgame, when my insides tingled and I was just nervous enough to stay focused but not nervous enough to come unglued. The difference was that I knew what my objective was when I played baseball, so I could click the engine into gear and move forward. But it wasn't at all clear what my objective was right now. That worried me some. But it felt good to have that hum going. It felt like I was plugged into something.

And even though I didn't have a job to go back to, actually I didn't really have much of my old life to go back to, it felt kind of good having a clean slate. Good, but scary, too. What was I going to do?

113

That's a scary question, but it's also a question I haven't had to ask for my whole adult life. I've always known what I was going to do every day. Life might have been pretty awful, but at least it was simple. I didn't have to give it much thought. I knew my life. Now I didn't know it that well, at all.

Of course, there also was my father. He was definitely a "known commodity," as they say. He was part of the simple but awful side of things. He's been what he's been for as long as I can remember. Like an old song that you know so well you can't stand hearing it anymore, and yet the radio plays it over and over and for some reason you keep tuning in. Maybe I was hoping that just once the words would be different.

"What was the address again?" I told him. "My wife was in there. She was so bad she wouldn't get out of bed. It was after our son died."

"I'm sorry to hear."

"Yeah, she was in an awful way. Just couldn't move on. She wouldn't change anything in his room. I'd find her in his closet smelling his clothes and crying. I didn't know what the hell to do."

"Must have been…"

"Yeah, it was bad, I tell ya. Her doctor said she should go in for some treatments. I didn't know what he meant but I said okay. Well, come to find out, they wanted to do them shock treatments, you know, where they shoot the electricity through your brain, scrambling it all up. Jesus, I thought, what the hell kind of thing is that.

"Uh huh, that."

"But then I looked at her, and I thought, if it will help her, I'm willing to try anything. And you know, she had a whole bunch of these treatments and they worked. I couldn't believe it, but they worked. She started to get better. I mean she didn't exactly pull out of the dumps quick, but she started to, and she started to talk. And after some months, she laughed and I knew things would get better."

"What happened to your son?"

"Hung himself."

"Oh. How did you ever."

"I don't know. It was pretty bad. I mean he did it one night in the garage. We knew he had been depressed after his girlfriend broke up with him, but we never suspected anything like this. I mean we were out for the evening. When we came home I pushed the button to open the garage while I turned around to back in. I like to back it in so I can just drive straight out in the morning. So I backed it in quick like and heard this thud. I mean I could feel something hit the car and I thought, what the hell, so I looked again in the rearview mirror and all I could see were two legs and his sneakers and I knew right away what it was. My wife went nuts, I mean she started to scream and I tried to get him down, but I couldn't. I wasn't strong enough. So I held him there while she called 911, I held him, but I knew…"

"He was already gone."

"He was already gone."

"My God…"

"Yeah." He wiped his eyes the way men often do, not like they're crying, but like they got some dust or dirt in their eye. I didn't know what to say, so I just looked at him through the mirror and finally his eyes caught mine and he laughed a little.

"Jesus Christ. What a fuckin' welcoming committee I am. Here you are just gettin' out and I'm tellin' you my tale of woe. I mean, sorry."

"No, no, that's fine. I mean, I'm sorry you had to go through all that."

"Yeah, I guess that's why I take these calls when we get them from the hospital. I know someone is going home and they're going home alone, you know, because no one is picking them up. No offense, but that's right, right?"

"Yeah, that's right."

"So, it's like, shit, no one should have to go home alone like that. There should be someone there who knows what the hell it's like. Not that I know what it was like for you, but I know, you know what I mean?"

"Yeah, I do."

"So, that's why I came."

"Thanks. I'm glad it was you."

"Okay, so here we are. Are you sure this is it?" I gave him the address of the hardware store a few blocks from my home so that I wouldn't just suddenly be there.

"Yeah, this is fine." I started to get my wallet out.

"Hey, no, really, this is on me."

"Thanks."

"You gotta make me a promise, though."

"What's that?"

"You gotta make sure you don't end up doing something you shouldn't, you know what I mean?"

"Yeah, okay." There were more Uncle Harold's in the world than I realized. I wonder what kind of promises my mother made after her brother died. Which ones she could keep and which ones she couldn't? Did she promise to stay alive? She couldn't have known what was coming in her life. You can't know what's ahead although mostly you try to figure it out through hoping and worrying and guessing. That's what promises are, I suppose, kind of a hope about what you will do in the future.

If you were a bird flying over this neighborhood, you would see that my house is one block off the main drag, hidden on a sycamore-lined street. When I was a kid, I used to pick the bark off those trees and throw them like skipper stones across a pond. I'd lean over so that my arm would be perfectly parallel to the ground and I'd launch the bark into the air and pretend that if it reached the other side of the street I'd hit a game winning homerun. Other times I'd play war with some friends. I was the best because I figured out how to make the bark curve when I threw it so I could hit someone even if he was behind a tree. I was always good at games that involved throwing something.

Our front yard was dirty and dusty in the summer, perfect for playing marbles or war games with our tiny plastic soldiers, all frozen in permanent postures of combat. I remember that my mother warned me about playing in the dirt. She worried about us breathing in the dust and catching polio. If I close my eyes I can still see a neighbor kid, a year younger than me, standing in the front yard with his gleaming stainless steel crutches propping him up, a smile on his face, a bunch of us kids swirling around him. I can still hear him call out and see him falling, his body twisted in the metal. We watched and didn't know what to do. He cried and could not get up.

The sidewalk out front was like a super highway, a road to friends' houses and back. A good place to run and a great place to ride bikes. I lost my two front teeth on that sidewalk, falling off the back of Billy

Hamilton's bike when I was seven. There was a VFW next door, a bar for WW II vets. Still there. That's where my dad spent some time each night. He'd be laughing loud when he came out of the front door with his friends, but that was all gone by the time he made the short walk across the yard to our front door. His sense of humor had fallen off of him like a marble off a table top and all that was left were sharp edges and corners and I knew I'd better stay clear.

There was a fire escape on the side of the building and I remember one time that some of the older kids in the neighborhood collected a giant jar of maple tree seeds. They went up to the third platform and opened the jar and out flew all of these tiny helicopters, turning, turning in the breeze, twirling so fast and falling so slow. I had never seen anything like it. To me it was the Fourth of July right there in my backyard and I laughed out loud when they reached my upturned face.

Beside the VFW near the railroad tracks was a flagpole rising from a concrete base. I would walk round and round that base, balancing myself by holding onto the pole and hoping that a train would come by soon. Whenever a train did come I'd pump my arm up and down furiously, signaling the engineer to blow the whistle. Obediently, he would reach above him and pull the chord. The whistle's mouth would burst with howling steam. I would smile with satisfaction at having such influence in the world.

There was a tiny box of a house on the other side of the tracks. That was where the crossing guard stayed. His door was always open and when I would walk with my mother to Shuler's grocery store, he would always speak to me. I couldn't imagine having a more wonderful job. He knew when a train was in the block and traffic needed to stop. He would walk out into the middle of the tracks, blow his whistle and hold up the sign—Stop! And everyone did. All the rushing cars would halt. Everyone would wait. No one moved until his sign came down. Then he would walk back to his little house and sit in his well-worn leather easy chair until the next B&O train came through town.

The fire escape is gone. And so are the flagpole and the crossing guard and his house. And so are the tracks. That was the best world I ever knew; even with my father's craziness, it was the best. When my mother died, it was like the shades were drawn on that world and when they were finally opened again, it was all gone, all the color, all the light, gone.

Our house is huddled and small and gray from wear, with all the blinds closed; it looks like a stray cat asleep in the dirt. There is a small porch with a green and white metal awning that shields the house like a protective hand. A single lawn chair for my father. Above the porch is a gable. That's my room, with its slanting walls.

I took out my keys, but the door was unlocked. As I entered, I called out to see if he was home, but there was no answer. Entering the living room, though, I saw him there in his chair, asleep in his flannel shirt and work pants and white socks with his shoes tossed to the side. His head leaned over to the right and his mouth was wide open, sucking air, his cheeks slowly vibrating in and out against his toothless gums, his teeth beside him on the table. He smelled stale, like a closet you haven't opened in months. And he looked different, but I wasn't sure why. Maybe he wasn't different at all. I hadn't looked straight at him like this in God knows how long. Maybe I was just seeing him as he was, but still, he looked different.

I started up the stairs and he began to stir. I kept going and then he called out, "Is that you?"

"Yeah."

"You're home then."

"Yeah, I'm home."

13

In the first couple of weeks after I came home, we fell into a comfortable rhythm. I was asleep when he left for work and when he came home I was out or in my room. He slept in front of the TV until bedtime. Once he was in bed, I came down and watched TV until almost dawn. Dinner was the only part of the day that wasn't perfectly choreographed. Our paths crossed in the kitchen, but our lines were well rehearsed:

"How's it goin'?" I'd ask.

"Okay."

"How was work?"

"Okay. They got me haulin' stuff again. I'm not supposed to, you know."

"Uh huh."

"Yeah. Killin' me."

"Hungry?"

"No."

Then he'd stand there for a few minutes while I made a sandwich or got a bowl of cereal. He'd watch me, but say nothing. Then he'd go upstairs and I'd hear his bedroom door close. By the time he'd come out again, I'd be back in my room and we would settle into the evening. Once he asked how I was doing.

"So, did they help you?"

"Who?"

"The hospital people."

"I don't know. Maybe."

"You okay now?"

"Uh huh."

That was it, though. I must admit, I didn't even expect that.

It took a while before I figured out the real difference, though. I realized I hadn't seen any beer bottles or cans around the house since I'd been home. At first I figured he was out and waiting for a delivery. But it never came.

This wasn't the first time he'd done something out of the ordinary like this. In fact, he used to do it routinely when I was young. Sometimes it was very dramatic. He would come home with flowers for my mother and some new toy for me and announce that things were going to be different. He never said he'd stopped drinking, but we knew what he meant. Sometimes he still had beer breath when he made these declarations, but he'd make them anyway, all full of a blustery kind of hope. Other times, we'd just notice that he wasn't drinking. Usually this was after a particularly bad fight with my mother. Maybe he'd hit her or for the one-thousandth time she'd threatened to leave. It was his way of saying, "I'm sorry. Give me another chance." He couldn't just apologize. He couldn't say the words, so he'd stop drinking for a while to clean out his system and with it, he hoped, everything else. Didn't last very long. Sometimes a matter of days. Maybe even a week, as I recall. But never long enough to shift the balance of daily living to a new kind of normal. It always felt like we were on vacation and that soon we would get back to the routine.

I wasn't sure what he was apologizing for this time. Maybe for what I did and what he didn't do. Maybe for not paying more attention and for leaving me so long before he called someone. Maybe for all the other times he didn't do what a father is supposed to do. Who knows? I told myself it didn't matter, but I couldn't stop thinking about it. Why had he stopped? How long would we be on this vacation?

It was another week before I went into Wilson's to clean out my stuff. The door to the blue print room was closed. I had never seen it closed before. It was always propped open because there wasn't any reason to close it. It was always being used and people were always coming and going with their orders, but not anymore. They had gone ahead with their plans. No hum of machines, no rhythmic stamping, no smell of chlorine, no muffled conversation. It was good that Don was dead, because seeing this would have killed him. It was his life, his little kingdom and his stool, a thrown. It was still there behind the copy table, the leather seat cushion the shape of his skinny butt. The floor was worn smooth in front of the machine from my constant shuffling from the copier to the table. There were still some unopened packs of paper in the corner, but all the chlorine was gone. There were dust bunnies in the corners as big as fuckin' cats. The place was wasted.

I stood in front of the empty deck that used to hold the copy paper and the prints. The prints would go on the top shelf and the copy paper on the shelf below it. That way I could pull one print out on top of a sheet of copy paper all at once. Then I'd turn to the machine, where the rollers would be going, settle the two sheets on the shelf, line up all the edges and feed her in. That's what I did all day long. Over twenty years. When I opened the stash drawer underneath, there was some old gum, a few pens, a couple of paper backs, my coffee mug, and some rubber thumbs for when I covered Don's job. I kept the mug and one rubber thumb. The rest went in the wastebasket.

It was so quiet. Not a sound. Not a movement. Everything still, like it was a museum after closing time. And I was part of the display. It was never supposed to be a lifetime, but it was all I really knew for years, the only place where I felt okay to be myself. I think Don did that for me. He could give a shit what I did or didn't do. "None of my fuckin' business," he'd say. But not like he didn't care. More like he understood that what I did was up to me and no one else. He kind of assumed that I could pull it off, my life that is, that I could make my own way. It was good to know that there was someone out there who had some confidence in me.

It was all gone for sure now. My father couldn't give it to me. I mean, even if he wanted to, I don't think he would have a clue how to do it. Neither do I, for that matter. I don't know how to kick myself in the ass and get going. Mostly I'm just scared to death all the time.

I haven't felt like ending things since I left the bin, but I haven't felt much like starting anything either. I feel like a man with no arms and legs. I can't seem to take a step and I can't seem to hold onto anything either.

I've been to the welfare office and they sent me to a work-training place where I took some tests to see what I might be good at. They were going to look into a couple of programs for me, but I haven't heard anything yet and I wasn't too impressed with what they had to offer. Seemed mostly like piecework for retardeds and stuff like that. But the guy acted hopeful—"We'll find you something!" One of those smiling guys who make you wonder what he knows that you don't. I've been checking the paper, too, and I even went on a couple of interviews. But, nothing. I only have one skill, really.

My dad put some money in my account while I was "away." He didn't tell me about it, but when I made a withdrawal and saw my balance, I was surprised. It took me a few days but I finally thanked him. He just shrugged. So, for a while I'm covered.

The only good thing that has happened so far is that I had lunch with Lorraine and I found out why she wanted to get together. We met at Mena's, a little diner in our neighborhood. I got there first and when Lorraine walked in, she looked a little unsure and suddenly I realized that Mena's was more of a dump than I remembered. She saw me and smiled. Her hair was longer than the last time we talked.

"Hi, how are you!" she said with a slight laugh, like she was glad to see me.

"Okay, fine," I said with surprising enthusiasm. She slid into the booth. I hadn't noticed her green eyes before. I looked at them and felt myself falling in somehow and it was hard to hear what she was saying because her eyes took up all the space I had inside. I leaned back, needing more room, but I couldn't say why. I started to perspire and my face felt warm. I hoped I wouldn't repeat my hospital performance.

"I'm sorry, what did you say?"

"I asked if you were okay? You look…"

"No, I'm fine. It's just a little warm," I said as Lorraine wrapped her jacket around her shoulders. The ceiling fan was blowing steadily on both of us and the fly that was assigned to our table just arrived. "No, I'm fine. You look great." And with that her eyebrows raised and I couldn't find a way to reel in my words. They just jumped right out of my mouth and I could almost see them heading directly towards her ears, but there was nothing I could do, no fail-safe system to recall them or blow them up in mid-air.

"Well, thanks," she said with a smile. "I've been better, but thanks for saying that."

"How are the kids?"

"Oh, they're doing okay, I guess. My son misses his dad, but he seems to be doing well in school. Nighttime is hardest for him. Sometimes when I wake up in the morning I have a guest in my bed. He just has a hard time being alone. He never says so directly, but I can see that he's hesitant..." I couldn't stop looking at her eyes. I felt uneasy and wanted to look away, but I couldn't. I mean I seldom look at someone when I'm talking or even when they're talking, but I couldn't look away. She kept talking about her daughter and then her son, who sounds very messed up, although she didn't seem to see it. He was withdrawn and hanging with some kids she didn't know, but she was just glad he had some friends. It didn't sound good to me, but what do I know, I've never been a parent, I've never even had a pet.

"And, so, how are things with you?" She tilted her head and looked at me with an expression that said, "Are you still totally fucked up?"

"I'm still here, that's the good news, I guess," I said with a laugh, and then I realized it wasn't that funny. She smiled like she understood that I really was still fucked up but she was going to overlook it and be nice.

"You look better. I mean you look more rested."

"Sleeping all the time will do that, I guess." Good. That should really impress her? Impress her? Am I trying to impress her?

"Well, you've been through a lot yourself in the last several months. I mean..."

"Nothing compared to, you know, Don and all." There. I sounded almost like a human being. Almost like I could take someone else's feelings into account. "Hungry?" Almost.

I ordered the chili and a dog. She ordered a house salad and a tetanus shot. What was I thinking asking Lorraine to meet me here? She just didn't fit. There was a spider on the wall for God's sake and luckily enough we couldn't see behind the counter. Who knows what was living back there on the old chili encrusted floor. Fine for me, but, Jesus. She didn't seem to mind, though. She said the salad was good, fresh, that is, and for some reason, I felt complimented.

I launched into the weather.

"Something, isn't it, the weather we been having. I mean, it's been warmer than I can remember. Like a drought for the farmers. Although it's almost fall, now, so it probably doesn't matter. Although, some stuff doesn't really 'come in', as they say, until now, but even if it rained, I don't know if it would make a big difference. Sure been hot, though. I like it I guess, although it makes sleeping hard. I mean I don't have an air conditioner. I got a fan, but it isn't worth shit. I mean, I'm sorry for the 'shit,' I mean I'm sorry." That went well.

"Yes, it has been hot. I lived on a farm when I was a girl. My stepdad would have hated this. He would walk out every day on hot, dry summers and look at the corn and just shake his head. He wouldn't say anything, but even as a little girl, I knew it wasn't good when he shook his head."

"Your stepdad still alive?"

"No, he died when I was 17."

"I'm sorry to hear that."

"Yes, he was a good man. I mean I loved him. It took me a long time to get over it. Sometimes I still miss him."

I wasn't sure what to say.

"How did he die?"

"He had a heart attack. At least that's what they think. We found him in the barn, just lying there. It was…"

"That sounds terrible. I'm sorry I brought it up. I didn't mean…"

"That's okay, really. It's been a long time, but I guess it all came back with Don dying and all. I mean the losses seem to pile up and all the feelings that I thought I put to rest wake up and it feels like it all just happened yesterday."

"Yeah."

"What about you? Is your father alive."

"Yeah. That's who I live with."

"Oh, that's nice."

"Well, not really. We aren't that close at all. I mean we live in the same house but we don't really live together, if you know what I mean?"

"Oh."

"Yeah, he and I haven't ever been close. He's kind of a drunk and it's all just messed up."

"That's too bad. What's your mother think about it?"

124

"Not much. I mean. She died when I was a kid. I guess I know a little what you went through and your kids, in a way."

"I'm so sorry. What happened?"

"I don't really like to talk about it." The food, such as it was, came. "I mean, let's just say she died unexpectedly."

"That must have been very hard on you. I'm sorry, really."

I liked that she was "sorry," that she felt something for me, or for what I went through. She seemed to understand. At least that's what her eyes said. I didn't want to go into my long sad story, because I was afraid she would wilt under the heat of my feelings about what happened to my mother. It would be like opening a blast furnace on someone when they least expected it. She might get severe burns all over her self. So I didn't say anymore. Instead I called to the waitress and asked for some ketchup and mustard. That seemed to end the conversation.

Next we ran right into the long embarrassing silence part of our visit. Luckily, we were eating, so it didn't seem to matter. I guess that's why people meet over food, so that when there's nothing coming out of their mouths they can put something in. She ate her salad delicately and barely drank any of her soda. It was easier to look at her now because she was paying attention to what she was doing. There was a shadow under her eyes, a shadow that had been broader when Don was ill. That must have been where she kept her sadness. If you looked only at her smile, which came quickly and broadly, you would miss her sadness altogether. It was well kept, hidden there behind the green.

"I brought you something," she said as she searched through her purse. "Here, I thought you would want this." She handed me a single white chess pawn. At first I didn't know what it was, but then it donned on me. The missing piece. "It has to be from Don's chess set, the one he had at work." She held out the pawn for me and I just looked at it. "You and Don played chess together, right?" I still didn't know what to say and I didn't know why. It seemed so odd to see this piece of my relationship with Don here at Mena's, completely out of place. We had played so many matches together over the years. Mostly in silence, sitting over coffee with the machine humming behind us, one hand reaching out over the board and then another, back and forth in a slow rhythm of friendship. And then everything stopped when he couldn't find that damn pawn. Wouldn't let me replace it. He wanted that one pawn. So many pieces and yet if you're missing even one, you can't play. And so we didn't. Ever again.

125

"Thank you," I said as I felt the soft wood on the rounded tip. I looked up at her. "Thank you. Where did you ever find it?"

"When I went to the office to get his things, it was there. It was right in his briefcase, at the very bottom, under some other things, but right there." I had forgotten that Don carried a briefcase. Always did and I never knew why. I never saw him open it and in later years it never left the office. Maybe it made him feel like a real someone walking in in the morning with a brief case like all the suits upstairs. So the piece was there all along. Now the set was complete. Nothing was lost after all.

"That is so strange. I mean he looked and looked for this damn thing. He was so angry. And he wouldn't let me replace it or get another set. He just completely shut down about it."

"Well, that was Don, too. When he wanted things to be a certain way and couldn't make it happen, he just stopped, dug in his heels and wouldn't budge."

"Yeah, that sounds about right. I guess there was a lot he couldn't control, huh."

"Yes."

"I want to thank you Lorraine. Really. You have been very nice to me and you don't hardly even know me and what you know about me came from Don, so who knows." We both laughed.

"Well, I'm glad I could do this for you. I thought you would want it. I knew he would want you to have it."

The check came and we stood up and headed for the door. I opened it for her and she touched my shoulder as she walked through and said, "Thank you." I couldn't get that out of my mind and I didn't know why until later. I couldn't remember the last time that a woman had touched me, I don't even mean sexually, I just mean on purpose, like she meant to, like she reached out specifically to me and touched me. And it wasn't much. A light touch on my shoulder, not even her whole hand, just the tips of her fingers, maybe not even all of them, just a few, but still I felt it. I felt the touch and when I walked away I felt different for a while, like I belonged or something.

When I got home I went upstairs to my room and got the chess set out from under my bed. I opened the box, cleared a place for the board and set up the pieces, placing the pawn last, making each of the rows complete.

14

I moved my bed back to its old spot near the window. It was warm and I liked the feel of the night air, steady and cool on my skin. Even as a kid I used to lie near the window, my arms wrapped around my pillow, looking out at the southern sky, tracing the line of Orion's belt, searching for one of the dippers and listening to the leaves of the maple tree brush the house. There was a metal roof on the porch below my window and when it rained it sounded like bacon frying, a sound so steady and so soothing that my eyes just naturally closed and when I'd wake up I wouldn't have moved a muscle.

Of course, in those days my mind was full of kid thoughts. In the summer that meant baseball. How would the Pirates do this year? They were my team. They had beaten the mighty Yankees in 1960, but nothing very exciting happened during my growing up years. I watched them in the standings, but if I had to watch one player more than any other, it was not a Pirate, not even the great Clemente. Instead it was Mr. Willie Mays. "How did he do last night?" was the question I woke up with each morning. I checked the box scores each day to see how my hero had done. My mood went up and down with his batting average and homerun count. When he went on a spree or had a game winning catch I felt a little lighter and the world seemed easy. If he was in a slump, I was too. That's the kind of loyalty he deserved.

I even created a baseball game I could play by myself bouncing a rubber ball off the front steps. If I missed the ball it was a hit. If the ball reached the sidewalk on the fly, it was a double. If the ball reached the street on the fly, it was a homerun. I don't know how I managed it, but Say Hey always did well in my front yard league. He could do it all, as they used to say. He could run, hit, hit with power, field and throw. That's all you can ask of any ballplayer and he did it better than anyone before or since.

When I was that young, I assumed that kind of perfection was out there waiting for me, that I would naturally grow into it and one day someone would be playing bounce-ball off their front steps using me as their star player. It's hard to recapture that frame of mind once you have been in the world for a few decades. Hard to think back to what it was like to be so naively hopeful and expectant about life. What it was like to look forward, instead of always looking backward, like driving a car by looking in the rear view mirror. You run off the road a lot and never quite know where you are heading.

I am surprised that I felt like that even with all the problems we had. Somehow I put the problems away in a little container when I really needed to so they couldn't spill out onto my life quite so easily. Not that I didn't hurt, I did, but I could put them away from time to time and think about the world clean and crisp like a newly chalked foul line and a freshly trimmed infield. I wish I still had that in me, that capacity to set it aside, to set aside all the noise and the disappointments and the loss.

I would love to sit down with that little boy and ask him how he did it and when exactly he lost it. Was it when his mother died, or just before or sometime after? Did he really believe she was dead, as in gone forever, or did he think she was dead like things die on TV and then come back? Was she like Road Runner? When did it dawn on him? Was he lying in bed looking out the window one night when he realized she was utterly and completely gone? Gone as gone could be. Is that when it happened? Is that when something stopped? Is that when he knew he would never be Willie Mays?

I thought about lunch with Lorraine. Even after a few weeks it stayed with me. I couldn't remember much of what we said anymore, but I could remember the angle of her eyebrow, her left eyebrow, when she listened closely, the way it peaked and fell away. And I could remember a tooth, a slightly crooked tooth that made her smile imperfect, which made it seem all the more perfect to me. I tried to shake these thoughts from my mind. What would Don think if he knew I couldn't get his wife out of my head? "Jesus Christ," he'd say, and look at me sideways like he couldn't believe his eyes. What was I doing? I had to stop thinking about her. It didn't do me any good. It just frustrated me, but nevertheless I found her creeping into my mind in those long dark hours after the lights were out and dad was settled and the house stopped creaking and I lay staring out the window at a world that made less and less sense with each passing day. Thinking of her took me away. She was a soft place in a hard world.

I wanted to call her to get together for lunch or something, but I couldn't think of a reason to meet. I felt like I did when I was thirteen and wanted to call a girl. Now, as then, I sat staring at the phone, hoping it would ring and I wouldn't have to be the one making the call. I spent a lot of hours staring at the phone when I was a teenager. And when I made that rare call, it never went the way I wanted it to go. In my fantasy the girl would say:

"It's you! I was hoping you would call! I was thinking about you and wondering why you never talked to me in class. I figured you were just shy."

"Yeah, I am."

"You don't have to be shy with me. I think you're pretty cute…"

You can fill in the rest.

The real calls went something like this. After I'd say hi and tell the girl my name, she would say:

"Who?"

I'd repeat my name.

"Do I know you?"

"Yeah, kinda. From class."

"What class? I don't remember anyone by that name."

"Math. Math class. Mrs. Baldinger."

"Math class? Are you sure? I think I'd remember."

"_____"

"Who is this really? Did you make up that name? Is that you Frankie? You really had me going. Is that you?"

"_____"

129

"C'mon. Is that you?"

"_____"

"This really isn't that funny, you know."

"_____"

"This is not funny at all! Don't you ever call me again, whoever you are! Creep!" Click!

Finally I decided, fuck this, and I tried to put Lorraine out of my mind. But "putting-Lorraine-out-of-my-mind" became a new thing on my mind.

In the meantime, my life was heading flat out towards nowhere. I couldn't find a job I wanted. I couldn't bring myself to flip burgers at McDonald's or any of those other fast food places that are run by pimply-faced kids all named Heather and Sean. Wilson's was running ads for janitorial staff but I didn't want to crawl back there after everything that had happened. So I sat on my dead ass most of the day and all of the night and did nothing except watch time pass and wonder where the fuck I was going. I even called the therapist that Jake had recommended and got on a two-month waiting list. I stopped taking the medicine.

When I left the hospital, I was scared, but I wasn't what you'd call desperate. I mean I didn't want to kill myself, or anything like that. Although sometimes I wasn't sure why.

15

I sat bolt upright. It was about 3 am and at first I couldn't figure out where I was. What the hell was that noise? I sat in my bed, quiet, listening as my eyes adjusted to the darkness. Nothing. I didn't hear a thing and decided it must have been a dream. But it seemed so real, the sound. Like someone struggling or gagging, or an animal wounded and crying out. Must have been a nightmare. Which wouldn't have been unusual. I had been having nightmares for as long as I could remember.

The first time was after my mother died. Maybe a half year or so later. I dreamed that she came in my room and there was blood all over her face, but she acted like there was nothing wrong, like she was coming in to wake me up for school and tell me that she had made pancakes for breakfast. There was a deep gash in her side, but she didn't seem to feel any pain. For some reason I knew that if I mentioned what I saw, it would become real for her and she would panic and then die, so I tried not to say a thing, but the bleeding got worse and I became afraid and finally I said one thing, just one thing, "Mom?" And she immediately realized what was going on and she started to scream and she ran from my room and I followed her and found her in a pool of blood at the bottom of the stairs. She was dead and I screamed and woke myself up. I was sweating and breathing hard like I had just run the whole way home from school and I was afraid and I started to call for my mother and then I realized that the dream was true. Even though my mouth was open there was no one to call. I lay back down. I didn't even cry. In a while I heard the first bird of the day, a morning dove.

That was the first time, but not the last time, and so I assumed I had had another nightmare; one, thank God, that I couldn't remember. I was awake now, so I decided to take a piss. When I opened my door, I could see that the bathroom light was on. "Dad?" I took another step into the hall and I could see something on the floor of the bathroom, something sticking out from behind the door. At first I couldn't tell what it was, but then I could see that it was a foot. "Dad?" Nothing.

I stepped into the bathroom and he was lying on the floor beside the toilet. He had thrown up all over the seat and on the floor. His head was lying on the porcelain base of the john. His eyes were closed but he was awake and breathing. He opened them, but didn't turn his head. He stared and panted like he was trying to catch his breath. He was only wearing his boxers and he looked gray as a November sky, his ribcage looked like a xylophone. I hadn't noticed before, but he was an old man, curled into a backwards 'S' on the floor.

"Dad?" He still didn't answer, but his eyes moved back and forth like he was getting his bearings. He took a deep breath and stretched out his legs. He put one hand on the edge of the toilet like he was going to pull himself up.

"Don't move just yet. It's a mess everywhere. Let me." I reached for a towel to clean up some of the vomit.

"I can't."

"That's okay. Just lay there. Don't do nothing." I got more towels as he laid back down on the floor. He was shivering now, so I got his robe and draped it across his back.

"Jesus, how much did you drink?" He didn't answer. He was still breathing deep and staring at the floor. His mouth was wide open and he didn't have his dentures in so it looked like a black hole in the middle of his face, like a Halloween mask, and his eyes were wide and moist and scary, actually scared was more like it. He rarely got sick from drinking beer, but since he hadn't been drinking for a while, maybe it hit him harder than usual.

Once I got things cleaned up, he was breathing more even and I tried to help him sit up. He really struggled to turn over and when I finally was able to pull him up to a sitting position, he didn't want to go any further. He looked exhausted.

"Let me sit here. Okay?"

"Sure." I didn't know what to make of this. He never got sick. He never missed work and never complained about feeling ill. He used to make fun of my mother because she went to the doctor's almost every week, sometimes more often than that. He was proud that he never had to go, except to get a work physical every few years, and then he put it off as long as possible. He thought going to the doctor's was a sign of weakness.

"You wanna get up?"

"In a minute. Just let me sit." He was edgy so that was probably a good sign.

"Fell off the wagon, did you?"

"What do you mean?"

"I know you haven't been drinking lately. I haven't seen Ben make any deliveries since I been home. I figured you must of tied one on to get this sick."

"That what you figured?" He looked at me for the first time and his eyes looked odd. They were sunk deep into his head and his forehead hung over them like a cliff.

"No, I ain't been drinking, but thank you for your concern." The sarcasm was back so the nausea must have been gone. I wanted to say, "I give you concern equal to the concern you give me," but I held my tongue because he looked so different. I couldn't figure it out.

"What made you so fuckin' sick then?"

"Don't know. Just got sick, that's all." He sounded like my question was of no interest to him at all.

He tried to stand up on his own. I could tell he didn't want to ask me for help so I watched him, but his legs were still rubbery and there was no denying that he couldn't get up on his own. I didn't say a thing. I just reached out and put a hand under his armpit to give him a little more leverage. He still struggled and I almost toppled over on him. I reached down and placed my other hand under his other armpit and tried to pull without pulling so hard that he would realize that he wasn't contributing anything to the effort. At that point, though, he didn't seem to care. He rested both arms on mine and held onto my elbows with his hands.

I couldn't remember the last time I had touched my father. Somewhere along the way he had turned into a little glass figure that had to be held just so, or he would break. There was almost no meat on his arms and legs. His upper chest had disappeared completely. I was amazed that he had anything to throw up at all.

We were quite a sight as we navigated to his bedroom, me walking backwards with him holding my shoulders as he shuffled forward. We looked like a couple of ballroom dance rejects. He didn't say a thing and he didn't look at me. He looked at the floor, concentrating. He no longer had hair on his head, just hairs, barely covering anything, pasted down from the sweat.

He sat down on his bed with a sigh. He tried to prop his pillows up, but couldn't manage it.

"Could you?"

"Sure." He leaned back and closed his eyes.

"Do you need anything?"

"No."

I started to walk away but then I stopped.

"Are you okay?"

"What do you mean?"

"Are you okay, is what I mean. You stopped drinking. You look like hell. I find you lying on the bathroom floor in a pool of puke. Are you okay?"

"Not as okay as I'd like. But I'll be fine."

"Maybe you better stay home tomorrow. It's almost morning as it is."

"I'm not going in." His response was too casual, to I'don't-really-care. Not him at all. Work was life.

He didn't say a thing about it the next morning. I found him at the kitchen table in his robe nursing a cup of coffee. He didn't look up while I poured myself a cup. Usually I went back to my room, but I sat at the table, instead, and this seemed to startle him.

"What?" he said.

"Nothin'."

He looked at me and then back to his paper.

"Did you sleep?"

"A little."

"Must not have been much. I mean it was almost dawn when we went to bed." I waited but he didn't say anything.

"What was that all about last night?"

"What do you mean, what was that all about? I was sick, that's all."

"Hell, I know you were sick. I was there. Remember?"

He didn't say anything. I sat for another minute and decided this wasn't going anywhere so I went upstairs.

Three nights later we were at it again. I woke up again and could hear him retching. This time, though, he wasn't in the bathroom. He was in his bedroom with a pan he had brought to bed with him. He was on his hands and knees on the floor, sweat pouring off of him. His arms were trembling from trying to hold himself up so that he could get sick. I knelt beside him and put my arms under his stomach to hold him up.

"Don't touch me!" He was in pain and his face was drawn up tight, erasing his eyes completely. Nothing was coming no matter how hard he tried. I turned on the light and I could see some blood in the pan. His skin was yellowish, although I wondered if it was just from the light, but his eyes were, too.

He still knelt although nothing more was coming. Finally he sat back against the bed. I offered to help him up but he shook his head "no." I stood beside him. He looked small. He had always seemed big to me, not so much because of his size, he wasn't tall at all, but because of everything else about him. I always felt small beside him, even long after I had passed him in height.

"Dad?" He didn't answer.

"Dad?"

"I got nothin' to say."

"What's goin' on? I mean this is crazy. Every night you're sick as a dog. Look at you. You look like death warmed over. This can't be no bug, for crissakes." He still didn't say anything. "You gotta go to the doctor's. This isn't right."

"I been to the doctor's."

"You been to the doctor's?"

"Yeah."

"When have you been to the doctor's? You never go to the doctor's."

"Well, I been to the doctor's." He started to get up, like the conversation was over, like he had told me everything I needed to know. But this time he couldn't walk away. He couldn't even walk.

"Here," I reached out and helped him lean back on his pillows.

"Goddam, I don't want this," he said.

135

"What do you mean, you don't want this, want what?"

"This! Pukin' my goddam guts out all the time and not being able to get up and, shit, I can't work, can't work at all. They're gonna know that soon enough and then what? What will I do?"

"What are you talkin' about? How long has this been going on?"

"For a while."

"How long is 'a while'?"

"Long enough. You been gone, you know." He said it like I had been away to Hawaii and had left him with nothing to eat or drink.

"Whadaya mean, I been gone? What's that got to do with anything?"

"A lot has happened. I been sick."

"Is that why you aren't drinking? You know, I noticed that right off, I mean not seeing beer cans and bottles around is like not seeing furniture in the house. Did you think I wasn't gonna notice? Jesus. I just figured it was one of those things, like the old days, you know. You'd stop for a while and then you'd start up worse than ever."

"Fuck you."

"Fuck me? Fuck you."

"You hate me don't you?"

"What?"

"You hate me. I know it. You've hated me all along. Ever since you were a little snot nosed shit. You hate me. Say it." He was right. He was absolutely right. I hated him. But hearing it out loud like that, hearing it come back at me in his voice was unsettling, not untrue, but unsettling, like he was stabbing me with my own feelings.

"No, I don't hate you. I don't have that much feeling for you anymore."

"Well, good, then it won't matter when I'm gone."

"What do you mean, when you're gone? What's the doctor telling you?"

"It ain't no he. It's a she."

"What's *she* tellin' you then?"

"She's telling me the truth, that's what she's telling me. She's telling what's comin'."

"What *is* wrong with you? You know, don't you? Tell me what it is."

"I'm on my way out, that's what it is."

"What?"

"I'm dying."

"Whadaya mean you're dying? Since when did she tell you that?"

"It means your wish is finally gonna come true."

"What did the doctor say?"

"She said my time is almost up."

"When did she tell you this?"

"Been a few months ago."

"You've known and didn't tell me?"

"You went nuts, remember? And you wouldn't let me come visit you, remember?"

"You could have written me a letter or left me a note. You could've told me what the fuck was going on!" He had to be wrong on this. It couldn't be me. He was always the one who fucked up.

"It wasn't worth it. I figured you'd hear it sooner or later so it didn't matter. I was too tired to try and get through to you. You weren't gonna let me, so why try. I had other things to worry about."

I stayed angry, but I felt guilty. Not sure why. I mean I didn't owe him anything. He owed me, for chrissakes. He owed me a lifetime of consideration and yet I felt guilty, like I had done something wrong or had missed something that was impossible to miss, something that I should have noticed. How did I miss this?

"You shoulda tried," I insisted lamely. He looked at me for a long moment, long enough that I felt uncomfortable. Not the old squirming feeling I had when I didn't know what was coming next, but uncomfortable because I sensed what *was* coming next.

The waiting room smelled like people who had been lying in their own urine and sweat for weeks. There was an old woman beside us who stared out the window to the parking lot and breathed heavy like Darth Vader. I could see that this was a full-time job for her, that she was staring so she could keep her concentration, so she could focus on each breath or she might stop breathing altogether. There was a young couple across from us, must have been teenagers. They had a tiny baby buried in a mountain of homemade blankets. The mother was about 16. She was chewing gum and looking at her baby. Her nose and lip were pierced and she was wearing black lipstick. Her boyfriend was playing his Gameboy and listening to his CD player.

This girl's mother was on her constantly about the baby, "Hold him up, no, up, don't let his head bob like that, he's gonna break his goddam neck!" "Ma!" the girl would say and look at her mother like she was an asshole. The boyfriend-father-kid just kept listening to his CD player. Never looked at the baby once.

"How long does she usually make you wait?" I asked.

"I don't know. A while."

We sat for another 20 minutes. The old woman's place was taken by a guy who looked like he was about 60. He had wild hair that stood almost straight up and he had a handmade pocket purse that hung from his belt. He wore an old corduroy jacket and a tie that was as wide as his head. He talked very intelligent but nothing he said made sense. He talked to anyone who looked at him and to some who didn't, maybe even some who weren't actually there, for all I knew. I tried not to make eye contact.

"How long you been comin' here?" I asked dad.

"I don't know."

"Jesus, what a fuckin' hole."

Next came a woman with five kids, one in her arms that was dripping snot as steady as a broken faucet. She had a stroller and a couple of bags and some toys and the kids were flying off in every direction and she took her time with each one and tried to make them settle down and when they didn't, she just smiled. What the hell else could she do with that many kids? She wasn't much older than the other kid with the kid-father and the baby. I was amazed she could even get to the doctor's at all. The littlest one started crying for no reason and I thought I was gonna have to kill him or me. Thank God the nurse called my dad when she did.

Of course, this didn't mean we were going to see the doctor anytime soon. It just meant we were being moved to a tiny examination room to wait some more. The nurse weighed my dad and joked with him like he was a frequent flyer and I guess that's what he was. He even joked back like he was a regular person who made regular conversation with regular people. There was a particularly gross chart on the wall that showed every possible bad thing that could happen to someone with diabetes. There was another sign written in Spanish. It had a picture of a woman huddled in the dark with a shadowy figure standing over her. There was a small wooden table with a stool on wheels, a table to lie on with stirrups, and two chairs. Finally there was a knock on the door and in she came.

"Hi, I'm doctor Buckley." She reached out and shook my hand. She said I must be "the son." She smiled at my father and asked how he'd been and he said fine. He seemed to puff himself up for her; wanting to impress her by saying he was doing okay.

"That's good," she responded, but with a tone that said, "I know you're not."

She asked me about myself, what I did for work, or used to do, and how I was, which seemed like an odd question, until I realized that my father must have told her I had been in the bin. She said she was glad I was able to come. She asked me if I had any questions about my father's "condition."

"What exactly is his condition? I mean, he throws up a lot and looks like he's lost weight, and he's all yellow, but he hasn't told me what exactly the problem is." I didn't say that he told me he was dying. After he told me the big news, I thought about it and wondered if what he told me was true. It wasn't beyond him to lie if it would benefit him in some way. He always lied to my mother, at least that's what she told me. He would lie about his pay; he would lie about where he had been or where he was going; he would lie about things he promised to do. As far as I knew, it was unreasonable to expect a truthful statement to ever come out of his mouth. So why should this be any different? The only problem with this theory was that I couldn't figure the angle. I couldn't figure out what he was getting out of lying about this.

"What has your father told you so far?" She leaned forward with an earnest look on her face, her stethoscope draped around her neck.

"Like I said. Not much." And then I added, "He said something about dying, but I didn't know what he meant. I figured he was just so sick he felt like he was dying, you know what I mean, you can feel so awful that you think you're dying?"

She smiled, "Yes, I know what you mean." I smiled back figuring we were on the same wavelength about my father's lies.

"You should know that your father is very ill. I had hoped he would have told you more." She glanced at him, as if to say, "Remember that talk we had?" My father stared at his feet.

"Your father came in with some belly pain a few months ago. He complained that he had been losing some weight and didn't have

139

much energy. At first we thought it might be flu, but it didn't go away so we began to consider other things. Were you aware that he has been drinking pretty heavily for quite some time?"

I wanted to say, "Of course, I know, for chrissakes. It's been the story of my life. Do you want me to tell you how I know that my father drinks? Do you want me to tell you the stories or show you the scars or what? What would convince you that I know?" But I didn't. In fact, her question was asked as if to say, "If you did know, you should have done something and if you didn't know, you're an idiot."

"My father's been drinking for as long as I can remember."

"Oh," she said, looking again at my father. "Well, I started wondering if that might be part of the problem. So I ran some blood tests and didn't like what they showed, so I sent your father for a CT scan. Do you know what that is?"

"Uh huh." Don had told me everything I ever wanted to know about CT scans. It seemed like he had them every week.

"Well, the scan showed a mass in your father's pancreas. That was about a month or so ago, wasn't it?" She looked at my father for confirmation. He shrugged his shoulders, looking humiliated by the conversation. My father never liked being the center of unwanted attention.

"So."

"What do you mean by a mass?"

"A mass is a tumor. We found a tumor."

"Like cancer?"

"Yes, exactly, cancer."

"You found cancer in his stomach."

"Pancreas, actually, and so we…"

"How long ago was this? You said a month?" I was in the hospital. Had just gone in a while before that. I tried to remember if he seemed sick before I went in, but I couldn't remember anything about him, any real contact, no talking, I couldn't remember even looking at him. Had I heard anything at night? Had he been sick and I didn't hear him?

"Yes, it was about a month ago."

"I wasn't, I was away at the time.""Yes, I know," she said. Again I wondered what he had told her.

"So we decided to do an endoscopy to take a biopsy of the mass. Your dad didn't like that much," she said smiling at him. He was still looking at the floor. "We had to put a scope down his throat and into his abdomen to get a small piece of the tumor so we could test it and see what we had."

"And?"

"And I'm afraid it was malignant." At this she stopped and looked at me for a long time and then at my father. When it became apparent that we weren't going to say anything she asked if we had talked about this at all.

"No," I said.

She smiled and we sat another few seconds in silence. My father continued to stare at the floor. The doctor shifted on the rolly chair.

"So what's next?" I asked.

"What do you mean?"

"I mean what's next, what will you do for this? Does he need an operation or some medicine or something? How sick will that make him? I know that people can lose their hair and…"

"Well, I see that the two of you haven't talked yet."

"No, we haven't."

She looked at my father again. This time he sighed and looked up at her. "I told him you said I didn't have a lot of time."

"Well, that's not exactly what I meant when I asked you to talk to your son. I thought you would explain."

"Doctor, my father and I don't talk."

"But you live together, isn't that right."

"Yes, we have lived together for a long time, but we don't really spend time together."

"Oh, I see."

I never thought of our arrangement as terribly odd until I had to explain it to someone else and then the conversation usually ended with, "Oh, I see."

"So let's pretend that I am hearing this for the very first time, which actually I am, okay?"

"Okay, well, your father is very sick."

"He did tell me that."

"And it is taking a toll on him. He's losing weight and as you know he's very nauseated all the time. We're trying to help with that by giving him medicine. We are trying to treat the pain, too, so that he can be comfortable, but…"

"Does this thing have a name?"

"What?"

"Does it have a name? What's he got?"

"It's pancreatic cancer."

"Bad cancer?"

"Yes, bad cancer."

"How bad is bad?"

She looked at my father. "Do you want to tell your son or shall I?" My father looked up and started to move his lips, but his eyes filled and he couldn't speak. Finally he said, "He don't care anyway."

"Whadaya mean, I don't care? I'm here. Just tell me how bad it is." He wouldn't say anything. "Doc, tell me."

"Well, it's not good."

"I think we've established that. Is he dying? That's what he kind of said at home, but I didn't know if I should believe him. You see, doc, he's been a liar for as long as I can remember. You can't believe much of anything that comes out of his mouth. If my mother were alive she could tell you lots of stories, but she's not, is she, dad?"

"No…"

"Now, hold on, let's not."

"She's not"

"That's right.

"Okay now."

"She's not alive."

"You say that like it's my fault."

"Now why in the world would I think it was your fault?"

"Gentleman, I can't have this…"

"You've blamed me all your life and you don't know the half of it."

"Gentleman!"

"What the hell is that supposed to mean?"

"Never mind."

"What the hell is that supposed to mean, I asked!"

"Stop it! Stop it." My father glared at me, and the room was suddenly warm. My palms stuck to my jeans. "I can't allow you to behave this way in my office." I was furious and embarrassed and confused. What did he mean? He had never so much as hinted anything about my mother or her death all these years.

"I know this is a trying time, but you have to be calm about this. You can't let things get out of control. Your father can't take it. It will make things worse."

"You never answered my question."

"What?"

"Is he dying or was that just one more lie?"

She looked at me and than at my father. She took a deep breath. "Well. Yes. Your father's prognosis isn't good."

"What does that mean?"

"It means that when he dies it will be because of this cancer."

"How long does he have?"

"This is what he really wants to know," my father said. "This is the big news for him. This is what will make his day."

"Please!" she said to my father and he sat back in his chair.

"The two of you must figure out a way to get along. This is too important to let your anger get…"

"How long?"

She took another deep breath, looked at the floor and then again at me. "It could be as long as a few months and as short as several weeks. We just don't know."

I didn't hear much of what she said after that.

On the way home we hit a traffic delay. Linemen were pulling cable for a telephone pole. The worker in the bucket truck maneuvered himself into a delicate spot between the pole and a tree as we watched, glad to have something to focus on. I glanced over at my dad as he sat quietly, his hands folded in his lap, his head turned slightly as he watched the workers. He always seemed too mean to do anything but keep going. But I guess it was true. While the lineman struggled to attach the cable, and his co-workers directed traffic, my father was sitting in the seat beside me dying.

I didn't know exactly what this would mean.

We finally pulled around the truck and started down the street again.

"Pull over," he said, and I did.

He opened the door, swung around in his seat and threw up in the street.

16

For a week or more he didn't get any worse. His appetite didn't come back entirely. He wasn't sleeping well, although he denied it. I heard him walking in the hall or down the stairs at night, which kept me awake wondering if he was getting sick again. Sometimes I went to the top of the stairs to listen, but usually I lay in bed waiting for him to come up again. If I asked him how he slept, he always said, "Okay, why?" like I was accusing him of something. "Nothing, I just thought I heard you last night, that's all," I'd say, but he wouldn't answer.

He never looked at me and he tried to avoid having contact with me in the house. Mostly he acted like I wasn't there, which wasn't entirely new. But he couldn't ignore me completely. He'd ask me to get the newspaper for him every morning because it was too hard for him to walk to the curb. And when he was hungry, he couldn't cook so he'd ask me to make him some eggs and toast. His dependence on me was grudging at best and at times embarrassing for him. One morning I heard him huffing and puffing in his bedroom. I called, "Are you okay?" but he didn't answer. A minute later he called out for me to come to his room. I could tell he hated asking me for anything.

"I can't get this," he said.

"What's that?"

"My shoe, for chrissakes!"

His right shoe was on his foot, although the laces were untied, but his left shoe was just sitting there beside his left foot because he couldn't keep his hands steady enough to put it on. I didn't know how long he had been struggling with this, but I could smell sweat. His hair stuck to his head. For a moment I felt bad for him.

"Well, are you gonna just stand there?"

"You want me to put it on for you?"

"No, I want you to take it and shove it up your ass."

"Look…" but I held myself. I got down on my knees, lifted his foot, slid it into his shoe and tied the laces. I stood up.

"What about the other one? You blind?"

I stared down at him but he wouldn't look at me. I kept staring at the top of his head and then I noticed his hands, palms up in his lap, creased and dry and useless, his left thumb rubbing his index finger. His nails were long and dirty yellow. I knelt down again and tied his other shoe.

"There, how's that?"

He didn't answer. He didn't thank me. He sat still and waited for me to leave. Once I was in the hall, his door closed and I didn't see him again that day.

He hadn't thrown up for several days and I counted that as progress, although I reminded myself that it didn't mean that he was getting better. He was sick, even if he didn't get sick. I'd tell myself he'd never be well again, but I didn't really know what that meant. I had never been around someone who was dying. My mother was never really dying. She was alive and then she was dead. And I didn't see Don enough toward the end to appreciate what was happening to him. This was different and I wasn't sure how I felt about it. I found myself not going out much and yet not knowing why. He stayed in his room and I stayed in mine. I don't know what he did. I just listened, waiting for the sound of him throwing up or struggling with some small thing that he could no longer manage. But some things stayed the same. He was mean and angry most of the time and he never had a good thing to say. I think he was in pain, but I wasn't sure because his face looked pained for as long as I could remember. I always thought it was hate that made him look like that.

I didn't like being in this situation at all. Not just that my father was sick and I didn't really understand what to expect, but that I would have to care for him. No one asked me if I wanted to do it. It was just assumed. The doctor didn't ask if I cared enough about my father to look after him while he died. She would have thought I was the worst son in the world if I had said, "No, I can't do it." And it would have taken too much time to explain why my "no" made complete sense in the longer history of our relationship. I'm sure it's hard to imagine that someone could have done so many bad things that he didn't deserve his son's support during his dying days, but that was the case with my father. And yet, there I was, lying awake at night listening for him in case he needed me.

One morning Lorraine called because she had heard the news that my father was sick. I was surprised to hear her voice and a little tongue-tied.

"Uh huh, yeah. He's, yeah. He's been not, he's not so, he's not been feelin' so, too good."

She asked if the doctor had told us anything and I explained that it was something with his pancreas. She seemed to understand that this was not good and asked if it was serious. I told her it was. There was a long silence.

"I'm so sorry to hear that."

"Yeah, well, he's hanging in there."

"It must be hard."

"Yeah, he has his days."

"No, I mean for you. It must be hard for you. I know you and your dad aren't real close."

"No, but, well, I'm trying to help him when I can. He's pretty tough though, you know, he doesn't like to be helped a lot, so most of the time I'm just here in case he needs something."

"I'm sure he appreciates it."

I didn't answer. Sometimes I wondered if he'd rather be alone even if it meant sitting for a week on the side of the bed with only one shoe on.

"Well, I just wanted to see how you were doing."

"I'm okay. How about you? How are you doing?"

As it turned out she was doing pretty well. She got a job as an office manager at an insurance company.

"Yeah, it's been great so far. I'm learning a lot. Don would laugh to see me working like this. You know he always wanted me home. He thought it made him look bad if I had to work. But now I realize I should have been working all along."

She was right. Don hated the idea of her working. Sometimes she'd take a part-time job around the holidays to help out and it bothered him no end. He felt like it took away from him being the breadwinner and yet they needed the money and there was no way he could work a second job. He could barely work a first.

"Sounds like you're doin' good."

"Yeah, well, actually I mainly wanted to see how your dad is doing. I'm so sorry."

"Well."

"I know what…"

"Yeah, you've been through…"

"Not exactly the same, but I know it can be hard. You know you can always call me if you need anything. Could I make you and your father a meal sometime?"

"No, that's okay."

"No, I mean it. Why don't I bring something by for the two of you? Not a big deal."

"Well."

"I'd like to. It would make me feel good to do something for you and your dad."

"Okay, that would be nice actually. I'm not much of a cook, that's for sure, so, yeah, that would be nice."

When I told my father that Lorraine was going to bring us a meal, he got pissed.

"I'm no shut-in for chrissakes. What's she pokin' her nose in for? And how'd she find out anyway?"

"I don't know. She's just trying to be nice, that's all. What's the big deal?"

"I don't like what she did to Don."

"Whadaya mean, what she did to Don?"

"You know as well as I do what she did."

"No, I don't. Enlighten me." He didn't answer.

"You mean all that bullshit about Conner? Is that what you mean?"

"What the hell else would I mean?"

"That's none of your fucking business."

"I'm surprised to hear you say that. I didn't even like Don. But, you, you were his best friend. I'd a thought you, of all people, would be pissed. Jesus, there's Don working his ass off while his wife is fucking his boss."

"You don't know that." I felt angry and confused, and I hated to hear my father, of all people, jumping on this bandwagon.

"Jesus, he used to brag about it to us guys on the loading dock. Some of the guys told me someone saw her go in and out of his office several times and when she'd leave, he'd come out with a big shit eating grin on his face."

"You don't really know nothin'."

"Don't tell me you never heard it?"

"I heard it plenty, but I don't believe it. She's not like that." My father looked at me for a long moment and then started to smile.

"You're sweet on her ain't you?"

"No, now…"

"Yes, you are, aren't you…"

"No, I'm…"

"…Jesus, you finally got a hard on for somebody."

"Stop it!"

"Wow, what would Don think? Here he ain't been dead a year even and you're scratchin' at the door."

"It ain't like that, it ain't…"

"Have you got in her pants…" Something snapped like it had snapped a thousand times before. I felt him pushing me into a corner, pushing to see how far he could go. I grabbed him by his shirt and lifted him out of the chair. He winced in pain. I could have broken him right then and there. I could have crushed him.

"Let go of me," he said, not angry, but pleading. I held him a moment longer and then I let him down gently in his chair. He pushed my hands away. He was panting for breath. I reached for his bucket and he threw up as I held it for him.

"Goddammit, dad," I said in a whisper. "What the hell are we gonna do with you?" He was trying to catch his breath between bouts of vomiting. He couldn't get up and it was too hard to reach the bucket so he threw up all over himself as he sat in his favorite chair. I watched, not knowing what to do. Finally he stopped and I helped him stand up so he could go to the bathroom. Again he held my arms as I backed slowly up the steps. He had to sit on the john for a long while, completely wasted from the climb. I ran water for him and helped him get undressed. I stood in the tub as he lifted each leg into the water and I helped him sit. He didn't speak and he didn't look at me.

"I'm sorry," I said. He just sat. I put his clothes in a garbage bag and threw them away.

I was still angry about what he had said about Lorraine. It was hard for me to believe the rumors, even though I had heard them all and had also judged her, joked about her, and prevented anyone from even hinting to Don what was going on. Conner never denied anything that was said and my last meeting with him didn't do anything to sway my thinking about what had been going on in his office.

But nothing in all of my times with Lorraine supported the rumors. The distance between the stories and the person I sat with over coffee seemed so great that they might have been drawn from two entirely different books about two entirely different people. She seemed good to me. I couldn't think of another way to put it. She seemed like the kind of person who did the right thing, not because she sat down and tried to figure out the right thing to do so everyone would notice, but because it came natural. Maybe that's why the stories started. Maybe she was too unbelievable. Why would someone as attractive and likable stay with someone like Don? Why would she put up with all of that? Maybe she wasn't putting up with it? Maybe she had something going on the side. Who could blame her?

Or maybe I was blind? I couldn't judge these things. I had no experience with women at all. She could be running some game with me like she did with everyone else. But that didn't make sense. How could I feel this way about a lie? She had to be true.

Dad hadn't spoken to me in two days when Lorraine came with a meal for us. He didn't move from his chair when the doorbell rang.

"Hi, how are you," she said, smiling as she entered the house.

"Hi. This is very nice of you."

"Glad to do it."

"Did you have any trouble finding the house?"

"No, your directions were great. I think I've actually been in this neighborhood before, but I can't remember why."

He still sat. He didn't turn his head to greet her. He stared at the TV instead.

I ushered Lorraine far enough into the room that he couldn't avoid looking at her.

"Dad? This is Lorraine. Don's, she was married to Don. Remember I told you she was going to bring us a meal."

"Hello," she said, holding her hand out.

"Uh huh," he said. "Excuse me if I don't stand. I've been sick." Lorraine's hand hung in the air.

"She made us a meal, dad."

"I hope it's something I can eat."

"I'm sorry that you have been so ill." Lorraine put her hand back in her coat pocket. "It must be very hard on you. I know that you are used to working. Don always said you were one of the hardest workers he'd ever seen."

"That what Don said, huh. That was nice of him to say it. I was sorry to hear he died. Don't get me wrong, we weren't that close but you work in a place that long and you kinda know everyone, you know what I mean."

"Yes, I think I do," said Lorraine.

"You kinda know everyone and everyone's business, too." He looked up at her with a smile.

"Yes, I'll bet you do," she said, not understanding his smile.

"So, something smells very good," I said. "Wouldn't you say, dad?"

"Yeah, something smells."

Lorraine looked at me and squinted as if to ask, "What's that about?" But then she laughed.

"Well, let's hope it tastes good too."

"I'm sure it will, Lorraine. This is great." I felt like I was treading water and the only chance I had to reach for the side of the pool would be when Lorraine left. And yet, I didn't want her to leave. Besides Carla, I couldn't remember the last time a woman had been in our house.

"I made meatloaf. And there's some potatoes and carrots and some salad. I hope that's okay."

"I'm sure it will be delicious. We never get to eat a real home-cooked meal, so this is special for us. Right, dad?"

"Huh?"

"This is special. We never get to eat like this do we?"

"Haven't eaten it yet, so I can't say." I wanted to reach down his throat and pull his heart out. But that seemed impractical at the moment.

"You'll have to forgive my father. He hasn't been himself since he's been so sick."

"I'm sure it's hard on both of you. I know when Don wasn't well, he often didn't feel like having anyone around. It just got on his nerves I guess."

"Too bad about Don," my dad said. "Too bad he had to go through so much for so long. It must have been hard for you, a young woman like you, I mean. Hard to have a man just wastin' away like that."

"Dad, Lorraine has been through a lot. She doesn't need to talk about this now."

"Oh, I'm sorry, Miss. I didn't mean to…"

"That's okay," said Lorraine, "you're right, it was very hard, but…"

"So how did you handle it? I mean what kept you going?"

"Dad." I could feel the car skidding off the road but I couldn't get control of the wheel.

"Well, I had my kids and my family stayed in touch and would visit…" She remained pleasant and polite.

"But they couldn't have met all…"

"Dad stop!"

"…your needs. You're a young…"

"Stop it!"

"…woman."

"That's enough! Lorraine isn't here to…"

The pleasantness and every hint of color left Lorraine's face. She took a step forward and stood directly in front of my father. He tried not to look at her.

"What are you referring to?" she said, steady, intent, her color was back.

"Oh, nothing. Why, did I say something…"

"Lorraine, I'm sorry. My father is…"

She regained her composure with a deep sigh. The smile came back although she didn't look at me when she spoke.

"I think I know what your father is." She looked at me. "I think I understand what's going on here. Good luck to you with all of this. Enjoy the meal. No need to return anything."

151

"Lorraine, I'm sorry."

"There's no need for you to apologize," she said as she glanced at my father. And then she was gone.

All the air left the room when she closed the door and I stood in a vacuum with my father, fighting to breathe as he crinkled the evening paper in front of his face.

"What the hell was that all about?" He didn't answer. I ripped the paper from his hands. "You couldn't just let it go, could you?"

He didn't answer.

"You don't know nothin' about her."

"And you do?" He turned his head slowly and looked at me, his eyes narrow and hard. "I know her kind."

"What the hell is that supposed to mean?"

"Never mind what that's supposed to mean. Just believe me, she's no good. Stay away from her."

"Who the fuck are you to tell me who I should or shouldn't see?"

"You're seeing her?"

"No I'm not. You know what I mean."

"You are sweet on her, aren't you?" I didn't answer, but his question made me realize for the first time that I did have feelings for Lorraine, feelings that I couldn't put into words, feelings down in the center of my chest that made me hum inside.

"You are aren't you? Jesus Christ!"

"We're just friends, that's all. What business is this of yours anyway? When have you ever given a shit about what I do?"

He didn't answer at first and looked like he was in pain. He turned slowly in his chair. His hands were brittle looking, just skin pulled tight over bone. His eyes were yellow.

"I don't want you to get involved in another man's troubles, that's all." He said this so quietly that I could barely hear him and yet the words were measured and thoughtful, like they had been inside him for years waiting for the right moment to come out.

"What do you mean?"

"That's all I want to say." I asked him again, but he was adamant that he didn't want to talk about it. He got up from his chair and walked slowly to the stairs. I could tell he needed help, but I wanted him to ask. I wanted him to say he needed me to help him up the steps, but he didn't, and he wouldn't. It wasn't like him to ask for anything that might make him look less than a man. So I watched him disappear up the stairs and listened as the bathroom door closed.

I called Lorraine but there was no answer, so I left a message saying the meal was delicious and that I appreciated everything she had done. I wanted to say I was sorry for how my father had acted but I couldn't find the words. I was afraid that by saying anything I would be telling her that I knew what had happened between her and Conner and I didn't want that between us, so I said nothing. I hoped that by being pleasant on the phone she would understand that it didn't matter to me.

My father was right. I felt something for Lorraine that I hadn't felt for a woman in years. Something I hadn't let myself feel, because there didn't seem to be any point in it. I had never felt comfortable around girls or women. Couldn't talk to them in grade school, which hardly mattered since my friends couldn't either. In middle school they found their voices but I didn't. So I pulled away, acting like it didn't matter, like I didn't care about girls anyway. I wasn't friendly even if a girl spoke to me in class. I missed biology regularly because my lab partner was Sheila Cross and sometimes we had to work so closely together that our hands would touch or our shoulders would lean against each other. I would start to sweat and get tongue-tied. I worried that she would notice and tell the other kids. Sometimes I walked out of class for no apparent reason. I would sit in the stall in the boy's lav and try to stop sweating. I would take deep breaths and tell myself it was okay.

Women were like magnificent alien beings that both attracted and frightened me; whose needs I didn't understand and assumed I could never meet. Around them I felt transparent as a jellyfish and just as attractive. I learned to move away when they came near so that I wouldn't be stepped on and squashed. I watched them from a safe distance and wondered about them and wished I could cross the great invisible divide I had created to separate us.

I didn't have sex until I was twenty three. I stopped at a bar one night coming home from work and there was a woman drinking in the corner. I was picking up a six pack for my father and she started to talk to me. She must have been in her late 30s, maybe older. She wore a red dress that must have fit her once and spiked heels and her lips were as red as Lucille Ball's. But she took an interest in me and before I knew it I was giving her a ride home because she felt too drunk to drive herself. Before she got out she leaned over to give me a thank you kiss, first on the cheek and then on the lips. And then her tongue was in my mouth, searching and warm and then she leaned against me, sighing.

She asked if I wanted to come in for a drink. I didn't answer, but got out of my car and followed her. We drank and she told me about her husband who was a tuck driver and how he didn't appreciate her and how she was lonely a lot of the time because he was away and how I was such a "cute boy" and soon we were in her bedroom and she was on top of me and then it was over. It was as romantic as attaching a hose to a faucet, but it also felt good, good in a way I had never felt before. And so I went back. We didn't talk much. Sometimes she had been drinking and sometimes she was just sad. And once when I went to her apartment she was gone and that was it.

There were a few others along the way, mostly one nighters, sometimes hookers from a local strip club. Nothing that would have qualified as a relationship.

It was odd being around Lorraine. She wasn't like anyone I had ever met before. I couldn't put her into any category. I didn't really feel sexual towards her, although she was attractive and I liked to look at her. But that wasn't it. It was more that she seemed like a real person and around her I seemed like one too.

17

My father didn't eat Lorraine's meatloaf. In fact, he wasn't eating much of anything in the weeks after her visit. Sometimes I'd make him a milkshake or he'd eat some pudding or maybe some soup, but nothing that needed to be chewed or seriously digested. Mostly he stayed in his room or in the bathroom. I would knock on his door to see how he was. Sometimes he'd answer, but just as often he wouldn't. I'd hear him going to the bathroom at night. At first I thought he was turning the faucet on and off, but then I realized it was him. The smell reached my room and I slept with the window open some nights. The bottom of the toilet bowl was often dark with lava.

We fell wordlessly into the routine of his dying without acknowledging that we were on a journey together without a map and without a clear destination. The destination would meet us, I guess, and we wouldn't know when that would be or how to prepare for it. I didn't leave the house much either. Not because he was asking for me, but because I didn't know what else to do. I felt I should be there even if it didn't matter to him. In time it seemed like he had always been dying and would go on dying and that would be our lives.

We went to see Dr. Buckley. She told us "things were progressing," which, despite sounding positive, meant things were getting worse. The disease was taking over and was roaming through his body like millions of tiny cattle eager to find new pastures for grazing.

"Have you and your father talked about hospice care?"

"No," I said, not knowing what hospice care was. My father listened.

"Well, I think it may be time to give it some serious consideration. What do you know about hospice?"

"Nothing."

She then explained how hospice worked. Mainly these were places where people went to die. They were staffed mostly with volunteers although there were nurses who made sure the person was comfortable. I guess that meant all the drugs they could bear. Family could come and go as they pleased. You couldn't get into the program unless it was obvious that you were going to die soon. I guess the doctor would have to make a prediction of some sort. My father was not interested.

"Well, I can understand that you might not like the idea at first, but it would be good to think about it before making up your mind." My father looked away. "You need to think about your son, too. There may come a time when he won't be able to look after you at home." Still no response. "There's also the option of home hospice." My father didn't like the idea of strangers in the house. It was a no sale all the way around.

"Do you want to ask the doctor anything more about this stuff, about hospice?" I asked.

"No." I looked at the doctor and she looked at me, eyebrows raised.

"Well. How is your pain?"

Still no response.

"I think its worse. He doesn't say, but I can hear him sometimes at night. Sounds like he's groaning. And during the day…"

"What are you talking about? I don't groan."

"Dad, I can see you're in pain. Maybe something can be…"

"I'm fine. Everybody just leave me alone."

The doctor increased the dose of pain medicine and talked about a morphine pump and asked dad to think about hospice. She was definitely sold on the hospice idea even though she said it was "entirely up to him." Each time he said "no" she tried again, as if another explanation would make a difference. My father wasn't interested in leaving his home and I understood that, even if he couldn't explain why. I wouldn't want to leave either, not because home was a better place but because it was the only place I ever knew and I wasn't about to go someplace new to die. It didn't make sense. She told me to call if there were any changes. I told her I would, although I didn't know what she meant by "changes." What was I supposed to watch for?

It was hotter than hell when we hit the parking lot. Indian summer. He began to perspire and turned white as toilet paper. I told him to wait inside where it was air conditioned while I got the car. It had been a miserably hot summer, with triple digit humidity and warnings everyday that people with breathing problems shouldn't go outside. I bought a small air conditioner for his bedroom and fans for my room and the living room.

He sat back in the seat and I lifted his legs around so I could close the door.

"Why didn't you put the damn air on?"

"It's on, dad. It'll take a few minutes."

He stared out the window as I maneuvered through the now familiar parking lot maze. As I turned into traffic, he said, "Take me by work." I was surprised that he showed any interest in work at all, especially since they hadn't made any effort to contact him since he'd gone out on medical leave. I knew this must have hurt. For all his bitching, he was proud of working at Wilson's. It didn't matter that he never rose up the ladder very far. What mattered was that while others came and went he had stayed through good times and bad, through union votes and near strikes and wage cuts and bonuses and just about everything that marked the history of Wilson's. He gave them everything.

We turned down Orchard and then onto Fifth and there, stretched out like three ocean liners, were the factory and warehouses. Grey cinderblock and old asbestos tile roofs, grass grown high around the chain-linked fences. Their glory dry-docked. I drove past the loading docks, three of the four bays empty, their mouths open and hungry for business.

"I wonder who's taken over for you." He looked but he didn't speak. "Maybe Harry, you think?"

"Maybe."

We drove by the main office, which was a few blocks away. This is where I had worked. It was an old red brick building that had been converted from a community rec center into an office. I worked in the basement. The ads for janitorial help hadn't been in the paper for a few months.

"A lotta years in those buildings, huh?" I said.

"Yeah, I guess so."

"I think they really screwed you, dad. For what it's worth." I looked at him, expecting a response to this olive branch. "I mean you gave them your whole life practically."

"Never expect nothing back. That's what you gotta learn. You expect things. You hold on to things and never let go. It ain't worth it."

"What do you mean?"

"I mean holding on is a waste of time. It don't accomplish nothin'."

"I don't agree."

"Not surprising. Seems like that's all you do. Hold on."

"Maybe there's some things you gotta hold onto. Maybe there's some things you gotta hold onto because if you don't, there won't be nothin' there at all. Maybe there's some things you gotta hold onto because that's what you're here for."

"Nobody's here just to hold on. You can't hold on. It all goes away anyhow. Look at me." He gestured with his hands for me to look at his arms and his chest and his face. He was slowly disappearing. Everything about him was diminished in some way. He was a collection of black and blue blotches on skin as delicate as rice paper.

"What's to hold onto?"

I wanted to say, "Maybe if you had held on more when I was young, things would be different now, maybe if you had held on to me even a little bit, I would be different, maybe if you had held onto mom…" But I didn't. We rode in silence.

"Take me up the hill," he said.

"What?"

"Take me up the hill to the Grove."

"To the cemetery?" I said.

"Yeah."

"What for?"

"Because that's where I want to go." What the fuck was this? I was the one who went up the hill, not him. That was my place, not his.

"Do you think this is going to make a difference? Going to mom's grave? Do you think that somehow that's gonna make things right?"

"There's nothin' I gotta make right."

"Excuse me. Where the hell have you been all these years? What world have you been living in? Because as far as I can tell there's a lot of things to be made right?"

He didn't answer. That was always the case. When he didn't like the question, he turned away, or walked away or ran away. I'd seen it with my mother time and again. Her voice trailing after him as the door closed.

We pulled down the narrow lane through the rows of stone. There was a fresh grave to our left. It looked clean as a newly planted garden. It was cooler on the hill. The wind always blew and a few clouds had rolled in to make a comforting shade. I stopped the car and before we got out, he turned to me again.

"You know, I wasn't all bad and your mother wasn't all good." With that he turned and struggled out of the car. He shuffled away as I watched, wondering what he meant. What the hell did he mean? He couldn't possibly be suggesting that he was the victim, that it was my mother who came home drunk, who threatened and terrorized us, who didn't care, that it was my mother that killed him, that let him die, that never spoke a soothing word to her son.

When I looked up, I could see my father sitting on the grass leaning against my mother's gravestone. His head was back and his arms were wrapped around his stomach. I hurried down the hill to his side. Pain was his constant companion. It was a commonplace thing, something that he tolerated, like bad luck. But sometimes it was more than that. It could take him across the border to a place that was intolerable, that pinched his face tight and curled his toes. It was a place that made me resent having to care.

"Dad, are you okay?" I kneeled beside him. He was gulping for air and couldn't speak. "Just breathe. Try to breathe slow. Just sit here for a minute. Just breathe. Don't move." He looked at me and his eyes were pleading, but I didn't know what for. "Just take a few minutes. I'll get you back home and you can take your medicine. You'll feel better if you can lie down."

We sat together beside my mother's gravestone waiting for the pain to subside, looking down into valley where new homes snaked across the hillside. We didn't talk for a long while. The wind cooled my father and whispered in the silence between us. My shoulder leaned against his and I realized I had never had this much direct contact with him in my life. We had never touched except in anger.

His stomach began to rise and fall slowly and I knew the pain was going away. But still we sat. I didn't want to talk, because words always got tangled between us. I wanted to pretend that we were father and son sitting together because we wanted to.

He began to stir.

"We better go."

"Are you sure? We can sit for a while until you feel better."

"I ain't gonna feel better," he said with a laugh. "Help me up." I stood up and reached out my hand and he grabbed it with both of his. I held firm and he pulled until he was standing.

"Sure you're okay?"

"Yeah."

"Do you want me to try and bring the car down here?"

"No, I ain't dead. I can make it."

"I know you ain't dead, dad. I was just trying to…"

"I know what you was trying to do. I know." He looked at me as if he understood that I was trying to help him, but he couldn't say so.

That was the last time he left the house.

18

The heat continued and I lay awake in my own sweat most nights, while my father tossed and turned and moaned and got up and laid down and slept and woke up again and so on and so on and so on. Sometimes I got up and walked into the hall to listen. Sometimes I even called to him, but he seldom answered. I sat in the hall, nevertheless, and waited to see what would happen. I wondered if I would be sitting in the hall some night listening to him die and not know it. I would think that his silence was rest, that his death was sleep. I couldn't imagine that he would ever be at rest or that he deserved to be at rest. But I also hated to see him in so much pain. He looked lost and small and inconsequential and afraid. And I couldn't do anything about it.

I called the doctor who listened patiently. She said that as long as my father refused hospice care, the next best thing was the hospital. When I couldn't take care of him any longer, we would put him in and that's where it would all happen. He hated the idea of going to the hospital almost as much as he hated the hospice idea.

"I don't want a bunch of damn strangers pokin' at me and comin' into my room all hours of the night." He wanted to stay at home. "Tell that doctor to go to hell. I'm staying here. I can take care of myself and no one else has to bother with a thing." This, of course, was bullshit. I found him in the bathroom again. He was moaning and he couldn't get onto the john, so he lay on the floor and that's where he did what he had to do. The floor and rug and he were an absolute mess. He was embarrassed, and said he could clean everything up and why the hell did I come into the bathroom anyway without knocking on the door.

"Dad, what about the other night?"

"What other night?"

"You know what I mean, the other night when I found you, you know."

"That wasn't my fault."

"I didn't say it was your…"

"You shouldn'ta come in. You shoulda minded your own business."

"Jesus, dad. What were you gonna do? Huh? Answer me. What were you gonna do? You couldn't even pull yourself up to sit on the goddam john."

"Yes, I could! You just didn't let me."

"Yeah, that's right."

"Damn right!"

"You can handle everything on your own, that's right."

"Don't be smart with me."

"You're invincible. You can handle anything and everything. Isn't that right, dad?" He sat in his chair staring at the TV. "You can handle this by yourself? Is that what you think? Can you?"

"If I have to. Yes."

"If you have to, yes. If you have to what? If you have to die, dad? If? There's no ifs about it, no ands or buts either, for that fact. You got that don't you? You're gonna die." I felt the old anger rising, like a sewer backing up and overflowing into a basement. I'd hated him for so long that I couldn't help myself. Even if the time wasn't right, it didn't seem to matter.

A fly landed on his hand. He flicked his finger, but the fly didn't move.

"I know I'm dyin'. I know it better than you."

"I guess you do."

"And I know you don't care."

"I'm sorry. But you're right. I don't care."

"Then why don't you leave me alone and let me deal with this my own way."

"Because someone has to be here. Someone has to sit with you and clean your shit and do whatever else needs to be done. Someone has to do that. It's just the way it is."

"Better you than me."

"Damn right, better me than you. If it was you lookin' after me, I'd still be lying on the bathroom floor in my own shit."

"Got that right."

"And you'd be yellin' in from your room, 'What's that goddam smell?', wouldn't you?"

He had to laugh. "Yes, I probably would."

I hadn't seen him smile or laugh since I don't know when. His face was different, softer, and his eyes had a glint, something alive that I hadn't noticed before. I felt bad that it felt good watching him laugh. And laughing with him. It didn't seem right after all these years to get any closer to him than was necessary. After all, if it weren't for him I probably wouldn't be sitting here in this house with a tired old man who craps his pants and never has a good thing to say about anything. I'd be out there somewhere. I'd be living. Instead I'm here dying.

Nothing happened for days. I got up in the morning and checked on him and he went to the john and I cleaned him up and fixed him soup and Jello and bought him some vanilla pudding which he didn't eat and I sat in the living room watching ESPN and Barry Bonds hit more homeruns and I thought about playing baseball and dad was so quiet sometimes that I'd look in to see if he was dead and if he wasn't moving I'd get real close and watch his chest and if I couldn't see it moving I'd get even closer so I could hear him drawing the air in and releasing it, not exhaling, but releasing it like he'd held it prisoner and didn't want to let it escape but had to and I'd back out of his room and watch some more TV or read the paper and eat a peanut butter and jelly sandwich and watch some more TV and listen one last time for dad and then go to bed. The next day I would do it all again. I did get a card from Lorraine.

It had an ocean scene on the front. Inside she wrote,

> *I am writing to say that I hope you are doing well. I am sure all of this is hard for you. If it is anything like what I went through with Don, I understand. I also wanted you to know that it wasn't because of you that I left so quick when I stopped by with the meal. Anyway, I am thinking of you in this hard time and hoping you are okay.*

I read this note many times because it was so rare to receive such a thing from a woman. My mother would stick notes in my lunch bag for school when I was little and afraid to go. They would say things like, "Hang in there, Tiger!" or "Have a great day!" Always with an exclamation point meant to lift my spirits or make me imagine that she was smiling somewhere for me. I never got a note from a girl when I was in high school. And certainly not as an adult.

So I read it over and over again and tried to imagine her going to the store and looking through a rack of cards deciding which one would be right. Why did she choose the ocean? Were there other cards with geese or golf clubs, the usual cards for men? Did she specifically decide to get me something that wasn't "usual"? Or was she in a hurry and just picked the first thing she saw? Or did she have an extra card at home in a drawer somewhere and she figured it was good enough? If she went to the store to buy it, she had to think about it for a while before she went. Did she make a special trip or was it something she threw on top of the pile when she was doing her weekly shopping, an afterthought. Maybe the card had been lying around for weeks and she finally decided to send it just so she wouldn't have to think about it any longer.

Did it take her a while to figure out what to write? Did she sit at a table thinking about me and wondering what was the right thing to say? Or was she writing her bills and tossed the card onto the pile, one more obligation taken care of?

She said she hoped I'm doing well, that I'm okay, and that she's thinking of me. Is she thinking "of" me or "about" me? Those seem to be different. When someone says they are thinking "about" someone, they usually can't get that person out of their mind, they are distracted by thoughts about the person. But thinking "of" someone sounds more like you could be thinking of the answer to an important question or thinking of a number between one and ten. Did she put as much thought into choosing the word "of" as I am putting into understanding it? Or did she just write it without a thought at all?

As I said, a letter like this was rare.

Whatever it meant, I couldn't stop looking at it, the perfect loops and distinct angle of each letter, the blue ink on off-white paper, how level each line was, not rushing off to one corner or another, just gliding across the page like there were invisible lines to follow that only she could see.

So between dad's puking and moaning I read Lorraine's note and felt like a man who had stumbled onto an oasis just feet away from the killing heat and parched ground of my father's dying. I drank in the cool water and leaned back on the gentle breeze of her words. And, of course, never mentioned it to dad. He still felt that she was a whore and didn't even want her dishes in the house, didn't want any evidence of her infidelity to butt up against his twisted sense of right and wrong. Who the hell was he to judge? And yet, I wondered if it were true; if the tales that they told around the office that last year were fact. Everyone loved to talk and it was hard to tell what was real and what was just a bunch of words made up on the spot to get a good laugh or to spark someone's fantasy about Lorraine. She wasn't bad to look at. Some guys shook their heads when they thought of gnarled up Don in bed with a woman as attractive as Lorraine. "What a waste of a good body" they'd say. I never thought much of it. I didn't really know Lorraine then. She seemed friendly enough when she brought Don his lunch from time to time, but I never gave her much thought. Others did the thinking about her and I just picked it up from them. Their thoughts were what I knew of her. And so I assumed they were right until I sat down with her the first time and looked into her eyes and saw that there was nothing there to hide, nothing that needed to be explained or denied, just her truth. And yet, I wasn't sure. If it weren't true, why did the stories about Conner and Lorraine hang on? And if it were true, did it really matter? I mean, I can't explain why a person chooses one brand of dish soap over another, so who am I to figure out the deeper workings of people's hearts.

All I knew was that thinking about Lorraine had become a real preoccupation. It made life more bearable. I thought about sitting with her at the diner and talking. She would listen to me like I really had something to say and I would listen to her because she really did have something to say. But she wouldn't act like I was below her. Instead she would act like she enjoyed being with me, like it was okay to be out in public with me for no other reason than she wanted to. And sometimes I thought of holding her and she would be warm as fresh bread, and soft. And she would smile and lay her head against my neck and I would smell lilac in her hair and I would look at her and she would smile again and I would kiss her. And she wouldn't pull away. And all I would feel was better.

It was hard not to think these thoughts, but I fought them because they made it harder for me to imagine actually being with Lorraine. I knew that she would see right through my outside to the pool of swimming fantasies inside and she would not understand and I would not be able to explain. So I fought them, hoping that when I was with her, I could be with her unembarrassed. But I welcomed the thoughts as much as I fought them, like a diver welcomes the first breath he takes when he reaches the surface again.

19

My father hadn't left his bed without my help in days. He hadn't come downstairs in longer than that. It seemed to happen slowly until you stood back from it and then it seemed like it all passed in a flash. One day he was an angry old man and the next day he was nothing much at all, just someone waiting. And I was waiting with him.

The doctor made a house call and said she didn't think he would live more than a couple of weeks longer, although she couldn't be sure.

"You never know about these things. Sometimes people go fast and other times, they hold on. They don't want to give up living. Everyone goes their own way."

We were in the hall outside my dad's bedroom. He was propped up watching the TV. I had moved it to his room because he had nothing to do. I bought a little set at Wal-Mart for my room, although sometimes I sat with him and watched the ballgames. The Pirates were making a run at their division. That was one thing we shared, a love of baseball, particularly the Pirates. It had been a long time since they'd won anything so we were both excited and it gave us something to talk about.

"What the hell are they doin' for chrissakes." he'd whisper.

"Just watch the game, dad. Don't get yourself upset. You know what the doctor said. Try to take it easy."

"But they should have had a hit 'n run on. What are they…" and then he'd have to stop because of the pain. For some reason he was refusing the morphine despite his doctor's urging. "I don't want to be fucked up all the time," he argued. But the pain almost lifted him right out of bed at times. It was like one of those train engines with the pointed front for cutting through ice and snow, but this was cutting through his organs and muscles and everything. But he still refused. He took Tylenol by the hand-full, which, as far as I could tell, did nothing.

"Dad, why don't you go back on the morphine? You didn't feel as bad…"

"I told you I don't want no drugs." I encouraged him to at least have a few beers so he wouldn't feel the pain as much. He didn't say anything but he did ask me to get a case from the grocery store. He started drinking again and at least it dulled him if not the pain. But when he got drunk and the pain hit, he was sick as a dog and had no control over where he was and what he did.

I could see he was afraid. He looked at me with his yellow eyes wide as hubcaps, as if to say, get me out of here. I did what I could. Held his head while he puked. Cleaned up what missed the bucket. Washed the bucket out so that the smell wouldn't make him sick again.

At the end of the day, I fell into bed exhausted and lay there thinking. What if things had been different? What if my dad hadn't been a drunk and my mother hadn't died and I hadn't stopped living so long ago? What if mom was still alive and my folks were still together? Dad would have stopped drinking, I suppose, that's the only way they'd be together. In that case, he probably wouldn't be dying right now. And maybe I'd have a wife and some kids and we would come to visit and my parents would be laughing on the front porch, their arms wide open for their grandchildren and I would be working somewhere with my own office, making good money and my wife and I would be happy. What happened along the way? How did things get so twisted?

When I was born my parents must have looked at the future in a similar way, hoping for similar things. What went wrong? I felt like whatever went wrong with them was the only inheritance I had, the only thing they passed on. And I didn't know what to do with it. How to change it or get rid of it or even how to understand it. None of it seemed fair and yet that's just the way it was.

Someone opened a new deck and dealt the cards and then must have shaken their head when they saw my hand. "Oh, my," they must have thought. At least I hope so. I hope that somewhere someone is taking note of this. It's awful to think that you could go from cradle to grave without someone noticing.

Sleep was hard for me but it was even harder for him. I could hear him moaning, sometimes for an hour or more. He never called. I rarely went in his room at night. When I did, he would get mad and tell me to mind my own business, but I could also see that he couldn't handle this on his own, so at least I would call to him from the hall to let him know I was out there, even if I didn't know what to do.

"Fine," he'd say.

"Are you sure?"

"Yeah. I'm fine."

"Can I get you something." Usually he didn't answer. Sometimes he wanted water, but got upset when I brought it to him.

"I can't drink that!"

"But you asked…"

"I can't drink it! Just leave it on the dresser." His moods changed so quickly that any response was too late. He was already on to something else, some other frustration or need or pain. But his moods were nothing compared to his body. My father was not a very big man. He was about 5'7", maybe 180 pounds, a beer belly that he winched up tight under old work jeans that never quite fit. He wore a ball cap all the time to hide his thin hair. There was nothing about him that would make you pick him out of a crowd. Like me, he was mostly background. As the cancer got worse, though, his body began to fade away and he stood out from everything around him like the sickliest pine tree stands out from the rest on Christmas.

His cheeks were sunk and hollow and a pool of water could have filled them. His eyes were hidden under the cliff-like overhang of his eyebrows. For some reason he couldn't breathe through his nose, so his mouth was always open, like the dark opening to a mine. His lips were dry and cracked despite the Vaseline I put on them repeatedly. His hands were thin and delicate, breakable like tiny breadsticks and they seldom moved anymore; he gestured with slight movements of his blackened fingers against the white bedspread.

I saw him looking in his mirror one morning wondering, I'm sure, where the rest of him had gone. His skin had great purple blotches all over, vast shallow pools of blood under the surface and it was dry like turkey skin a week after Thanksgiving dinner. His feet were cracked and sore.

"I can't find no place for my feet."

"What?"

"I said I can't get them comfortable, my feet, they're sore all the time just layin' there. Can you take the cover off my feet?" He said this with a grimace. I pulled the cover up and the sheet out from under the mattress so his feet were free.

"That's better," he said with a sigh. His feet were purple and black like a boxer's face after the short end of a long fight. His toenails were long and yellow and his heels were aching red and looked like they were about to bust open. And they smelled.

"They look pretty nasty, dad. How 'bout if I put some Vaseline on them?" He didn't answer.

"Maybe I'll wash them first." I left his room and went into the bathroom to look for the old basin that was usually under the sink. I ran some warm water and went back with a cloth and some liquid soap. I took the heel of one foot in my hand.

"Watch what you're doin'! Jesus!"

"Sorry." I held the heel in the palm of my hand. "There, is that better."

"Just watch it, would you? They're killing me."

I soaped the water and then lay the cloth in it. I wrung the cloth out and it was warm. I wrapped his heel in the cloth and held it, not moving it in case it hurt, but to my surprise he said it felt good.

"Man, that's good. That heat."

"I'm gonna wash them off a little." I slowly moved the washcloth over the top of his foot and soaked the cloth again, this time wrapping his whole foot in it, all the while balancing it in my right hand.

"How's that?"

"Good." I unwrapped his foot, laid it on the bed slowly and then soaked the cloth again. I took his other foot in my hand, careful not to rub the heel, and then I wrapped it in the warm cloth.

"You never expected this, did you?"

"What do you mean?" I asked.

"You never expected this. Holding my half dead feet and washin' them, having to take care of me." I soaked the cloth again and slowly ran it over then through his toes.

170

"No, I guess not."

He continued to watch me as I soaked the cloth again and gently worked his toes. It was quiet for a long moment. We were together. There wasn't any pushing or pulling. It felt good and uncomfortable all at the same time. I didn't want to start caring about him, but I had seen too much in recent weeks not to. I was holding his feet in my hands for God's sakes.

"How's that feel now?"

I took a soft cloth and began to dry his feet.

"Good. That feels good."

It was quiet again, but not the quiet of the cold war that had settled over us for all these years, but a peaceful kind of quiet, one you feel when things seem almost right.

"Good."

"Thank you."

"What?"

"Thank you. For this, I mean. Thank you for all this shit you're doin'."

I had never heard those words before. I had never heard him say that to me or to anyone for that fact, and it took me by surprise. I wondered if I had heard him right, but when I looked at him, I could tell that I had heard it right after all. I wouldn't say that there was love in his eyes. It was just that he was actually looking at me.

"That's okay, dad."

"I didn't want you to have to be in this situation. I didn't want anyone to have to look after me like I was some old fuck who couldn't do for himself anymore. But I guess that's what I am. Can't change that. I just always thought I be dead one day. I never much thought about the dying."

"Yeah." He was talking. Had the cancer reached his brain? Had it shook something loose and now the words were falling out?

"You know, I never knew my mother. My dad neither. They were gone before I knew anything. I was just small. Grew up with other kids around, but no parents. They tried to be like parents at the home, but they couldn't be, you know. I mean they went home at the end of their shift. Some of them were nice and some of them were mean. But they went home at the end of their shift. They weren't like parents really. Mostly we were on our own. I remember Christmas was a sad sort of time. People would come to look at us, you know, size us up to

171

see if they wanted to take any of us home. We'd get all cleaned up and put on something that didn't have holes and we'd smile and try to be hopeful about the whole thing, but mostly it was a show. After a while, I didn't bother. I could see what happened to the older kids. No one wanted them."

"What made you think about all this?"

"I don't know. I was just thinkin' about my mother, that's all."

It was quiet again. I looked at him wondering who he was and where these thoughts came from. His mother had been dead for over a half century and yet there she was, right in the middle of his mind.

"Dad?"

"Yeah."

"When we were up on the hill you said something to me."

"Uh huh."

"I didn't understand it. And I wanted to ask, but I was afraid you would get mad and we'd just fight."

"Yeah."

"But I want to ask anyway."

"Uh huh."

I squirted some lotion into my hand and began to rub his right foot. The lotion was cool and it made his foot feel soft again.

"You said that you weren't all bad and mom wasn't all good."

"I did?"

"Yeah, you did. What did you mean?"

"I don't know. I was probably a little nuts at the time, you know, with the cancer."

"No really, what did you mean? I gotta know." He looked at me a long time and then took a deep breath.

"Well, your mother and I had problems." Not exactly a news flash. I almost laughed. "We didn't have the best of starts. I mean we didn't have a long time to get to know each other and I was a little wild. But you have to know I loved her." I didn't answer, because I wasn't convinced it was true. "She was already, you know. She was."

"Pregnant."

"Yeah."

"That's not news. I knew that." I was starting to feel the old anger. He was telling me things that I had always known, but of course he couldn't possibly have realized that because he had never been a part of my life.

172

"Yeah, but..."

"You're not blaming all the problems on that, are you?" Was he trying to say that I was the blame for my parents' shitty marriage?

"No."

"Because if you are, that's the most unbelievable thing I've ever heard..."

"No, I'm not..."

"What about the drinking? Huh? What about that? What about the times you hit her? Huh? What about the million times you walked away, the times you weren't there, huh?"

"Listen."

"Listen to what? What could you possibly have to say that would make a difference?" I put the basin on the floor, picked up the cloth and towel and started for the door.

"She was pregnant before I met her." I stopped at the door, unsure of what I had heard, not sure I wanted to hear more.

"What?"

"We only knew each other for a few months. I loved her and I begged her to marry me the second time we went out together."

"What are you talking about?"

"But she kept saying 'no'. And I didn't..."

"Wait a minute."

"I want you to understand. I thought..."

"What the hell are you talking about? What is this? Some new lie to make you look good?"

"I thought she didn't like me. But she told me she did. She told me she loved me but she couldn't marry me."

"Stop."

"But I kept at her. I kept asking and asking and finally she told me the truth."

"Stop!"

"She told me she was pregnant to a guy she barely knew. She thought he loved her, but he went away."

"Stop this right now you fucking old man!"

"But I told her I didn't care. I told her I loved her and that I would be the father."

"No! What are you saying about my mother? That she was some whore and you were her knight in shining armor and that you saved her? Is that what you expect me to believe?"

"No, I'm no knight in any kind of armor. But it's the truth. I always wanted you to know. But she refused. She was afraid. She was afraid of what you would think of her when you were old enough to think about it at all. She was afraid you would reject her. I told her that was bullshit, but she didn't believe me."

"This is bullshit."

"So I didn't say anything. I tried to be a father. But I think she resented it. I think she didn't ever want me. She wanted you."

"Goddam you. Shut the fuck up about my mother."

"She kept you tied to her. She turned you against me."

"You turned me against you! Don't you remember the beatings? Don't you remember the times I begged you to stop and you wouldn't? Don't you remember what you were like? You were never a father to me and now I know why."

"I wanted to be your father. But I gave up. I just gave up. She loved you more than anything and there wasn't any room left for me. No, I wasn't a father. But it wasn't because I didn't want to be and it wasn't because you weren't really mine."

"Oh, c'mon. After all these years you're the one who was hurt, you're the one who got screwed? Give me a fuckin' break. Mom should have never married you. We both would have been better off without your sorry ass in our life."

"That's probably true, but..."

"Probably! No probablies about it. That's the *real* truth here."

"Maybe so, but there was a time, there was a time when I loved her very much. And there was a time when I loved you."

"Go to hell!" I slammed the door behind me and went into my room. Where did he get off telling me such a pack of lies? For chrissakes, how did he make all that up? And why? I was there all those years. I saw what it was really like. If she kept me away from him, it was because she knew what he was like. She was trying to protect me. Where was he when I needed him? Nowhere, that's where. And now he wants me to believe his fairy tale? No fucking way. Not this time. I heard too many stories along the way to believe this one.

What's he trying to do? Fuck me up for all time since he won't be around much longer to do it in person? I couldn't believe it.

The walls went up between us again. We didn't speak at all for several days. I mean, I didn't speak. He'd say "good morning" or "what's it like out today?" or any number of things to try to get me to say something. But I wouldn't. I didn't want to waste my breath. I knew it wouldn't come to any good if I did.

His damn feet were still sore all the time and I had to put lotion on them, but not like before. I just slapped the lotion on and left it at that. I did it because it seemed stupid to leave him in pain. But I was done with him now. I was just playing out the string till he died.

I couldn't shake what he said to me, though. It stuck. It couldn't possibly be true. That my mother was pregnant to someone else when she married my old man. Not that the thought of him not being my father was necessarily a bad thing. Although, in my mind, he was so much my father that I couldn't imagine it otherwise. It had all been very simple for such a long time. My mother had suffered through an awful marriage for reasons that still escape me, protecting me from my father, at times at great cost to herself, while my father came and went like a dangerous and unpredictable weather front. No matter how hard I looked, I couldn't see the love he referred to. For my mother or for me. It was invisible, a lie. It had to be. How could he expect me to believe it?

Maybe he *was* going crazy from the cancer and the pain. Maybe it turned him all around and upside down so much that it changed not only his prospects for the future but his recollection of the past. Maybe if he would take the damn medicine he would be his old self and he'd stop these lies and things would go back to the way they were. I don't need this in my life right now. I don't need it. No more lies.

Enough.

20

The next time I saw Lorraine it was at the grocery store. I was picking up a prescription and she was checking out the produce. At first I didn't know if I should go over and speak to her. She didn't see me, and it would have been easy to walk out. I hadn't been around her since she came to the house and just the sight of her made me feel awkward and embarrassed about my father and all he had said. I took a couple of steps toward her and then stopped, watching her inspect some lettuce. She looked all wrapped up in what she was doing, so I turned to leave when I heard her call my name.

"Hi," I said with false surprise.

"How are you?" she said not quite looking at me, not quite smiling.

"Okay, I guess. What about you?"

"Busy. That's for sure. With the job and carting the kids everywhere," she sighed a laugh. "I feel like I'm on the go all the time and yet at the end of the day I couldn't tell you what I've been up to." She laughed again and looked at me. "How are you doing?" she asked, meaning it this time. I wasn't sure what to say. I wanted to say, "Well, my father did it to me again. This time he said my mother got knocked up by someone else and he's not really my father. In fact he says he's the good guy and my mother was the bad one." But that seemed like too much for the produce section.

"I've been better," I said, trying to match her laugh with one of my own, but it came out as a kind of groan, something you might hear from a sick cat.

"Your father?" she asked to be polite.

"Not so good. He's just getting worse each day and he won't do what the doctor wants him to do. He's not gonna go easy." I wished I hadn't said that. At least not to her. Made me sound like I didn't care. Not that I did care, but once again, not something for the produce section of the grocery store.

"It's hard. I know. Must take a lot out of you."

"I'm getting by, I guess."

"Good. I'm glad to hear it." Now we both smiled and there wasn't anymore to say. I felt like my father stood between us, and it was hard to push him out of the way once we got past pleasantries.

"Would you like to get a cup of coffee," she said. "My treat this time."

Sure! "Okay."

There was a coffee shop in the plaza. The air conditioning rattled over the front door and you had to sidestep the constant dripping when you entered, but the place had a good, clean Formica look about it. Better than where I had taken her. The waitress had a dirty apron and a warm smile. We ordered something to drink and settled into a silence that was broken just in time by the delivery of coffee and the saving sounds of opening sugar packets and pouring cream and stirring. She looked at her coffee.

"You know, I've been meaning to talk to you ever since the thing with your father."

"Don't need to say a thing. He's just a mean old guy. He's always been like that. I'm just sorry that you had to get in the line of fire."

"Thank you. I appreciate that. But still. I mean, I knew what he was referring to. And I knew that you knew and I didn't want to get into it there. I didn't feel I needed to."

"Right. No, you don't have to answer to him at all. You don't have to answer to no one."

"I know I don't have to answer to anyone. It's not a question of having to answer to someone, it's more needing to talk to someone about it. I always hoped that Don wouldn't hear anything. I don't know if he did or not." She looked at me as if she were asking me a question. I didn't know how to answer. "He never acted like he knew anyway," she said. This was getting confusing. What was there to know?

"You know, Lorraine, this is none of my business. I mean you don't have to…"

"Believe it or not, you may have been Don's closest friend. Maybe that's why I'm talking to you. I've never talked about this."

She looked at me again. Her eyes were asking more questions that I didn't know how to interpret. What did she want me to say or do?

"He never really talked to me. You know what he was like. By the time he came home, he was in so much pain that it seemed like talking was even too much. He sat on the porch in the summer and listened to his ballgames and the rest of the time he slept in his lounge chair in the living room. At night, too. Don't get me wrong. I loved Don. And I miss him. But I lost him a long time before he died. As his arthritis got worse, I slowly stopped being his wife. I became his mother and finally just his nurse."

She paused and looked down into her cup again. I always wondered why someone as attractive as Lorraine would stay with Don, but I never expected to hear an explanation. I wasn't sure I wanted to.

"All the rumors. They were mostly lies. I never felt I was unfaithful to Don. I was trying to help. Seems foolish now, looking back, but all I wanted to do was help."

"What do you mean?"

"The whole thing with Conner. As Don got worse, he began to worry that he might be fired because he was missing a lot of work and sometimes he couldn't do his work. I mean, you used to do it for him, I know. He always appreciated that you never said anything to anyone."

I guess I knew Don appreciated it, although he never really said so. He never asked me to keep my mouth shut either, but I never thought of saying anything. I was just helping him a little. And I liked working on the other side. I couldn't tell Lorraine that partly I was practicing for what I thought would be my job anyway, so it didn't bother me to step in.

"I told him they couldn't fire him because of his arthritis. It was against the law. But he didn't believe me. He said they could figure out a way to do it so it wouldn't look like it was because he was sick. That's why he started to panic when he couldn't go to work, when he was just in too much pain. I didn't know what to do. He'd complain to me and when I'd suggest something, like disability, he'd get crazy angry. He'd yell at me for talking like he was an invalid and he'd say he was still a man. It was bad."

The waitress came by to see if we wanted to order some breakfast. We got refills.

"So that's when I thought I'd call his boss. I'd met Conner before and he seemed like a nice man. I thought I'd call and ask for his help, ask if he could do something about the disability. I thought that if the company was supportive about it, maybe that would make it easier for Don."

I thought, "Jesus, how dumb was that?" Conner was a prick from the get-go. He wouldn't help anyone with anything.

"Did Conner help?"

"Well, I had a good talk with him on the phone. He asked what Don thought and I said he didn't know that I was calling. That's when he suggested we get together to talk some more. I asked when he wanted me to come by and he said he didn't think it was a good idea for me to come to the office. He said Don might find out and get upset." She looked me in the eye. "I thought that made sense. Don would have been upset. I thought he was being considerate. Stupid as that must seem."

"No, that wasn't so stupid. I mean, you were doing what you thought was best."

She smiled. "I know it was stupid. But I didn't then." Her eyes narrowed and her mouth turned thin and determined.

"I have to tell you what happened."

I didn't want to know. I didn't like the idea of Lorraine even being with Conner. I sure didn't want to hear what happened.

"So we met in a restaurant in Henrietta. He said it was best not to meet where someone from work might see us. That made sense to me so I went. He got there before me and was waiting at a table. He was very kind. He listened to my story and he said that it was very complicated and that he would do the best he could and that we should meet again. I felt relieved. He really seemed to care about Don. When we left the restaurant, he walked me to my car and he reassured me that he would do what he could and that I shouldn't talk to anyone about this. And then he hugged me and told me Don was a lucky man. He joked and said, 'and beautiful, to boot,' and hugged me again. It felt good and I didn't think anything of it."

I felt myself getting angry. Angry at Conner for being such a fuck. But angry at Lorraine, too. What was she thinking? How could she not see right through someone like him? I kept telling myself she was only trying to help Don and if Don hadn't been Don she wouldn't have been in such a mess to begin with. Being Don's wife must have been a real burden. But still. Conner was such an ass. How could she not see that?

"That's how it began. He started calling me at home. Mostly to talk about the disability issue and what he was trying to find out and whether or not to tell Don. After a while, he would just call to talk. We met again for lunch and then another time. The lunches got longer and I found myself getting home late and the kids would ask where I was and I couldn't tell anyone anything. He made me feel that getting together was very important, that this was taking a lot of extra time for him to figure out and he had to talk to people in the home office and they were giving him the run-around. I felt the least I could do was meet with him."

I could see her shoulders clenching. She didn't drink any of her coffee even though she held it with both hands.

"And I enjoyed it. I enjoyed someone taking an interest in me and listening to me and thinking I was okay to look at. I admit that. So I kept going and kept it all to myself. And one thing led to another and I found myself sitting in the car with him after lunch one time. He kissed me and I kissed him back and it felt good so we kissed some more." She stopped. "I'm sorry. You don't need to hear all this."

"It's okay. Really."

"I never slept with him. I can tell you that. I mean, it went too far, maybe, but it didn't go that far. Almost. We did go to a motel. But when we started, I began to cry and I couldn't stop and he tried to comfort me at first and then he just got angry. And then there was nothing. I mean he didn't speak. And I cried. He got dressed. And that was it."

She couldn't talk. Her mouth fell open at mid-phrase and her eyes were red. She looked at the table as if she were miles away trying to figure out some puzzle that she didn't understand.

"Have you ever had a moment when you suddenly could see things the way they really were? I mean, like you saw everything one way and thought it was true and then you realized you had been standing on your head the whole time?"

I didn't know what to say. I thought of my father's story about my mother. I wondered who was standing on their head. I couldn't help seeing Lorraine in a motel room with Conner. I wanted to ask her where it was. And I hated myself for wanting to know, for feeling so disappointed in her, for not being able to understand her better. All I could think was, "Why?"

"I felt foolish. Ashamed. I never talked to him again. I never saw him. I don't know how all the rumors got started. All the lies. I don't know what he said. I don't know what Don heard. If he did hear something, he never let on. Do you know?"

"I don't think he knew. He never said anything to me about it." She began to cry. Her hair stuck to her cheek and as she rubbed it away, her hands looked small and pale.

"I think he would have told you, or he would have acted some way that would have made you suspect something. He didn't?"

"No. He didn't."

"I'm glad."

She opened her purse and pulled out a small pack of Kleenex. I wasn't sure what to do now. I wasn't sure what to say, what to think, what to feel. It was like I had stubbed myself on this conversation and I was numb. Nothing made sense anymore. Not just about Lorraine, but everything. Was there some chance that my father was telling the truth, that my mother wasn't who I thought she was? Everything seemed twisted into knots that I couldn't untie. Why had Lorraine decided to tell me this? Was I really that close to Don? I don't know. We worked together for a long time, but we often went days without saying one meaningful thing to each other beyond deciding what orders to fill first. Is that enough to qualify me as a friend, let alone qualify me to sit here listening to his widow's confessions?

I wanted to leave. The place was getting smaller and the air was getting thin.

"What's wrong?" Lorraine leaned forward, her face lined with concern. She had stopped crying.

"Nothing."

"You don't look so good. Are you alright?"

"Yeah, no, I'm okay, fine."

"This was too much, wasn't it? Too much for you right now with everything else. I mean your father and all. Maybe I shouldn't have…"

"No, really, I'm okay. It's just…"

"It's just what?"

I wanted to tell her that I thought she was special, that she wasn't like everyone else. I wanted to tell her that the few times we had spent together made me feel different, made me feel like it was okay to be alive. But now I wasn't sure what was okay. I wasn't sure how I felt about anything.

"I feel bad that you went through all that. I really do. But I don't know what to do."

"I don't want you to do anything. I don't need you to do anything. I just wanted to tell someone. Someone who knew Don. Someone who might understand. I needed to get this out of my head. I needed to hear myself telling this story. I needed to hear what it sounded like. And now I know."

"What do you know?"

"I know that if I was listening to this story I would think I had made a big mistake, but I would also think I was just a person trying to figure out what to do when there's no rules to follow, trying to do the right thing when it isn't clear at all what the right thing is."

I stood up. I had to leave.

"I'm sorry, Lorraine, but I have to go. It's my father…"

"Okay." She stood too, looking befuddled.

"I'm sorry that you had to go through all those things. I'm sorry about what happened to you. I'm sorry that I can't help. I'm sorry for everything."

"You don't need to be sorry. There's nothing to be sorry for."

"Yes, there is. I'm sure of it. I just don't know what to do about it. I don't know what to say." I turned to leave and she took hold of my arm.

"You can talk to me. I mean, I can listen. I won't judge. You didn't judge me." But I did judge her and I hated my judgment but I couldn't escape from it. It was all I had. The only way I could make sense of the world was to judge it. There was good and there was bad and I needed to see the difference plainly or nothing made sense. My father was bad. He was the definition of bad for as long as I remembered. There was something comforting in that. When things were unclear or confusing, I could always count on him to be who he was at the core. On that I could be certain. And my mother was good. That was certain as well. If that wasn't true, then what?

"Thank you. I gotta go now." And I turned and walked out of the restaurant. I never even paid. I don't even know how she got home.

I walked straight to my father's bedroom when I got home. He was laying still, his head rolled over to one side, the TV on, his eyes closed. He opened them.

"Why the hell did you tell me all that crap about my mother? What the hell were you trying to do and did you for even a second think that I would believe one fucking word you said about her? Listen to me you sonofabitch, you can't do this. You can't wait all this time and then tell me your damn lies and expect me to swallow them. Mom may have listened to your lies and believed you and given you a million fucking second chances, but I'm not! You got that? No second chances! You can't change the past now that you got no future. You gotta die knowing that you failed as a husband, as a father and as a man. You can't re-write history and make the bad guys good and the good guys bad. I won't stand for it. I won't! You got that?"

He didn't say a thing. He looked at me with his sunken eyes. He stared at me and he didn't move and his chin held firm even though his eyes were moist and his hands fumbled with each other. He didn't speak. He just stared at me like he was seeing me different, like he hadn't seen me before and was seeing me for the first time. And he licked his lips and took a deep breath like he was lifting something heavy off his chest, but he still didn't speak. He opened his mouth but no words came out. He nodded at me like he wanted me to wait. He opened his mouth again, but the words were mumbles and they fell out of his mouth and onto his chin and were gone.

"What!"

He tried again.

"You…are right. I have failed." What was this bullshit? What was he trying to pull now? I was furious at him and afraid of what he was saying because I didn't know what it meant. He swallowed several times as tears settled into the hollows of his face. He spoke once more.

"I'm sorry."

"No! You cannot be sorry. You cannot. It's too late for you to be sorry. I won't listen to it! You can't do that. Not now. Not after all these years. You can't."

21

There's an old Crosby, Stills, Nash and Young song where the singer is talking about the past and the future and he says he's "24 and there's so much more," meaning more to his life, more ahead. When I first heard that song, I was about 24 years old. It was a time when I wondered if there was much more. At least for me. I wondered and hoped that the future would include "more," even though I couldn't say exactly what I meant by it. I just thought that despite everything that was behind, what was in front of me was so much bigger that eventually the future would swallow up the past and I would have a different life. I thought things would heal up and somehow time itself would make things different. All I had to do was take one step after another and things would close in behind me and the fingers of the past would slowly loosen their grip on me.

It's been almost 20 years since I first heard that song and time just stopped somewhere along the way. It didn't carry me up in its flow and whoosh me away into the future. It kind of made an exception and allowed me to stay just where I was. Just where I am, which is nowhere.

The past has been the most important part of every single day of my life. All the memories, all the questions, all the anger and disappointment. These are the things that have made my life worth living and, at times, made me not want to live it at all. It's almost as if time only has meaning when it's slipping away.

Sometimes when I close my eyes, I can still see my mother's face, her tired eyes and her hair pulled back, her sad smile, more clearly than I can remember a single thing that happened yesterday. When I look over my shoulder, I find my life. I see everything that was and I can dream of what might have been, what might have happened for me, but never did. It was not a happy life even before my mother's death, but the final die had not yet been cast. When she died, though, it was as if the world itself shuddered, and even though others may not have noticed, everything in it was thrown off kilter and nothing would be the same again, and nothing that had been promised would come to pass.

I tried to stay away from my father, but it was difficult. His needs grew each day. He was throwing up more often now and oftentimes he couldn't make it to the bathroom. Sometimes I couldn't bring myself to go into his room, to look after him and clean him up. It was awful smelling when I did, but he didn't complain; he seldom said a word even though I knew he was suffering. When I wasn't in his room, I could hear the sound of him, the moaning, low and rumbling like a train in the distance.

Once when I went in his room there was a picture of my mother on the table beside him. It must have been from when they were dating, because I didn't recognize it. They are with another couple at a restaurant. There are drinks on the table in front of them. My father has a cigarette in his mouth and a squinting smile on his face as he looks at her. She is leaning back in laughter, her mouth open and teeth like pearls, happy and unaware of the mistake she was making. They were young and stupid. Was she pregnant in the picture? I couldn't tell. I couldn't see her stomach. Was I in the picture, too?

"Your mother could laugh, you know." His voice startled me. "This picture was taken up in Carleton at Nino's. Jesus, that was a long time ago. A guy came around and snapped your picture whether you asked for it or not. She wanted us to get it. We had just met, but I said okay. I bought it for her and when it came in I called her and she invited me over. She had a little apartment and was working somewhere, I don't remember, and she made coffee and we talked a long time and she told me about the problem she had and I didn't know what to think except when I left her apartment I knew I loved her and the rest didn't matter."

I had never heard my father say he loved my mother. The words sounded odd coming from him, not because I had never heard them before, but because he said them so easily, like there was never a doubt.

I didn't know why he was telling me this story although when he mentioned the "problem" I knew exactly what he meant. When it no longer made me angry, I realized for the first time that I believed him. My father was not my father. He was someone else who had become my father because my mother fell in love with him or because she needed a man when she was carrying this baby. I felt a little numb as the past started to change.

"We got married pretty fast. Let me think. It was only a couple of months later." He looked at the ceiling as if the memory was floating there above him. "I don't know exactly, but it wasn't long. And your mother was happy."

He looked at me when he said this.

"She was already pretty far gone then, with you I mean. She got bigger and bigger and then she got sick and the doctor said she had to stay in bed. She got scared and sometimes she didn't want me around and she acted like I was a stranger. I didn't know what to do. I went to work each day and came home and she would be on the couch and she looked all pale and sickly and I thought she'd be better off not having a baby at all, but when I said that to her, she really got angry and told me I was wrong and that she wanted the baby more than anything and that if I didn't like it, I could find the door."

He paused for a long time trying to take in his own words, looking like he was surprised by the sound of them, or maybe by what they meant. I felt like I had found a box high on the top shelf of a forgotten closet and it was being opened. I wasn't sure what was inside or if I wanted to know, but I felt helpless to close the lid again.

"So I stayed out of her way. I felt like I was just a bystander watching this thing happen. She didn't want me to do anything for her. She wanted me to leave her alone. And so I did. I don't know if that was right or wrong, it's just what I did." He paused again. I didn't know if he was waiting for me to judge him or let him off the hook.

"What happened when I came along?" I asked.

"I came home from work one day and her water and stuff had broke and there was all this blood and she was hysterical crazy and I was scared to death. I thought she was dying and I called the ambulance but I couldn't wait so I carried her out to the car and drove like hell to the hospital blowing my horn and runnin' all the lights. She was in a lot of pain. The doctors met us right at the entrance and took her away and I sat there in the waiting room."

He took a deep breath and looked away.

"I really thought I was gonna lose her. But they came out after a few hours and they said she was okay and they said she had a baby boy. Up till then I hadn't even thought about the baby. I just worried about her. I kept thankin' them for saving her and asking if I could see her and they said I could look at her through a window while she tried to feed the baby. I felt like I was on cloud nine, cause she was okay and I thought 'this will be a new start.' So I went up there to the baby area and stood by the window and she barely even looked at me. She wouldn't take her eyes of that baby. She wouldn't look at nothing else. After a while I went home. Mostly it stayed like that. It was the two of you and then there was me."

"Jesus Christ, dad, you talk like she did something to you. Don't you remember what a fucking bastard you were. For chrissakes, I don't know why mom stayed with you at all. You tell it like 'poor me' but that ain't the way I remember it. That ain't the way it was. What about all the times you were drunk? Are you gonna blame that on me and mom too?"

"No. I was drinking long before your mother came along. We met because of drinking. Both of us drank a lot in those days. We met in a bar. Nothin' bad about it, but that's where we met. I mean she wasn't no drunk but she wasn't afraid of drinkin' either. After a time she drank less than me, that's all. I kept goin' on I guess."

"You don't remember what you were like, do you? You were too drunk to remember weren't you?"

He didn't answer and I wasn't expecting him to.

"Do you remember the times you'd come home late from work stinkin' drunk and smack my face just because I was standing at the door? Do you remember that? Do you remember mom standing at the door crying and begging you not to go out and you'd call her a fuckin' whore and you'd leave us? You know what it was like for a little boy to have to figure out what to do with his mother who couldn't stop cryin'? Do you remember any of this or is it all lost in one of your bottles somewhere?"

"I said I was sorry."

"Don't start with that again! Just don't!"

"What do you want from me then?"

"What do I want from you? I wanted a father. I wanted you to give a shit about me."

"I'm sorry. I wasn't allowed to be."

"Bullshit."

"She made it clear. It was the two of you, like I said. I tried hard to love you like a father should love a son. I did. And I never stopped loving her."

"You had one hell of a way of showing it."

"Yes, I did." He wouldn't fight with me.

"Why all of a sudden are you talking to me about this? I mean, why now? Huh? Why did you wait so damn long? I mean, it hardly even matters now, right? Times up. So why are you telling me all this?"

It was quiet for a moment as the words settled to the floor like so much dust.

"You know the first thing I do in the morning when I wake up? I don't even have to move and I can see a corner of the window there. And just outside the window is that maple tree, just the end of one branch, just a little bit of it stickin' out with barely a handful of leaves on it. A few months ago there was just some scraggly twigs. Nothin' more. And then after a time there were some green buds. Just little nothin's, really. And then there was the start of some leaves and then these whole big leaves came along that look like they always been there, just waving in the breeze permanent like. But they ain't always been there. And they won't always be there. I look hard at them every morning because I know what they don't. I know they'll be gone in no time. They'll be laying all gold on the ground and then brown and then just a little bit of dust. Gone. Most of my life I didn't know any more about life than an empty branch waiting in the dead of winter. Dyin' makes you know stuff whether you want to know it or not. It kinda clears up your vision. The lies don't seem to be worth the effort any more."

"What makes you think you can tell the difference now? I mean you been so good at lying as far as I can tell, that I don't know how you'd be able to just turn on a dime and see the truth of things. I been trying to see the truth of things all my life and no matter how hard I look, I can't exactly tell. Don't get me wrong, I think I know the truth, but I don't know it exactly. I don't know it the way two people know it when they're looking at the same thing at the same time and then they look at each other and they can see in each others' eyes that they've both seen the same thing and seeing it together makes it true. But sometimes one person sees the truth and knows the other person's seen the same thing, but the other person just decides they've seen something else, the other person just decides they seen something else and the longer they believe it the more it becomes true. But it ain't true at all. It's just a lie to look like the truth.

"But that first person knows what he seen and he knows what's true and he ain't about to be tricked by someone who's convinced of a lie. He just ain't, not after years of holding on to what's true."

My father looked at me and his eyes met me in a way they'd never done before.

"It never was the way you thought," he said.

"What was never the way I thought?"

"You know what I mean."

"No, I don't. I want you to tell me, Mr. Truthteller." He looked at me like he was afraid to answer, like the words were there but he didn't want to turn them loose. And I was afraid, too. We had never come this close to actual talking. It was like we were stepping into a wilderness and neither of us had a compass and we had to figure out where to go but neither of us could do it alone.

"I don't think you want me to tell you nothin'."

"Sure I do! I want you to tell me everything. I want you to tell me about how much you loved my mother and how much you stood by her and how you were there for her. Right to the very end."

"That's enough. I don't want to talk anymore."

"Now there's a surprise. You don't want to talk to your son about his mother. I wonder why?"

"I don't want to talk."

"Maybe it's because you don't want to face that truth."

"I said I don't want to talk anymore." He was trying to turn away, but he couldn't move much. He couldn't leave anymore. He had to stay. He had to listen no matter what I said.

"Then I'll talk. Let me tell you my truth. My truth is about a 10 year old boy who got up in the middle of the night..."

"Stop this!"

190

"...when he heard his mother's cries for help. So he went to his father's room, but he was afraid to wake him up. Afraid what might happen. But his mother still called and so he woke his father up and he went downstairs and then the world just plain ended."

"Don't."

"A boy who went down those stairs and saw blood everywhere and his mother curled in a ball and his father yelling at him and the next thing the boy knew his mother was gone. Dead gone."

"Get out!"

"You killed her didn't you?"

"Get out of here!"

"Didn't you!" He laid his head back on his pillow, tears in the corners of his eyes, gasping for breath, pale as the sheets rumpled round his face.

"Please get out," he said in a rasping voice, more pleading than anything else. I stood in the quiet of his room and then turned to leave. I looked back and he was rolled up like a baby, his back as round as a hard-boiled egg.

Tears filled my eyes as I closed the door to my bedroom, and then something broke inside and I began to sob and I couldn't stop. I opened my mouth but my breath was gone, leaving only a silent scream behind. I lay on my bed not able to stand. The floor was full of blood again and this time, like the first, I couldn't clean it all up. It was just too much and it would always be there in the corners and near the cracks and along the baseboard.

I went to the bathroom and opened the cabinet and took what I could find, which wasn't as much as before. Anything to put me to sleep. I went to bed and lay there looking at the ceiling and watching the shadows cross with each passing car. I traced the ceiling cracks from one corner to the next. In a short time the room began to sway and I was floating. Everything that had held me so tight was letting go and I was light as a falling leaf. Even my mother slipped out of my grasp and she retreated into the mist that surrounded me. I felt safe. I felt good. Soon I fell asleep.

22

I threw up out of a deep sleep and lay across my bed tossing everything that was in my stomach and God knows what else. I had a horrible headache, too. It was just before dawn and the first morning dove was calling by my window. I just laid there, letting my weight sink into the mattress, my arms dangling almost to the floor, my chin buried in the comforter.

In all these years I had never asked my father if he killed my mother, but both of us knew the question was there waiting for words to express it. It was impossible to ask when I was a kid. In fact the question was just an unformed mass at the back of my throat then. I didn't want it to turn into words, because the idea scared the shit out of me. But in time, the words began to form and they settled in my heart and mind and finally formed the lens through which I watched my father's every move. I know he felt it. I know he understood that my whole life was a kind of accusation. His silence about my mother over the years was the best evidence that I had of his guilt. Why else would he not talk about a mother to his son? Why else would he avoid the topic? Why else would he never speak her name? He was burying it all. He was hoping that it would rot away under the soil of silence.

I didn't even try to clean up the mess I had made. I rolled up the area rug by my bed and threw it in the garbage. When I came back up the stairs, I could hear my father coughing. I stood by his door, listening. I couldn't tell if he was choking. The coughing stopped but

I stood a moment longer. I could hear his voice, faint and weak, not really calling but talking or mumbling. I couldn't tell what he was saying. But it sounded like he was talking to someone because he would pause and then start again like he was answering someone. After a time, he stopped again. I continued to listen. When I heard his heavy breathing I figured he must be asleep so I went back into my room.

I washed the floor. My stomach ached like it had been turned inside out and I could barely stand the light that was hinting its way into my room. I rolled my head slowly, hoping to relieve the ache. I lay down on my bed and in no time I was asleep.

The next thing I remember was the phone ringing. It was Lorraine and I didn't feel like talking at all and I'm sure she could tell. She asked how I was doing.

"Fine."

"How's your father doing?"

"Not so good."

"Not so good?"

"No. He's just getting worse."

"Are you getting any help?" My head was pounding.

"No, not yet. I may go ahead with that hospice thing. I don't know."

"That would be good. Maybe that will give you some relief."

There was a long pause like we had concluded this part of the conversation and we didn't know how to build a bridge to the next part.

"Well, I hope you're okay."

"I am."

"I couldn't tell when you left the coffee shop. You seemed to change. I didn't know if you were upset..."

"No, no I wasn't upset. I was tired, that's all. With my dad not sleeping and having to be here all the time..."

"That's what I thought but I wasn't sure. I didn't know if what I told you bothered you."

"Why would you think that?"

"I don't know. You just got different."

"Maybe I got different because I have things on my mind too. I don't know."

"Okay." She paused and I didn't know what to say.

"Lorraine, I know you did what you felt you had to do. It's over now anyway."

"What are you upset about?"

"I'm not upset. I just don't know…"

"Don't know what?"

"Nothing."

"Don't know what? Don't know if I did the right thing? Is that it? You don't know if I did the right thing."

I didn't answer.

"Or is it that you feel I did the wrong thing? Is that it?"

I still couldn't answer. I really liked Lorraine but I couldn't shake the feeling that what she had done, no matter how well-meaning, was wrong and that she should have known better.

"I don't know, Lorraine."

"You don't know. I don't think that's the problem at all. I don't think that's it. I think the problem is that you think you do know. That's it, isn't it?"

Yes, that's it.

"I'll tell you what. When you think you don't know or when you think you aren't quite so sure about other people and the decisions they make, then why don't you call me, because I think we could help each other out. You know? It's no fun going it alone. But don't bother as long as you're so sure about everything and everybody. Not as long as it's so easy for you to judge. I just don't need that right now. Think about it."

She hung up before I could say I didn't know anything anymore.

I lay back on my bed again. My eyes ached. The sun shone sharp on the wall and the outline of the window was crisp. The line between shadow and light was clean and clear and unmistakable. I could have gotten up out of my bed and traced it along the wall. But then it moved a little and then a little more and by the middle of the afternoon it would be gone altogether.

I felt sick again. But this time I made it to the bathroom.

Lorraine being gone would be more difficult than Lorraine being right. Most of my life was in black and white, but she brought some color. She was different because she treated me like I was okay, like I was a regular person who had something to say and was worth listening to, like I had some value. As soon as she said goodbye, I

194

realized all of this. I felt closer to her than I did to anyone and somehow I had managed to blow it. I managed to push someone away who had actually tried to be close to me.

I felt sick again.

And again.

I sat on the bathroom floor for several more minutes wondering if I should call Lorraine and apologize. Should I call and tell her I was stupid and that she shouldn't care what I think about anything she did because I had been so fucked up for so long that nothing I said or thought really mattered anyway?

As I came out of the bathroom, I could hear my father stirring so I looked in on him. He was struggling with his pillow, which had gotten under his back somehow. He pulled at it without realizing that each time he tried, he was putting all of his weight on it as well.

"What's the problem?"

"Nothin'."

"Can't get your pillow?"

"It's okay."

"I'll get it out for you."

I walked over to the bed and with one arm pulled him forward so I could reach the pillow. His hands were wrapped tight around my arm, like he might fall into deep water if he let go. I fluffed his pillow and set it back where he wanted it. I leaned over to settle him slowly back onto the pillow. He sighed with relief once his head was down, the pillow engulfing it. He weighed nothing. I could have picked his whole body up with one arm, remade the entire bed while holding him, placed him down again and not have felt any strain at all.

His bouts of pain came and went. The medication helped for the most part, but recently he found it hard to swallow the pills and he refused the doctor's recommendation of an IV. He refused everything that might have made it easier.

I was still angry at him. But here I was, still his son.

"Do you want something to eat?"

"No."

"You know what the doctor said about eating."

"Fuck the doctor."

"Okay then." I hadn't noticed before how bad he smelled. I was ashamed that I couldn't remember the last time he had washed.

"How bout we give you a bath?"

"What?" He looked startled and confused by this as if I had asked him to perform an unnatural act with some small animal.

"A bath. Maybe you'd feel better."

"I can't take no bath," he said, emphasizing with his tone that I was even stupider today than I was yesterday.

"Sure you can. I can help you."

"I'm tellin' you I can't. It's too hard."

"Well, let's see." I left the room and ran some bath water and in a few minutes I was back. I didn't say anything. I pulled his blankets back and picked him up before he could complain and took him into the bathroom. This was the closest I had ever been to having a baby. He was helpless in my arms. He had to depend on me and I could see in his eyes that he was not confident in my dependability.

"Don't worry, I won't drop you. Unless you piss me off." He smiled. I guess it was just him and me now. That's all either of us had left.

I leaned over the bathtub and laid him in the water. He jerked as he entered, saying the water was too hot. The water wasn't hot at all to me, but it seemed like everything was more intense for him, so I added some cold water until he felt comfortable. Then he was too cold. I ran hot water and so it went, back and forth trying to keep him comfortable. He said his ass ached sitting in the bathtub. No wonder. He didn't have any meat on him at all. None. He kept one arm on my shoulder like he was afraid he might disappear down the drain if he let go. We found the right temperature as I filled the tub to above his waist. He seemed to relax and if the tub had been a few inches deeper he would have been floating.

"Well," I said.

"Well, what?"

"Can I get you...I mean do you want the washcloth or anything."

"Sure."

I handed him the cloth and a bar of soap. The wet cloth fell across his spider hands and he just looked at it.

"Here's the soap," I said holding it out for him. He looked at the soap and then he looked at me.

"I don't think I'm gonna need that." He sat for a minute more studying the washcloth.

"Do you need some help?"

196

"No. I'm fine." He sat some more.

"What's the matter?"

"Nothing."

"So why don't you wash?"

"The cloth, I can't..." His voice trailed off like he didn't want to explain how weak he was.

"Here." I took the cloth and wrung it out. I rolled the soap in and began to wash his back. He winced.

"Don't rub so hard! Jesus, do I look like a washboard?"

I held the soapy cloth at the base of his neck and squeezed. The warm water ran down the knuckles in the middle of his back. There was a large purple sore near his left hip and his ribcage looked like one of those xylophones. His skin was blotchy and didn't feel much like skin at all.

"Oh, man. That feels good," he said. He ran his wet hands across his face while I soaked his back again and again. The water was getting cool so I ran some more hot.

I soaped the cloth again.

"Here, let me wash you some." I supported his back with one hand and washed his chest and arms with the others. Gone, all the muscle. His elbows looked like small clusters of walnuts. I reached quickly down between his legs and washed as best I could. He looked at me.

"I don't know if we know each other well enough for that."

"Sorry." He laughed low and deep in the back of his throat. And then he started to cough and couldn't stop. This scared the hell out of me the first time it happened. He would start slow and gain momentum until he could barely breathe and his eyes were full of tears. All I could do was wait it out, so I kneeled there beside him on the floor as he worked his way through it. I wondered if this was how he would go. Would he have one of these spells and not be able to pull himself out? Would I be sitting beside him like I was right now and not realize that he was actually dying? What would I do if I were there when it happened, when he died, that is? It wasn't like I didn't know he was going to die, but I hadn't thought about the actual moment very much. I hadn't thought about being with him. I know it sounds odd, but we had gotten into the rhythm of him dying so much that I hardly thought about him actually being dead. Did I want to be there? I had never seen someone die.

He finally got control of himself.

"You okay?"

"Yeah. Now I'm all better," he said, a little of his old sarcasm showing through.

"Great, maybe you can give me a damn bath now."

He smiled and so did I and for a moment it felt good being with my father. Even with the news that he wasn't my real father, he remained my father. In a strange way I felt protective of that fact.

"Did I ever tell you about the first time you came to me?"

"The first time I came to you?"

"Yeah, when you were little."

"Not that I remember."

"After you were born, you're mother took you with her everywhere. She even slept in the room we had for you. She was always afraid you would die or something if she wasn't in the room. She had a friend, I think, whose baby died, or maybe it was because of her brother, I don't know, but she was frightened all the time. She would hardly leave the house and she didn't even like it when I held you. She'd hover over me until I got too nervous to hold you and then she'd take you away. And that's pretty much how it went. I got sort of used to it. I watched you with your mother but I never was really with you that much. I always told her you were gonna be a mommy's boy if she didn't watch out, but that just made her mad. Anyway, I stopped trying. I worked and came home and went to bed and got up and worked and that was pretty much it. Then one day when I came home I opened the door and I was hanging up my coat when I turned around and there you were, watching me. You musta been about two. And I looked down at you. And you held out your arms and walked toward me like you wanted me to pick you up and you said, Daddy."

I had never heard this story and wondered if it were true, but the look on his face, a faraway look of a man who had hunted a long time to find something important, convinced me that it must be true.

It was quiet between us for several minutes. I soaped the cloth again and wrung it out so I could wash his head without the soap getting in his eyes. He closed his eyes and his face looked peaceful, like he wasn't feeling any pain, like he wasn't feeling nothing at all.

"And after that you would meet me at the door after work almost every day. And we would play with stuff. Like your Lincoln Logs."

"Jesus, Lincoln Logs."

"Yeah. Lincoln Logs."

I took one leg and held it out straight and ran the cloth down its length, my hand wrapped finger tip to finger tip.

"And Tinker Toys, too."

"Hm, Tinker Toys."

I took his other leg and washed it as well.

"What do you think? Ready to get out?"

"Uh huh."

This was a little more challenging. I helped him to his feet and realized immediately that he couldn't stand on his own at all in the slippery tub. I didn't have a towel in my hands, so I had to have him sit down again. Of course the water had all but drained out and it was cold.

"Jesus Christ!"

"Just a minute." I quickly reached for the towel.

"Hurry up for chrissakes, I'm freezin' here."

I wrapped a towel around his shoulders and hoisted him to his feet. He was shaking now, more afraid than cold. I dried him quickly and helped him with his robe. I asked if he wanted me to carry him back to bed.

"Hell, no. I'm not a damn invalid."

"Okay." I stepped back and watched as he shuffled forward first holding onto the sink, then the doorknob and then there was only the hallway ahead. He hesitated. I came up behind him.

"Here, let me get in front of you." He didn't want to take my arm, but he held onto my shirt and we shuffled together across the hall and into his room. He backed slowly to his bed like one of the trucks he used to direct on the loading dock, sat on the edge and breathed a sigh. I could see that he was beat.

"Need some help?"

"I don't need no help." Then he looked up at me. "Thanks anyway."

He lay back in bed and I helped him pull his covers up.

"Sure you don't need anything?"

"No."

"Some pudding or something."

"No."

"Okay." I started to walk away.

"I wanted you to know."

"What?"

"I wanted you to know."

"You mean about the..."

"Yeah. I wanted you to know that you used to come to me. That we used to play when you were little."

"I didn't know that."

"No, I didn't figure you did."

"Now I know."

"Yeah, now you know."

"Get some sleep." I walked to the door and turned to look at him again. He had already turned on his side and was probably already asleep.

I didn't know much about my very first years. I was too young when my mother died to even think that I had a past. Everything was today. There wasn't even a future, just one long today. I never asked about when I was a baby, although my mother often told me the story of my birth. As I thought of it, those stories never included my father. It was always my mother and me. It was like her stories included a big eraser that kept everything else from view. I never even thought it was odd that she didn't talk about him being a part of things when I was very little. It just seemed normal that he wouldn't have been. I mean, he wasn't a part of things that I remembered, so he must not have been a part of things I didn't remember, as well.

My father was changing. And it wasn't just his body. It was like the cancer was eating the poison that had been in him so long. The meanness was almost gone and in its place was this other person that I didn't know well at all, this person with memories of things beyond my recollection, this person who seemed to notice. And, once upon a time, cared.

23

It became more regular as the days passed. My father would wake up in the middle of the night not knowing where he was and sometimes who he was. The first time it scared the shit out of me.

"Pa!" he screamed. It must have been 3am. I was sound asleep and at first I didn't know what was going on or who was yelling. For a moment I didn't hear a thing and figured I had dreamed it. But then the yelling started up again.

"Pa, watch out! Watch out!"

"Dad!" I called, but he didn't respond. "Dad!" Nothing. "Shit." I got up. It was winter and my toes curled as my feet hit the floor. I was angry. What the hell did he want? What was so damn important for him to be screaming out like that in the middle of the night?

"Stay away from there! Momma!"

It was the strangest sight. There he was standing in the corner clutching a pillow to his chest, his eyes bugged out of his head.

"Dad? What the hell's…"

"Don't do it, Pa! Don't go. Momma, stay here. Don't leave me!"

"Dad? What's wrong? What's going on?" He acted like he didn't see me or hear me. It was like he was watching a movie on a screen that I couldn't see. "Dad?"

"I can't stay here by myself alone! Get out of the car! Get out of the car right away! No, don't! It's bad, it's a bad thing that's gonna happen! No you won't be back, you won't. Don't go!"

I didn't know what to do. I went to him but I spooked him and he pulled back and cried out.

"Go away! Go away! No, no, don't take me! Momma! Don't let them take me! No! Pa, where are you?"

I stepped back. I didn't move. He looked at my face. His eyes changed like he realized he was all mixed up and confused but didn't want to let on.

"Dad? Are you okay? You were yelling and I didn't..."

He took a couple of steps forward and stopped. He looked all around the room as if he were getting reacquainted. He put the pillow on the bed but he didn't sit down. He stood there and didn't say a thing.

"Are you okay? You scared me with all the yelling."

He rubbed his face, his hands making the sound of fine sandpaper.

"Can I get you something?"

He looked at me again for a long moment and I could see his shoulders sag. Then he began to cry. He stood in the darkness, a silhouette against the window shade and his shoulders jerked forward over and over again and the tears rolled down his face like water through a dry gully.

I took a step forward and reached out to touch him, but I couldn't. So I stood there beside him while he cried. I stood and didn't say another word. I just watched, hoping that it would end and that he would calm down and go back to bed. He looked up at the ceiling with his mouth wide open but no words came out. He sat on the bed.

"What's wrong dad?"

He wiped his face with his hands again.

"Nothing. Nothing's wrong."

"But you were awful upset. I mean, you were calling for your parents and you..."

"I'm okay now. I'm okay."

"You sure?"

"Yeah, I'm sure. Go to bed."

I turned back at the door and he was still sitting there on the edge of his bed looking cold and alone as a statue. There were other times, as well. Once he called out and when I got to his room, he insisted there was an alligator in the corner and when I told him he was crazy, he said it had been on his chest. He demanded that I get rid of it, that

I stop tormenting him. I got so pissed off, I just left the room. He was still calling to me when I closed the door to my bedroom. And then there was the time that he thought a building made of needles and pins was falling on him. He could feel them pricking his arms and he wanted me to do something to make it stop. I didn't know what to do so I covered his arms with his sheet and for some reason that did the trick.

Those times he was afraid, but not nearly as afraid as he was on the night he was begging his parents not to go, not to leave him. He had never talked about his parents with me and I had always assumed that he was too young to really remember much about them. But I was wrong. A few days later I asked him about the dream.

"I didn't want them to go that night. Not like they had never gone out before and left me with Mrs. Crowley, the neighbor lady, but there was a big storm that night. Lightning and thunder. I was always scared of thunderstorms ever since my friend's house burned down from lightning. I wouldn't even go near a window if there was a storm. Sometimes my father would make fun of me. He'd stand by the window and say, 'Here it comes, here it comes,' but my mother would yell at him and tell him not to scare me. She would sit with me until the worst of it passed and then I'd be okay. But that night they wouldn't stay. They had a party or something and they were all dressed up and my father was in a hurry because they were running late. He told me that I was a 'little man' now and that I would be okay. My mother sat with me as long as she could. Then Mrs. Crowley came. They were in a hurry now. I tried to get them to stay, you know, making things up about being sick, but my mother just smiled and said I would be fine. Then they were gone. And that was it. They wouldn't even let me go to the funeral. They said I was too young, that it wasn't a good idea. It was awful hard, you know, being just a kid and all."

"I know what it's like, Dad. I know."

"No, I mean you didn't have to go to no orphan's house."

"True."

Eventually, I got used to these late night visitations. After a while, I usually didn't even get up, although when his voice reached a certain pitch, I would go to him and try to help him come back from wherever he was.

This was one of those times. I wasn't asleep this time. I was just lying in bed, unable to sleep, when I heard some muffled sounds coming from my father's room. I didn't think much of it until he started calling my mother's name over and over again.

"Margaret? Margaret?"

It sounded like he was looking for her, but then his tone changed. I couldn't understand what he was saying but I could tell he was all upset again. I went into the hall and listened.

"Margaret! No! Here, no, let me...Margaret! What have you...What do you mean?"

I pushed his door open slowly and there he was sitting up in bed, gesturing to the darkness. I could see his eyes in the light of the street lamp, wide and afraid.

"Dad?" I spoke quiet, so he wouldn't be startled. His head snapped round as he looked at me.

"Get to bed! Go away!"

"Dad, what's..."

"Margaret, don't do this, why are you...what's the matter...what is that...what did you do? What did you do? Here, no, just stay there, let me take it...My God, you're all wet, you're...lie down, lie down, don't move..."

"Dad, what's going on for crissakes? Dad!"

"Get out of here boy! Get!"

"What are you talking about?"

"What did you do? Margaret, Margaret, can you hear me? Help! Something's wrong! Don't get up, don't get up! Don't cry! Margaret!"

"Dad, stop!"

"Someone help! I can't stop it...I can't stop."

He was lying on his pillow holding it tight and rocking hard back and forth. His face was wet with perspiration now and he was crying. I went to his bed and tried to shake him out of it. He was afraid and when I touched him he cried out, "NO!"

"Dad, stop it! Dad!" I shook him hard and he let go of the pillow, which was wet as a sponge now. He became limp, his arms fell quiet to the bed, his chest heaved for breath as the tears continued.

"What the hell is going on?" He didn't answer.

"You were calling for mom. What was going on?"

"Nothing."

"Tell me what you saw."

"I didn't do anything."

"What do you mean? You didn't do what?"

He couldn't speak. He wouldn't even look at me.

"Dad. Tell me what the fuck you were dreaming."

"I can't talk. I don't know."

"What do you mean, you don't know. I was right here watching."

"It's gone. I don't remember."

"Goddammit, why were you calling for mom? What was going on? You saw something. I know it. Now what was it?"

"Leave me alone. Just leave me alone!"

I got in his face.

"What do you got in there? What the hell did you see? I have a right to know what that was all about."

"Go away." He was still. His breathing was shallow now. He stared at the wall as he lay on his side. I wanted more but I could see that he couldn't give it. I felt helpless. He saw something. For a moment my mother was in that room. And he was afraid. And I needed to know.

"Rest," I said. I pulled the covers up over his shoulders. "Do you want anything?" He didn't answer. I left.

One day passed into the next without so much as a hint of difference. My father was confined to his bed except twice a day when I lifted him out and took him to the bathroom. Even this became a useless ritual because he often didn't make it. Sometimes he told me and sometimes he didn't until I could smell it in his bed or he would complain of soreness on his skin where he had been lying in his piss.

As the days passed I got afraid that time would run out and I would never get an answer from him. There was no point even asking now. He was in pain and the medication wasn't touching it and some days he didn't speak at all. Not because he was angry. It was just too much bother. He needed his energy for other things, like trying to turn over in his bed or sitting up. And he never complained. He was a whole different man, someone I didn't know. He was all wrapped up in death and it was changing him, but not in the way you'd think. You'd think his meanness would come out full bloom under the circumstances, but it didn't. It was gone and what was left was a stranger, someone I didn't know well at all. And here I was in charge of his dying or at least making it possible for him to die, if that makes any sense. Before this we had never really done anything together. This, this dying, was all we had. It hung on the wallpaper and it was ground into the carpet. It lay on the furniture like old slipcovers and it left a film on the windows that you could never quite wipe off. I could taste it. I could feel it down deep in my lungs. I felt it like I had never felt my mother's death. Her death just came in the night. It swooped in and took her away. I felt it in my stomach like a sucker punch. I never saw it coming like I could see my father's.

24

I heard thumping in the night. No yelling. No calling. But thumping. Like someone was trapped and struggling. Kicking hard against the wall. I ran into his room and found him on the floor. He was shaking hard like he was having a fit.

"Dad? Dad!" He couldn't answer me. He couldn't get up. I tried to help him but it was impossible. I couldn't get my arms under him. I couldn't pick him up.

"Dad, can you get up? We gotta get you back in bed. Jesus Christ, you're burning up." His nightshirt was soaked and it clung to him like saran wrap, but his jaw chattered furiously like he was freezing to death. I finally propped him up and rolled him into bed where he lay sideways.

"I'm feezin' to death goddamit. I can't breathe." He was panting like a dog.

"Okay, okay, let me see what I can do. Just lie there."

"What the fuck else am I gonna do."

I ran to the hall closet and pulled out every extra blanket I could find. I piled them on him, but now there was a whole mound of blankets shaking. Meanwhile he was sweating like crazy.

"I'm gonna call 911."

"What?"

"You heard me. I'm gonna call 911."

"What for?"

"Jesus Christ dad, for an ambulance!"

"I don't need no ambulance!"

"What do you mean you don't need no ambulance? Look at you. You're freezing to death but you're sweating a damn river. You can't hardly breathe. I'm calling 911."

"No, I'll be fine!"

"The hell you will."

When the ambulance came he acted like the whole thing was his idea.

"I knew something was wrong. I knew I needed to get some real help." Meaning, of course, that I wasn't a help at all.

When they carried him out of the house, I was tempted to stay behind. I was sick of the whole thing. Here I was taking care of someone whose only claim on being my father was that he married my mother when I was in her belly. Outside of that, he had no credentials whatsoever, and yet, here I was, sitting with him through his goddam dying.

They took him right away. X-rayed his chest. Turned out he had pneumonia, probably from laying in bed all the time. Whatever it was they admitted him and by morning he was settled into his room. They had him hooked up to some antibiotics, dripping their way into his body. He calmed down and soon he was asleep. I realized I hadn't slept in about 24 hours. I curled up on the chair beside his bed and closed my eyes.

When I woke up, dad was still asleep. He was still as a baby. His breathing was slow and even. I stood beside him and pressed my palm to his forehead. He didn't seem warm any longer. I pulled the covers up to his chin and left his room looking for a vending machine.

A young doctor met me in the hall and asked if I was "the son."

"You know, your father is quite ill."

You're fucking kidding me! He's ill? I thought he was just faking all this, all the puking and the diarrhea and the wasting away to nothing. I thought it was all some game he was playing.

"Yeah, I know he has cancer."

He said they ran this blood test and that blood test and then he talked in numbers for a while and then he described how the cancer was moving from one organ to the next and then he talked about managing the pain.

"I think we will be able to manage his pneumonia. He seems to be responding already. But he also has heart failure."

"What?"

"Heart failure." He explained that my dad's heart wasn't squeezing out enough blood, which caused fluid to back up all over the place.

"We're going to add some lasex and put in a catheter. Do you have any questions?"

I didn't know what to say. Is this heart failure going to kill him? Is the pneumonia going to kill him? What's going to kill him? And when?

"No."

"Well, if you do, Dr. Washington will be on in an hour or so and you can ask for her or you can talk to your dad's primary nurse."

"Okay."

"We're going to do everything we can to make your dad comfortable." He patted me on the shoulder, which felt odd since he was probably ten years younger than me.

When my father woke up, he was confused.

"Where am I?" he said, squinting from the stark light in his room.

"The hospital."

"The hospital?"

"Yeah, remember, you were really sick…"

"Why'd you bring me to the hospital?"

"Because I was bored and couldn't think of anything better to do."

He looked away, frowning.

"Look, dad, don't you remember, you were freezing and you had a temperature and you could hardly breathe."

"Probably just a cold, that's all."

"A cold."

"Yeah, a cold. No need for this. I got cancer for God's sake. A cold ain't gonna kill me."

"It's a little more than a cold, dad."

"What the hell is this?" He had found the catheter.

"Trust me don't pull that thing. Look, dad, you've got pneumonia and you've got some fluid build up or something that's affecting your heart and your lungs."

"What?"

"Yeah. They're giving you stuff that should help, but for now you gotta stay here."

"I want to go home."

"I'm sure you do, but that's not possible."

"You can take care of me."

"Not this time. Not with this stuff going on. The doctor said they should be able to get it under control. Maybe then you can go home."

Once the medicine kicked in, my father started pissing like a racehorse, which drew praise from his nurses.

"1600 CCs, that's great! You're doing a great job." He was a damn hero. Film at 11.

"They seem awfully excited about my ying-yang."

"It's not what you think."

"A man can wish, can't he?"

"Yeah, a man can wish."

When the doctor came in later in the day, he wasn't as excited about dad's ying-yang as the nurses had been. In fact he was concerned that my father was not putting out enough fluid. He tried to explain the problem.

"You see your dad's blah blah blah heart blah blah blah blah weakened condition blah blah worry blah blah infarct blah blah trying different meds blah blah to prevent blah blah. Do you have any questions?"

"That doesn't sound good."

"Well, we'll do everything we can to clear him."

When the doctor left, my father asked what she was talking about.

"I'm not sure, dad. It's something about the fluid and your heart."

"Never had no trouble with my heart."

"I know."

Dinner was salsbury steak, green beans, one slice of bread, a thimble of salad, tapioca pudding and skim milk. Dad seemed overwhelmed by all the plates and covers and wrapped utensils. I put things in order.

"There you go. Hungry?"

"Not so much."

"You gotta eat something."

"Why?"

"Just because."

"But I'm not hungry."

"Eat something. How bout some bread and butter?" I cut the slice in half and buttered it with the frozen pat of butter. I held it to his mouth.

"Put it down. Jesus, I can pick it up myself."

"Suit yourself." I dropped it on his plate. He looked at it and reached for it with his right hand, but he couldn't steady his hand enough to pick it up so he tried both hands. I looked away. He couldn't do it.

"Look, dad, that bread doesn't look so fresh anyway. How bout some of this pudding? You like tapioca, don't you?" I pulled back the aluminum cover. I tasted the pudding.

"Mmm. Not bad. Here, try it." I reached the spoon to his mouth and he took a bite.

"Not so bad."

"How bout some more?" I gave him about ten small spoons of pudding before he said he was full.

"I don't know why but I am tireder then hell."

"Okay, well, why don't you get some sleep."

"And why don't you go home."

I had always thought of the place we lived as a house, but I never considered it a home. But hearing him refer to it as home gave me an odd feeling inside, like we had been sharing a home together all along, in spite of ourselves. Maybe it was the oddest kind of home, held together as it was, by all manner of bad feelings and secrecy, but it was still the place we came back to at the end of the day. I took his advice and went home.

But no sooner had I gotten home than the phone rang. It was my father's nurse. She said I should come back to the hospital. That something had happened. When I asked what it was, she said she would prefer for me to talk to the doctor when I got there.

"Is he dead?" I asked. I felt a flutter in my stomach like I didn't want to hear the answer, like I wished I could reach through the phone line and pull the words back before they entered her receiver.

"No, he's alive."

I felt relieved and surprised at my relief. I wanted to be there, if possible, when it happened. And yet, I didn't know why. It felt more like an urge than anything I could explain. I wanted to see him die. I

211

wanted to see what would happen. I wanted to make sure that if there was anything left to be said that I would be there.

When I got to his hospital room no one was there, which made me wonder again if he was dead already, but a nurse came in and told me he had been moved to the ICU. I was met by Dr. Pat-me-on-the-shoulder outside dad's room.

"Your father has had an MI."

"A heart attack."

"Yes. But we caught it early. It looks like a mild event. We are monitoring it very closely. The next 24 hours will be critical."

"Can I go in to see him?"

"Yes, but just for ten minutes every hour. He needs rest more than anything right now."

Dad looked like a science experiment. His bed was surrounded by several machines, each making its own clicking, whooshing sounds, and tubes ran to every opening in his body, including down his nose. I watched the jagged line run across the monitor. He didn't move. I stood near the head of his bed, my hands resting on the side guards. I leaned over to speak.

"Dad?" I said softly. His eyes fluttered and then opened. He looked the other direction not realizing I was standing beside him.

"Dad?" He turned his head to look at me. He smiled.

"You came."

"Yeah."

"Good."

"How are you doing?"

"They say I had a heart attack."

"Yes, that's right."

"And I'm still here."

"That's right, too. You need to rest, though. The doctor said…"

"It doesn't matter what the doctor said."

"Don't talk."

"I'm never going home again, am I?"

"I don't know, dad. The doctors haven't said that."

"They don't have to. I wanted to die at home. Not in some damn hospital with a bunch of sick people."

"Well, maybe you'll get your wish. We'll have to…"

"You gotta get me out of here."

"Dad, I can't do that. The doctors said your condition is very serious. The next 24 hours are real important."

"Why are they any more important than the last 24 hours or any 24 hours you can think of? If I'm living my life 24 hours at a time, I don't want to do it here. And you gotta do something…"

He was getting agitated now and his nurse came in.

"I think you better leave. Your dad needs rest. He doesn't need to get worked up."

"I'm not worked up. I just want to get the hell out of here."

"I'm sorry we can't let you do that." He looked at me again. "I'm going to ask your son to step out for a while. He can come back in an hour or so."

"I'll be back, dad. Get some rest."

"Where you gonna go?"

"I don't know. Maybe I'll get something to eat."

As I walked to the elevator, I could hear him arguing with the nurse. "I don't wanna" something, he was saying. All I could hear of the nurse was a determined tone. Dad was going to lose whatever battle they were having. But I knew he had to fight. He was like a dog pissing in a new neighborhood. He was making his mark, letting them know he was here before he was gone altogether.

When I went back, his nurse met me in the hall and suggested I wait a while longer. He said dad was sleeping. I could tell that he thought I had upset my father. I wanted to say "it wasn't me, it was him; he's always been like that, always angry and argumentative, always upset." But I didn't. Instead I took a walk around the grounds of the hospital, which sits on top of a hill overlooking the city. In the distance I could see the cluster of trees and rooftops that was our neighborhood. From the top of the hill it looked friendly and inviting and problem free like how the world looks from an airplane, so small and inconsequential. But the closer you get to ground it changes. The simplest thing is complicated and everything you can see clearly from above is hidden from view by all the clutter of daily life.

When I thought about the past, it was like standing on this hill. Everything was clear and it all made a kind of sense. My mother and father were like action figures that embodied what was good and what was bad in my life. As I looked at each one of them, the catalogue of evidence supporting my view of them flashed through my mind.

Based on all the evidence, I created an understanding of myself as a son. In the battle between my mother and father I was left behind to even the score, to fight a guerilla war against my dad, hiding in plain sight, always a reminder of his many crimes. My best weapon was just my being there, making the past present day in and day out. Letting him know that all was not forgotten.

But things happen when you make a home with the enemy. You share more than space and you get to know more things about the other than you want to know. You see him sick and weak and dying. You hear things you've never heard before and suddenly you're down off the hill and you're walking around on the ground where it's hard to see things so clearly. Everything looks a little different close up. And yet he's still the enemy, he's still the one who took your life away. How do you put those two things together? I thought I was here to look after my mother. But here I am looking after my father instead. And even though part of me doesn't want to, another part thinks I should, another part feels it's right somehow for me to be here with him at the end. I didn't think it would be like this, though. I thought I would be here for the laugh. I didn't expect to care. After everything that has happened, all the abuse my mother took, all the hurt I had, after all of this, how do you explain caring? It doesn't make sense.

When I went back to my father's room, it was dinnertime. His bed was raised so he could sit up. His face looked like gravity was trying to pull the skin right off.

"Hi," he said.

"How's it going? Did you sleep?"

"I guess so. That's what they told me."

"Hungry?"

"I don't know."

"Let's see what we got."

There was a thin slippery piece of meat. Some boiled potatoes, a little bit of gravy and a fruit cup. I took the fork and cut one of the potatoes in half and then mashed it into a pulp. I spooned a little gravy onto it and held the spoon to my father's mouth.

"There. Why don't you try a bite?"

He looked at me hard, eye to eye. He opened his mouth and I put the spoon in. He chewed on it much longer than was necessary and then he began to cough. He caught his breath.

"Do you want something to drink?"

He nodded. I poured some water from the plastic pitcher, opened the straw and bent the arm so he could drink it easy. I held it out to him and he drew from it like a bird. This must have taken five minutes. He didn't want anything else and soon it was time for me to step out again. The nurse came to help him back into bed. Both of us took an arm and raised him from the chair. He was like a puppet. His legs dangled to the floor but weren't doing anything. We hoisted him to his bed and I went to the waiting room.

Soon they wanted him to walk. They removed the catheter and insisted he get up to go to the bathroom. My father, who several hours earlier wanted to go home, didn't want to get out of bed.

"I'm too tired to go the whole way over there."

"C'mon dad, I'll help you."

I turned his legs around so they hung over the side of the bed and then I lifted his back. He was sitting without back support.

"There you go."

I stood in front of him and held both his hands as he tried to stand. After a few attempts and much cursing, he was up. He held my arm with both of his hands and then we shuffled as before to the bathroom. By the time he was back in bed, he was so exhausted that he went right to sleep.

Things were different the next day. The doctors said things were going well. They wanted him to walk and they thought he would be out of intensive care soon. They seemed very pleased even though they were only winning a small battle in a war that was already lost. I guess it made them feel better to have something they could fix.

The following day, though, dad had a fever. His pneumonia was back.

His fever came and went for a few days and he was released from the ICU even though he didn't seem much better to me than when he had entered. He was also experiencing more pain in his back and hips. They put him on a morphine IV and he calmed down. But he was a zombie. He just stared and groaned and slept. I sat in the room with him but I wasn't sure he even knew I was there.

When I arrived the next day he was shaking all over, not like he was cold, but like he was having fits of some sort. I rang for the nurse and she explained that it was a side effect of the morphine. She said that although it looked "troubling" it wasn't harming my father. I accepted this and watched him shake in bed for another hour or so. Although he couldn't speak, his face looked alarmed and he wasn't sleeping. Finally I went to the nurse's station.

"Hi. My father is in 208. He's on morphine and it's making him shake like crazy. Can you do anything about it?"

"Well, the morphine is for his pain. We can't do anything unless his doctor orders it. It's not a danger to him."

"He looks upset by it."

"I don't think so."

"What do you mean you don't think so? I'm watching him and I'm telling you he is upset. He's not resting and I want something done!"

"You don't have to raise your voice, sir."

"I'm sorry, but he shouldn't have to go through this. Can you do anything?"

"Like I said, sir, his doctor would have to authorize discontinuing the morphine drip."

"Well, is he here?"

"I don't think so. He rounded this morning and I'm sure he is having office hours now."

"You can call him, can't you?"

"In an emergency, yes."

"Well, guess what? This is an emergency, because if you don't call him about this I am going to raise my voice so loud that…"

"Okay, sir, calm down. I'll call him as soon as I can."

"When will that be?"

"I have a few things I have to do first."

"I don't think so. I don't actually think you have anything else to do before you call his goddam doctor." She set her jaw and I knew she was pissed, and I knew I was being an asshole, but I didn't care.

"Okay, then, I'll call him and let you know what he says."

"Thank you."

When I got back to his room, my dad's head was jerking and his legs were moving so much that his blankets were on the floor. His face looked afraid, but he still couldn't speak. He groaned, not so much in pain, but as if to say something.

"Dad, I told them to call your doctor. This is from the pain medicine. I asked them to do something."

About ten minutes later the nurse returned and said the doctor told her to discontinue the morphine drip.

"We will try to give it to him orally. But it may not be as effective. Especially if he can't swallow."

"Okay. Well, let's try it and see. Thank you. I just didn't want my father to…"

"I understand," she said, cutting me off. "Family members often get upset about these things. They don't always understand what we're trying to do. But since the doctor said to discontinue it we will. We will do everything to make your father comfortable, if you will let us."

"I don't want to get in anyone's way. I just don't want to see him shaking constantly like he's having some kind of fit."

"Well, let's see how he does with the pain."

In a matter of hours he stopped shaking and fell asleep. He slept all day and well into the evening. There were two meal trays stacked on his table when he woke up.

"Dad?" He looked at me but I wasn't sure he recognized who I was.

"It's me."

"Of course it's you," he said, his voice merely a rasp. He fell asleep again.

I came to the hospital early the next morning, hoping to see one of his doctors. His cancer doctor was at the nurse's station. I explained who I was.

"Yes, I was in to see your father this morning already. How can I help you?"

"Well, I don't know. How do you think he's doing?"

"As well as can be expected. His cancer has spread considerably and most of the major organs are involved. His heart is holding its own, even though we're seeing some more fluid. We've added more Lasex to drain it off. We're worried about the pain he was having, but he seems to be doing okay at this point being off the morphine drip. Oftentimes as we increase the morphine they drift into a coma-like state and then they are free from the pain. But I understand that you were concerned about all the involuntary movements you father was having on the drip, so we discontinued it for now."

"Okay. So what's going to happen?"

"Excuse me?"

"I mean what's going to happen next? How long will this go on?"

"We can never predict these things. But I can tell you that things haven't progressed enough for him to die." I didn't know there was a rule about this. It sounded like a hostess at a restaurant saying "your table isn't quite ready so we can't seat you." I didn't realize there were rules or steps to follow. What would happen if dad died before things had "progressed enough"? Would they rescind his death? Make him come back until the countdown officially reached zero?

"How do you know when it's progressed enough?"

"It's hard to say. It could be days or it could be weeks. I think it's safe to say that it won't be months."

"Okay."

"Your father *is* dying."

"I know that."

"Good. I wasn't sure if you thought he was going to get better. I wouldn't want you to expect something that..."

"I don't expect anything."

"Okay. Well. If you have any questions, just have your father's nurse contact me."

"Okay."

My father was sitting up in bed when I entered his room. His breakfast tray was gone. His head was tilted over. He was asleep. I settled into the chair beside his bed and started to read the paper. In a short time he opened his eyes.

"G'mornig," he said, his voice a fainter rasp, his words shortened like a child's earliest speech.

"How did you sleep?"

He turned his right hand palm up and shrugged his shoulder as if to say, "Not so well."

"Can I get you something?"

He opened his mouth and pointed at it with his hand.

"Hungry?"

"Na."

"Thirsty?"

"Ya."

I poured a glass of water and held the straw firm and tilted it to his mouth. He struggled to get the straw in straight so I guided it in. He

218

sucked hard but air came in through the corners of his mouth so the water was slow to come. He stopped and lay back against his pillow. He winced.

"Are you in pain?"

"Huh?"

"Pain? How's the pain?"

"Oh," he said scrunching his face.

"Where? Where does it hurt?"

"Ma back."

"Your back. Did you tell the doctor?"He shook his head, yes.

"Are you taking the medicine?"

He shook his head again.

"Would you like a pillow under your back?"

And again.

I took an extra pillow from the closet and folded it.

I tilted him over on one side and lay the pillow at the base of his back and then rolled him over again. He sighed and smiled.

"Ahhh."

"That feel better?"

"Yes," he said clearly.

He fell asleep again. I sat back in the chair and started to read the paper. In a few minutes I was following each of his Darth Vader-like breaths. They were slow and low and constant with a measured pause between them. Each pause filled the room with an uncertain silence. Would another breath come? And then it would. And I would settle into the comfort of a single breath until the next silence. And so we breathed along together through the day, breath by breath, silence upon silence.

25

In my dream a phone kept ringing and no matter what I did I couldn't find it. I went from room to room following the sound and as I entered each room I realized the ringing was coming from another. I became frantic because I knew that the phone call was important. I knew that I had to find the phone before the caller hung up, but how? The ringing got louder and my movements got slower. I could barely lift my legs when I saw the phone at the end of a long hall, a hall that seemed to get longer with each staggering step. I reached for it, but couldn't touch it. I stretched my arms out to their limits, but the phone was always just beyond my fingertips. I cried out as if the caller might hear me, but the phone just rang and rang.

I called out once more only to wake myself up. I was sitting in my bed. It must have been about 3am. I sat still waiting for the phone to ring. I was sure that as I woke up I had heard one final ring. I waited another second, long enough for another ring, but there was nothing. Just my darkened room and the sound of the furnace kicking on. I was breathing like I had just run a mile, my heart pounding against my chest, my face moist with sweat.

I got up to take a piss. I stepped into the hall and stood for a moment listening. Then I remembered that dad wasn't in his room. I was alone in the house. I clicked on the light to the bathroom and looked into the mirror. I needed a shave. My eyes were red and baggy and my skin looked like the paste we used to eat in kindergarten. I ran my hand through my hair, surprised by how much my forehead had grown. "Hello good lookin'."

I sat down on the john, my face in my hands as I stared at my feet. I worked on my batting stance again, shifting my feet a little. I moved them a part 18 inches or so, and then back and forth until I had them lined up just right, my left foot about two inches behind my right. An open stance. My father always told me I would have been a better hitter if I had opened up my batting stance. I never listened to him. I looked down at my feet.

"He was right."

It felt comfortable. And I would have seen the ball better and been able to turn on it more quickly. I always had trouble with that inside corner. I would break a bat or miss the ball altogether. Just two inches back and it would have made all the difference.

The phone rang. I startled and listened. This time it rang again and I ran for it. It was a nurse at the hospital.

"Can you come? It's your father."

"What happened? Is he alright or what?"

"No, it's nothing like that. I mean he's upset but he's not worse. He's alive."

She said he woke up around 1am and had been awake all night ringing the call button every 15 minutes or so because he felt afraid. She said she sat with him for as long as she could, but she couldn't stay with him any longer and she wanted me to come if at all possible.

"What's he afraid of?""I'm not sure exactly. He can't say. But it's not unusual. We see it in patients all the time. It's the darkness, I think. It's hard to be alone in the dark when your mind can wander."

"Yeah. I'm sure."

"So can you come?"

"Yes. I have to get dressed but I'll be there as soon as I can."

"I'll let him know."

Jupiter sat on the eastern treetops and there was a wide soft circle around the moon, its light casting shadows on the sidewalk. No bird sounds yet and the houses on the street lay sleeping, all in a line. There was one light on the next block down. I realized I didn't even know who lived there. The air was cool on my skin, but soothing. I loved this time of night, long enough before daylight that you could relax and not worry about what was coming, what might happen when everything woke up and the day got up a head of steam and problems started popping up here and there. There weren't any problems in the world when it was dark and cool and empty. For a moment I forgot where I was going.

Things were quiet at the hospital as well. Dad's nurse met me at the station and thanked me for coming so quickly. She said he hadn't pushed the call button in a while so she hadn't been back in to see him.

Even though his room was dark, I could see his profile against the window. I was surprised that he was sitting up in bed.

"Dad?"

"Yeah? Oh, it's you. They told me they were going to call you." He was talking more clearly than he had in days.

"They said you were having some trouble."

"Trouble?"

"Something was scaring you or something."

"Oh, I was talking to the nurse is all. Must have talked too long."

I didn't understand what was going on. Dad didn't seem to be afraid or anxious. He seemed calmer and more alert than he had been in days.

"You're okay then?""Uh huh." He pulled his sheet up. I was surprised that he could use his hands at all.

"Did you eat any dinner last night?"

"No. I ain't been hungry at all. They keep trying to get me to eat and I keep telling them I feel full. I ain't got an appetite. Nothing I can do about it."

"I guess they want you to keep up your strength."

"What exactly for?" He smiled.

"Yeah, I guess you're right. Can I get you something to drink?"

"Yeah, I'm dry." I poured some water into his glass, held the straw in place and lifted it to his face, but he held out his hand, instead, and took it.

"I can do this, you know."

"You couldn't yesterday." He took barely a sip and gave it back to me.

"I don't like the dark. Nothing good comes from it. Bad things mostly come at night for some reason. Maybe 'cause you can't see them coming so easy. They can sneak up on you while you sleep. Of course, I don't sleep so much. Especially at night."

"Uh huh. It must be hard sometimes. Not sleeping so well at night."

"It's better to stay awake. Not much time left, you know."

"You don't think so?"

"No, I don't. It's getting close."

"How do you know?"

"I can feel it. I can feel life sort of oozing out of me."

"Maybe you just need some rest."

"That's what they keep telling me. 'Rest,' the nurses say. 'Get some rest.' It's the advice of the living. Doesn't much matter to me if I sleep another minute. It's a waste really when you think of it. You spend a third of your life sleeping. And for what?"

"Uh huh." Neither of us said anything for a minute or so.

"Dad, do you want me to turn a light on?"

"No, this is enough light," he said, looking at the window. "The moon must be full."

"It is."

"Yeah, I could tell." He reached for the glass on the table and took another sip of water.

"I know you always thought I done something."

"What do you mean?"

"About your mother. I know you always thought I done something to her."

"I suppose you're right."

"I know you always held it against me."

"Right again."

"Do you want to know what really happened that night?"

"I know what really happened. I saw it."

"No, you only know what you saw with your little boy eyes, that's all."

"I know what I saw." We had never gotten this close to it before and I could feel old, old anger. I could almost smell it, taste it.

"Dad, don't go there, because I saw what I saw…"

"What did you see?"

"You know what I saw."

"Tell me."

"I don't have to tell you. You know, too."

"You saw your mother, right, curled on the floor. And she was bleeding, right. And I was beside her."

"And there was broken glass and she was cut and you screamed at me to go upstairs and so I went. I should never have gone upstairs."

"Yes, you should have."

"If I had stayed, maybe she would still be alive."

"No."

"Maybe I could have stopped it."

"No."

"Stop saying no."

"Do you want to know what happened?""What do you mean?"

"Except when she was with you, your mother was a very unhappy woman."

"That's your news flash. Of course she was unhappy with a sonofabitch like you for a husband. What could you expect?"

"More than that. More than my being a bad husband, more than all the things I did wrong, more than all of that, your mother had unhappiness in her bones. Just like you. And I made it worse. I know that. I didn't then. All I could see was her pushing me away. All I could see…"

"Was what? What could you see? Jesus Christ, you never paid enough attention to her to notice anything. What could you see?"

"I could see she was starved for something more."

"What are you talking about?" He turned his head and the moon caught his left eye in the half light.

"Your mother was pregnant when she died."

"What?"

"She was pregnant."

"That's what she was starved for? Another kid? What was the problem? Didn't you want it? Is that what upset her? Is that what led to…"

"She didn't want it."

"What are you talking about?"

"I always wanted a child with your mom. I always thought it would have helped us. But it never happened for so long I sort of gave up on it. But that day she told me she was pregnant when I came home from work and I thought, 'This is great, maybe things will turn around.' But she didn't seem happy at all. She didn't smile or nothin'. She said she had went to the doctor several weeks before. I asked why she hadn't told me and I guess I didn't listen to her answer because I was just so happy. But her face looked so strange when I looked at her that I just said, 'What? What is it?'"

He stopped talking. He was short of breath and he stopped talking and I didn't care if he could breathe at all because all I cared about was what happened to my mother.

"So what did she say?"

"She told me that I wasn't the father."

"Fuck you. C'mon, what is this?"

"That's what she told me. She cried and fell on the couch and said she was sorry."

"Wait a minute. What the hell are you saying? Are you saying my mother was fucking some other guy and got pregnant again? Is that what you're trying to sell? Huh?"

"Not like that. Don't talk like that. It broke my heart when she told me. And I hit her across the face with the back of my hand. And I called her a whore. And I grabbed the nearest bottle and I drank every ounce and then looked for more." He was crying now and he could hardly breathe. "She just laid there crying and saying she was sorry. I wouldn't listen. I couldn't. I went up the stairs and fell into my bed."

"But that's not the end of the story, is it? It didn't end there, did it? Something else happened? And you know what it was. I heard her calling and she wanted you, not me. And now I know why. She was trying to get you to forgive her wasn't she? And you couldn't do it, could you? Did you hit her again? Did you cut her up good, you fuck?" I grabbed him and pulled him off the bed. "You killed her didn't you? I knew it. You did, didn't you? Tell me."

"Put me down," he said, shaking, his eyes full of fear. I stopped. I laid him back on the bed. I fell back into my chair. I couldn't believe it was true after all. I had known it but now I realized I had always hoped it was otherwise. Maybe that's why I never asked him directly; maybe that's why I always stopped at accusations.

"I...did...not...kill...your...mother."

"What are you saying?"

"She called, remember? And you got up, right? But she wouldn't let you come down the stairs. So I went down, instead. She had been drinking and she was talking crazy about somebody not loving her and how she couldn't go on and I knew she wasn't talking about me and I asked her who it was and she wouldn't tell me. It was dark and she was lying on the sofa, curled in a ball crying. And I took a step towards her but I stepped on glass and cut my foot and I took another step and cut myself again, and then again. There was glass everywhere. Then I saw that her hands were bleeding and she had a sharp piece of glass in one hand and there was blood smeared all over her face and she looked up at me and said, I'm sorry."

"My God, don't tell me this."

"She said she was sorry and I didn't know what she meant. I went to her and she opened her arms and I could see that she cut through her dress and her stomach was bleeding. I never saw so much blood. It just ran and ran and I couldn't stop it. The hospital said she stabbed herself over and over, that mostly the cuts didn't go deep, but one did. One went too deep…"

"Stop!"

"It hit something. They told me but I can't remember. The blood was like a river had overflowed. I couldn't do a damn thing. I ran to the kitchen and got some towels but it didn't matter. She was breathing all shallow and she wanted me to hold her, so I sat there on the floor and then you came down the steps and I yelled at you to go back up and she cried and said not to let you see her and I held her. She was going too fast. I wanted to call the ambulance but I thought she was gonna die. I picked her up and ran to the car and…"

"NO!"

"…by the time I got there it was too late. I mean I tried but she was limp before I got there. I knew she was gone but I drove fast as I could anyway. I blew my horn and I went through all the lights but I knew she was gone. And she was."

"Oh, my God." I went to the sink and threw up. I could barely stand. "No."

"Everyone rushed and they tried to make her breathe but she stayed limp and they hit her hard on the chest and I was afraid they were hurting her but they couldn't hurt her. All the hurt was over."

"Stop!" I was crying. I felt like someone had kicked me in the stomach and then when I was able to breathe, they kicked me again. But he kept talking like he was in a trance. The words just kept coming.

"You were right about the police. They thought I killed your mother. They questioned me for a long time and they wouldn't let me see her and they treated me like a criminal. They kept coming around.

It was after the funeral that they decided I didn't do anything. But they never apologized. They never said, 'We're sorry about your wife.' They acted like it was my fault anyway. Maybe it was."

He stopped for a long moment considering his own words, wanting his confession to be heard.

"But your mother was so pretty when I first met her at that bar that I couldn't stay away."

I was in shock. I couldn't speak. My ears ached with everything he had said. I shook my head but the words wouldn't fall out. And I hated them because I knew they were true. I knew it from the bottom of my stomach. I knew it from the pain behind my eyes and the ringing in my ears and the sweat between my fingers. It was as true as a fist hitting you in the face.

I didn't know what to think. Did I really need to know this after all? Was this better than what I had always believed? I looked at him and he watched me, his eyes wide, waiting to see what I would do. I sat down, put my head in my hands and started to rock. I cried some more just as I thought I had it under control. I couldn't believe that my mother would do such a thing. That she would leave me without so much as a word.

"My God."

"I'm sorry."

"I always thought mom was the good one, the one I could believe in, who wouldn't…"

"Who wouldn't what? Be a plain old person?"

"I don't know what that is."

"Your mother was just a plain person trying to live her life. There's always some shit inside every life, inside every person. But it doesn't make 'em bad people. It just makes 'em people. Just people trying to make their way through the world. That's all. What your mother did doesn't change how much she loved you. Because she did."

"I just don't know anything anymore."

"No, you don't. Maybe that's not such a bad thing."

My heart felt like your elbow does when you hit your funny bone. I couldn't tell if it was going to pass or not. How could not knowing what's what be a good thing?

"You know your mother was about your age when she died. Think about how hard it is for you to live your life. How hard you struggle trying to figure out if you can go on. Now think about your mother. She was no different. She was just struggling along and she got to the point that she couldn't struggle no longer and she had to stop, but she didn't want you to know. She didn't want you to see. She didn't want you to have to face that awful thing. She protected you in her way even though she couldn't protect herself no more."

"Mom."

"Yes. Mom. Always."

I looked at this almost dead man and wondered how we had fucked things up so bad. He must have known what I was thinking.

"I don't know what went wrong with us exactly. All those years are gone now and we can't do nothing about it. I wish I could, but I can't. I wish I could bring your mother back, but I can't. I wish I'd been a better father, but I wasn't. I wish a lot of things, but all I got left to do now is this dying. I can't change all the rest, but I can try to do this okay."

"Yeah, I guess you can do that."

He reached out and took my forearm in his hand and shook it lightly and then let it go. My fingertips brushed his arm as it fell back onto the bed.

"You okay?" he asked.

"I don't really know. I guess."

"Dumb question maybe."

"I guess I never thought of mom as a woman, as someone who was separate from me. I guess she was. I don't know how to think about it."

"She was a part of you and you were a part of her, but she was more than that, too."

"And I never been much more than a part of her, I guess."

"Still got time."

The nurses came to the door and asked if it would be okay for them to come in and wash dad and change the bed. So I stepped out for about fifteen minutes and when I came back my father was asleep. I stood over him and he looked worn to the very bone. I reached down and took his arm in my hand and patted it. He didn't move. I stood over him for a minute in case he woke up but he didn't, so I pulled the chair up beside the bed and sat down. I opened the paper and started to read. But I put it down again and listened instead to my father's rhythmic breathing. I found myself breathing with him again, like maybe I could help him draw it in and push it out, help him stay alive a little bit longer.

26

When my father woke up, things had changed. At first I didn't notice. But then it was clear that he couldn't speak good at all anymore. He spoke in mumbles and syllables and sometimes he just used gestures and shrugs. Over the next two days we didn't really talk. I fell into a checklist of questions each time he mumbled something or groaned and I didn't understand what he meant:

"Uhh," he would say moving one hand and looking at me.

"What was that, dad?"

"Uhh uhh wa."

"You want what?"

"Uh uh wa!"

"Does something hurt?"

He'd shake his head.

"Do you want me to turn you over?" Often a request, since he had no padding left and laying on his bones hurt.

No response.

"Dad? Does something hurt?"

"Uh uh wa."

"Do you want some water?"

His eyes got wide and I knew I had hit the jackpot. I would then take the tiny foam tipped stick and dip it in cold water and hold it to his lips. He would press down on the foam with all his strength, trying to squeeze out the water. Sometimes I squeezed it into his mouth as he watched me like a tiny bird watches his mother.

"Do you want some more?"

"Na."

Then he would fall asleep.

His pain seemed to get worse, as well. He tossed and turned and moaned in his sleep. They decided on the IV again and he did better for another day.

He didn't have control of his bowels anymore and the nurses came in regularly to clean the bed and change the sheets. It didn't matter that my father used to be a boss who ran a loading dock, who never shit his pants in his life. That was all over. They were rolling him over on his side and wiping his ass while talking about problems they were having with the MI in room 207. He was turning into furniture. Not that they were mean or anything like that. It's just that they stopped talking to him. They talked to me or to each other about him and then yelled what they were going to do next without ever trying to get any response from dad. For his part, he gave up all efforts at trying to control any of what was going on. Mostly he closed his eyes when they came in.

"They're gone," I'd say, and then he'd open his eyes and look at nothing at all. His mouth was open most of the time, his dentures long gone. His mouth had shrunk so much he could never put them in again anyway.

Mostly I sat. There wasn't much at all for me to do and yet I didn't want to be anywhere else. I thought a lot about our conversation. In the end it came sort of easy, like two boxers who had fought fifteen rounds to a draw and then were too tired to do anything else but fall into each others' arms. Both bloodied and yet holding each other up. My father was not a good husband. He wasn't a good father either. But there was something more to him, if that is possible to imagine, something that had been hidden from me and maybe from him for a long time, something in him that felt all of the world's hurting and measured caring with each passing drink. He was a wounded guy who married a wounded girl, never thinking they might double the wounds they meant to heal.

And then I came along and inherited their wounds like some people inherit their father's riches. Of course, there was some love early on from my mother that I have held tight with my clenched heart. And maybe some love even now from my father, poured out like good medicine, tasting too awful to swallow easy. Maybe I'd been sort of lucky in the beginning of my life and lucky again at the end of my father's life. Like finding a couple of four leaf clovers in a desert. They look all the more green and alive for all the parched miles that surround them.

"He is getting close now," said one of the nurses.

"How can you tell?"

"Look how his ears are starting to curl and how his eyes have sunk in."

He was between worlds, gazing at the ceiling for hours, his eyes moving back and forth like he was watching something, like he was looking into another world. Who knows, maybe he was. Was my mother looking back at him? If so, I wonder what she was thinking? Would they try to make a go of it again? I had a hard time with the idea that you see people after you die, that you go to some place called heaven where everyone is kind of alive again and everything is okay. I just can't get my head around that. It doesn't make sense to me even though a lot of people say they believe it. I wonder if they actually do, or if they're just desperate to believe something. They want to believe life goes on. That part I can understand. I can understand not wanting things to end, even though I've tried to end my life. I guess I didn't want my life to end as much as I wanted the pain to end. Ending-the-pain is a heaven I could believe in. I don't think you should have to die to get there.

When I wasn't paying much attention, fall arrived. I looked out across the valley and most of the trees had turned those bright cartoon colors. It was sunny but the wind was stiff as a frozen chord and I leaned against it to keep my balance.

Alvie Coppler came around the shed.

"How the fuck are you, my friend?" He stuck out his hand for me to shake.

"Okay enough, I guess."

"Your old man dead, is he?"

"No. Not yet."

"Oh, I heard he had bit the bag and stepped out the door. Still hangin' on, huh? What a bitch. I'll bet you'll be glad when he finally kicks, huh?" I didn't answer and Alvie laughed and shifted his weight.

"Okay, so what the hell can I do for you? Were you lookin' to get another plot for your old man?"

"No, not another one. I came to find out if there's another one beside my mother."

"I don't know about that. Lemme check." He went into his office and came back after a few minutes.

"Yeah, says your old man bought two when your mother died. Surprising."

"Why's that?"

"Well, I mean…with all that happened with your mom…" He stopped as if I would say something, but I didn't.

"You know what I mean. They didn't exactly have a marriage made in heaven if you get my drift."

"Maybe not."

"I didn't mean nothin' by it. Just surprised, that's all."

"So there is a second plot where he can go."

"Yes, there is. I can show you others though. Unless you think it's okay for them to be together like that. I mean, I know they won't fight or nothing." And he laughed and looked for me to laugh as well.

"Actually, that's exactly what I want. I want them to be buried side by side, just the way my dad planned it when he bought these two plots after my mother died. That was his wish."

"Okay by me. I'm just surprised is all. I mean your old man…"

"You mean my father."

"Yeah, your father, well, he wasn't, I mean they didn't…"

"Is there anything I need to do, any papers I need to sign?"

"No, we'll make all…"

"Good. Alvie, take it easy."

"You too buddy, good to see you."

I called the minister who did Don's funeral and asked him if he would mind doing my father's.

"I mean, I know we ain't been much for going to church. In fact, I don't even know what my father thinks about church any more. But it's something I want to do. It seems proper and right to do it this way, to stop everything for a little bit and have people come and have someone say something, you know. It just seems like he should get a little consideration, that's all."

"Well, given the circumstances I would be willing to help you honor your father in this way."

"Thank you Reverend. Thanks."

"Okay. Is there anything else that I can do for you?"

"Not that I can think of?"

"Are there any hymns your father liked or scripture he would want us to read?"

Of course, I didn't have a clue. I couldn't even remember my father ever going to church. Hymns? I don't think he could name a single hymn even if he could talk.

"I'll have to get back to you on that. Okay?"

"Yes, that will be fine. I will keep you and your father in my prayers."

"Okay. Well. Okay." I wasn't sure what to say. No one ever told me they were going to pray for me. I didn't know if that meant I had to do something or that I had to start being a better person. If that was the deal, I didn't have the energy to be any better or worse than I was. I mean I felt lucky just making it through each day watching my father die inch by inch. That seemed like enough to expect from anyone. But it also felt kind of good to think that someone I hardly knew was going to be thinking of me and my father during this awful time. And tossing some words into the air for us was fine. I didn't know if Anyone would be listening but it couldn't hurt.

I walked to the corner to mail some bills. The morning air was cool and you could smell dry leaves and moist dirt, the smell of fall and football. In the field by the elementary school we used to play pick-up games. I remember scoring six touchdowns once. I could always run. Every time I touched the ball, I was as good as gone. I crossed the street and walked down the block to the old school. It had been an important part of my world during those years when my mother was alive. She would walk me to school on days she was feeling good and happy and we'd talk along the way and she'd point out the birds to me and name them all and we'd laugh at old Mr. Shelton who was always in his driveway swearing at his car. As I got a little older, she knew to stop walking with me when we reached the mailbox at the end of the block. I'd walk on from there, although every day I'd turn when I reached the school to see if she was still standing there. She always was. I'd lift my hand slightly to wave and she'd wave back as if we were both saying we'd be okay.

I don't know what happened each day after I entered the school. I could see our house from Miss Thom's class when I was in second grade. It felt good to look out every once in a while and see it there, and think about my mother inside the house, assuming she was thinking about me. What was she really thinking about? Why did she always go to the doctor? What was her suffering all about? What were those days like, alone in the house with me at school and dad at work?

I liked being in school where we were always busy and no one yelled and fought and cried. And yet I felt uneasy too, uneasy about how things were going down the street, uneasy about not being there and not knowing exactly why I felt that way. Usually, she would be at the mailbox when I came out of school in the afternoon. She would put a smile on her face once I got close enough and we'd walk home together, her asking me how my day was and me telling her who threw up during reading or who blew a fart in music. She'd laugh and I would too. Some days, though, she wouldn't be at the mailbox and I knew it hadn't been a good day. When I'd get home, she'd be lying on the couch in her robe watching TV. She'd ask about my day but it wasn't the same. It was like she knew the right questions to ask, but she wasn't really interested in the answers. I'd ask her if she was okay and she'd say that she was just a little tired. I'd sit and watch TV and soon she would be asleep. If her hair was over her face I'd brush it back or I'd cover her if she were curled in a ball looking cold. I'd watch her sleep for a while, her face all relaxed and smooth, sometimes a twitch at the corner of one eye.

It must have made her awful tired working so hard at being alive. I wanted to be angry at her after my father's story sunk in, but I couldn't. I felt sad, but not angry.

Do I wish I had known then what I know now? At first I thought, yes, but I don't know for sure. Maybe it was better having my father to blame than thinking my mother wanted to die. That way it wasn't like she left me. It was like she was taken away.

Mrs. Sanders was coming down the walkway as I headed back to the house. She was pushing her grocery cart and had a firm hold on her purse. She had been a neighbor for as long as I could remember.

"Good morning."

"Morning, dear. And how are you?" she said, reaching out to pat my arm. "How is your father?"

"Not so good."

"I'm so sorry."

"They don't think he will live much longer. But they've been saying that for a while."

"Oh, dear. Are you eating right? You look thin. You must take care of yourself, you know."

"Yes, I know."

"You must be just sick over all this, I can't imagine. You know your father has always been such a dear to me. When my Henry died, he was the first one to call. He came to the house and you would have thought he had lost his very best friend. He cried and cried and I had to comfort him. He told me he thought of Henry as a son might think of a father, which surprised me. I didn't think they were that close, I mean neighbor close, but not close like blood, but that's how he felt. And he would come by regular after that to see how I was doing and to fix things if I needed it." She shook her head and smiled. "Please tell him that I am thinking of him."

"Yes, I will tell him. Thank you." No matter how impossible it is or how long it takes, we keep looking for those who have left us too soon, like they are hidden in the world and by searching for what can't be found we can make it all right again.

I stopped at the house to fix a thermos of coffee. Went to the pharmacy to buy a paper. Got to the hospital around 9 AM. The tree outside my father's window was bright yellow now, shimmering in the breeze, holding to the last, before it would be bare again.

"Your father has had a hard night," the nurse told me when I reached the nurses station.

"What's up?"

"Well, he had a seizure during the night and things have gotten worse."

This was new. "What caused the seizure?"

"We're not sure. His fever was very high, but it's more likely it was the cancer. We're certain that it has spread to his brain. I think the doctor may have told you that."

"Maybe. I think so. I can't remember. So what do we do now?"

"Well, there's not very much to do. He's still on the IV drip because he seemed pretty uncomfortable during the night. He looked like he was in pain. He kept moving like his back ached. We turned him several times, but it didn't seem to make a difference." She pursed her lips and raised her eyebrows as if to say, Sorry.

"What's the doctor say?"

"All we can do is try to keep him comfortable."

"That's all? There's nothing else?"

"I'm afraid not." She reached over and took my arm in her hand. "You understand that your father is…"

"Yes, I know. He's been dying all along."

"Yes, he has. But now, he's dying. I think it is very close. You may want to be with him."

"Okay." As I turned to walk away she warned me.

"You should know that he is having the same reaction to the morphine that he had before. I'm sorry."

The breakfast tray came each day at the same time and sat on his table, cover in place, until it was cold and they took it away again. Yesterday's paper was folded on the chair and a candy bar wrapper was under the bed. The TV was on a music channel. Some orchestra was playing an old Beetles song. My father's watch lay on the nightstand ticking each day away as he lay dying through one endless moment.

I couldn't look at him at first. I looked at the pale green walls and the faded flowers on the curtains and his shoes in the far corner. They lay touching heal and toe, ready for his feet, ready for his step, to move and go and leave this place. The laces fell limp to the floor.

I was shocked when I finally looked at him. Not because he was so different than the day before or the day before that, but because I could see the whole thing at once, all the change, all the wasting away that had started months before.

"Dad?" I said, quiet as if I might disturb him, how silly.

"It's me. I'm here." The nurse was right. The terrible twitching was back. His arms and his legs jerked every few seconds like he was a puppet. He had kicked his cover off and his left leg was bare. His skin hung off the bone, bruised and angry looking. I covered him again. Between his head and his feet was an empty valley where once the mound of a person had been.

"Dad? Your tree is all yellow now. I can see the leaves through the window. And it's sunny today."

His eyes were open, dried tears at the corners. I leaned over him to be in his line of sight.

"Dad? Hi." He looked at me. I couldn't see it in his eyes before, not until he looked at me, and then I saw the only thing that was left, fear.

236

"Dad. I'm here now. I won't be going anywhere. I won't leave you. Okay?" He groaned, not the groan of pain, but a different groan, like there was a word inside of it, a response. He knew I was there.

"You don't have to be afraid. Okay? I'm here." He moved the fingers in his right hand slightly. His mouth was dry and cracked. I reached for the Chapstick on the table.

"Here, let's try this." I spread it on his upper lip. He was moving his tongue as if to speak and I leaned in close, but I couldn't hear a word. He was speaking in silence, a movement of his tongue, a gesture of one finger, a deep heavy sigh. His body continued to jerk and pull in every direction.

"I'm sorry for all this mess, dad."

I took a warm cloth and cleaned his eyes and nose. I filled the tiny sponge with water and pressed it against his lower lip so it would drip into his mouth. I couldn't tell if he could swallow it.

"Do you want the water, dad?" I don't know why I asked questions.

"Here let me try it again. You look so dry." I pressed the cool sponge to his mouth again and he groaned again. I took another pillow and propped it behind his neck so that his head was steady. I stood beside his bed, my hands on the rail. He was a shadow now, not quite a person anymore, and yet still here in the world.

I reached for his hand and took it in mine. To my surprise, I could feel his fingers trying to curl around mine. I squeezed his hand.

"I thought you were still here." Another deep groan.

"Jesus, dad, I hate to see you going through this." My eyes started to well up, but then I smiled. "I'll bet you're surprised to hear me say that, aren't you." He squeezed again. "Soon you're going to be okay. I don't think it will be very long." I tried to listen for the rhythm of his breathing, but I couldn't find it. Only the little bit of air that snuck through with each groan.

"You know, I saw Mrs. Sanders this morning and she wanted me to tell you she was thinking of you. She told me how much you helped her after her husband died and she said you were a good man and I thought to myself, she might just be right." I squeezed his hand. And he squeezed mine.

And then his eyes closed tight, wincing from the pain, thin lines across his lids, his mouth open and his head thrown back. His groans got worse, until it seemed like they weren't coming from his mouth any longer, but from every pore of his body. I didn't know what to do.

"Dad? Are you okay? Are you choking?" His face was beet red now and his groan became a moaning howl, like an animal, and the howl hit the ceiling and went right through it, and he howled again and again and he moaned and he pulled hard on my hand.

"Dad!" I wanted to run out of the room. I wanted to run out of the room and down the hall and into the parking lot and down the street and away and away.

"Dad!" I pushed the nurses call button and waited but no one came.

His mouth pulled closed into a thin line drawn from ear to ear, his eyes clenched tight and he gasped. I released the rail and leaned over him. His eyes were closed. I took him in my arms and pulled him to my chest.

"Dad, I've got you. I've got you." He continued to groan and I rocked him back and forth. But it didn't matter. There was no comfort, there was no way to relieve the pain. I held him tighter and tighter still.

"Nurse!" I called. And again. But it was just the two of us.

He wailed with the pain. It poured out of his mouth and across my ears and into my heart.

"My God, Dad!"

We were alone together and there was no one else. I pulled him into my chest. I put my hand behind his head and pressed his face deep into my coat. I held him tight so he couldn't move, so all he could feel was my hand on his head and I spoke to him low and soft.

"Dad, it's going to be okay. It's going to be okay. It's going to be okay." I held his face firmly into my coat.

The shaking stopped first. No more jerking and flailing. But I still held him close. I held him and I rocked him and I waited. And then I saw it. A small thing, but I knew. His right wrist fell back slightly, just a quarter on an inch at most, but with that movement his hand went limp, and I knew. I knew it was over. But I held on some more. I rocked him slowly now and I began to cry and I rocked him still and kissed the top of his head.

"That's it, dad. Over."

I leaned over and laid him into bed again. His mouth was open but his eyes were closed and gone was the grimace and gone was the pain. All of it. I took the warm cloth and wiped off his face and smoothed back his hair. I held his hand and looked at his fingers and took each one in my hand and let each fall like you might let a baby's fingers fall when they're asleep.

The nurse came in.

"What can I do for you?" I didn't answer and she could tell by the stillness of the room. "Did he…is he gone?"

"Yes. He's gone."

She walked over to me and put her hand on my back and gently rubbed it.

"Are you okay?"

"Yes."

"It's a blessing." I didn't answer, because it seemed too simple a word to sum up what had just happened.

"Your father fought hard. He did good with this last battle. He didn't lose it. He just didn't win it." She continued to rub my back while talking in low tones. "You know you did a good job, too. A very good job. He was very lucky." She continued to talk, but I wasn't listening any longer. I stared at my father and was amazed that he didn't move. His hand, which was warm a few minutes earlier, was already starting to cool. Nothing lasts. I was glad to be here at the end. I was glad it was me.

And like everyone else, I hoped that he had crossed over to something better where my mother was waiting, along with Howard and Don and together they were smiling and laughing at how foolish all of the heartache of living had been, and shaking their heads in amazement that so many miss the fact that being here at all is the blessing, and appreciating it is the point.

I stayed with dad for a long while. I sat beside the bed and looked at him and I held his hand again and said good-bye. And then I sat some more. Finally I went to the waiting area while they got dad ready for the funeral director. I had phone calls to make, the minister, some people at work. I picked up the courtesy phone and started to dial. The phone rang once, then twice and then twice more before someone answered. "Hi. Lorraine? Yeah, it's me. Randall."

Printed in the United States
30446LVS00006B/163-165